# Beyond the Palace Walls

**Amelia Hartley**

# Contents

# Chapter 1

-------------------------------------------------------------

They must have noticed I was missing by now so why weren't they looking for me?

What was the point of running away if no one came looking for you? I glance up again at the guards standing on the outer wall of the castle. I have been standing just outside the palace gate for nearly an hour now and the guards hadn't moved from their usual positions. I feel like such an idiot. After the argument I'd had with my father I really thought that he would have reacted. But here I was, standing in the middle of the entrance yard alone.

For the last hour I've felt the anger and frustration continue to build up at my father's complete lack of regard. I don't know why I'm letting it get to me so much. It really shouldn't be a surprise. My father has never seen me as anything close to a priority, there's always more important things going on than spending time with his only daughter. But he had promised and like an imbecile I'd believed him. Well, I reason, if my father doesn't care about me, if he isn't interested in keeping his promises, then I simply wouldn't go back.

Turning around slowly I face into the city. Thinking about it, I have lived in the castle my entire life and yet never set foot inside the city surrounding it. I have ridden through it on horseback and in various carriages but that was always directly down the main road to leave the city when we head out to the country or go on tour. One day I was going to be Queen and yet I had never actually set foot in my own capital city. Well that was all going to change now, I had nothing but time to kill and a very large city to explore, so carefully removing my tiara and letting my hair fall loose, I wrap my cloak tightly around myself and set off.

Picking a random street a sense of nervous excitement grows within me. This is probably the first time in my life that I have done something that was not written on an itinerary, and although I was scared as hell going into a world I knew nothing about with no guards or back up of any kind, there was also the thrill and independence of it all. I glance back at the guards to see if my movement has had any kind of reaction but it hasn't.

Cautiously at first and then with more confidence, I begin walking down a twisting, narrow, cobbled lane with tall rickety buildings on either side looking like they could collapse at any moment. I pass a few people but nobody pays me any attention, no-one recognises me, they just continue about their day. It's quite refreshing, not feeling like I'm constantly being watched. At the palace I always feel like I'm on show and always have to be perfect. Continuing down my path, trying to keep my head down so as to remain inconspicuous but also attempting to take everything in around me, I suddenly emerge into a large square bustling with people.

Everyone is standing around in small groups chatting and laugh-ing. People call across the square waving to each other as a mass of small children run around with a ball. I've never seen anything like it. It's so relaxed and free. It seems so natural. It's...strange. These people were happy! I'd always thought being poor was like a disease, everybody brutal criminals attacking and robbing each other, constantly miserable, living a half life. That was always the impression I got from my father and Lord Fagan when they spoke about people and life beyond the wall. Not that I spent much time thinking about them but when I did I felt sorrow and pity for these people, yet here they were laughing and smiling more than I think I'd ever done in my strict court life. Sure I've lived a life of luxury and pampering and I had plenty of stuff. I couldn't move in my palace suite for the amount of things I had. If I wanted something I only had to ask. But I've come to learn that stuff doesn't make you happy. Recently I've started to feel so isolated and alone, with no-one my own age, other than the horrible Joseph to talk to. There were other children and teenagers in the castle but they were tutored separately to me and when I did see them it was awkward, I was always the outsider within the group. Seeing these people smiling with family and friends only reinforces everything I feel I've never had. It was an odd bewildering moment that almost made me want to cry, until a loud shout from across the square startled me out of my brief bleakness.

There appears to be some sort of show about to start as a boy, only slightly older than me and standing on top of a rough platform, calls people to him; "...you ain't seen nufin like it folks n you won't never see nufin like it agen. Here for one week only in this bootiful city o yours for you the good people of Carrard. That's right folks, boy av I got a real treat for yous, gava round folks, gava round. A different show every night and tonight's show's about ta begin, n if ya like what ya see don't be shy to show yas appreciation by putting ya spens in the hats. N now kinds people allow me ta give ya Gallavanties production of 'The Pirates of Scroll!'"

# Chapter 2

---

He was right. I hadn't ever seen anything like it and it was brilliant. I'd never much liked the theatre at the palace. It was old and stuffy and full of unbelievably long songs and music I didn't understand, and in all honesty it was just plain boring. But this, this was alive. I cheer and clap as loud as anyone as the actors take their final bow and I find myself desperately wishing I had some coins on me to throw into the hats that were now being passed around and filled by other members of the audience, but I didn't think that going up and putting my tiara into the hat would be too good of an idea.

As people begin to drift away I become conscious of how darkness has fallen during the show, and it rather abruptly occurs to me that I must have been missing for several hours now. I'd better be getting back to the palace before my father becomes too worried, or angry for that matter. Then all hell breaks loose. Suddenly, where before people had been casually wandering off or milling around saying goodbye to friends, panic descends like a tidal wave and everyone starts running in different directions. Not having a clue what's going on I just stand stock still and within seconds the entire square is empty, with the exception of the travelling showmen who are frantically packing up.

It's then I hear shouting and the sound of horses' hooves from further away and I realise what is happening. Clearly my father has finally sent the guards out to look for me; although why this would send all the city folk running in such fear I have no idea. I am just mentally debating whether I should begin heading towards the soldiers who are searching for me, or stay where I am and wait for them to come to me, when a rough hand grabs my wrist. "Why are you just standing there? They're coming! Quickly! You can hide with us."

Before I know what is happening I'm being dragged towards one of the caravans belonging to the travelling showmen I have just finished watching. Despite my protests, the young man who has grabbed me pushes me inside, climbs in after me and shuts the door, at the same time turning off the lights. As I lie on the floor in near total darkness next to the young female from the play, whilst two of the men crouch protectively closer to the door of the caravan, I can hear the sound of hooves and shouts from the palace guards outside. They are only a matter of feet from me, all I have to do is shout out and they will find me and take me home. Yet I don't. My brain keeps telling me to just stand up and go out, to yell something, but for some reason my mouth wouldn't obey, and I just lie here in silence, listening to the heavy breathing of the others in the caravan with me as the horses' hooves, and soldiers shouts, begin to move away.

We lie in silence for another five minutes with no one daring to move or speak before the same young man who had pulled me into the caravan slowly stands up and glances out the window, "Coasts clear" he mutters, and all at once everyone relaxes, the lights are turned back on and then all six pairs of eyes turn to survey me. "What's your story then?" asks an older man who appears to be the leader of the group. I open my mouth to answer him but then can't think of a single thing to say and so quickly snap it shut again. The man sighs and rolls his eyes before saying, "Well do you at least have a name girl?"

"Cara" I blurt out without thinking, and then immediately wonder why I had given my middle name instead of my first name Elisa. Something to do with their reaction to the soldiers tells me that telling these people who I really am would be a bad idea.

"Hi Cara, I'm Risa" says the young woman who I have just been lying next to. "Are you alright? You seem a bit startled." She smiles at me in such a kind way I just stare blankly back at her, wondering why she is being so nice to a complete stranger. "I, errr, I have to go" I say simply and make to move towards the door before stopping suddenly when the same young lad who had dragged me into the caravan steps in front of me. "You can't leave, are you insane? Did you not hear the guards."

"But they've left now" I argue.

"Sam's right girl, you can't go walking through the city at night. It's dangerous for a young pretty thing like you, and if them guards catch you out after curfew you'll be enslaved quicker than lager than turns to piss."

"Enslaved?" I ask aghast, choosing to ignore the man's vulgar language.

"You're not from round here are you?" the larger man replies with a wry smile and shake of his head. "Trust me girl, best to stay here until daylight, at least if ya know what's good for ya."

"Come on love, I've made my famous stew." The woman Risa says as she puts her arm around me and leads me to a table set up at one end of the caravan. "You'll be alright here with us until morning and then you can return to wherever it is you came from."

Not feeling like I have much choice I sit down at the table whilst everyone else begins bustling around grabbing bowls and spoons. Soon all seven of us are sat around the one tiny table and I am presented with a chunk of bread and a bowl full of stew. Hesitantly at first I slowly sip a small spoonful of the broth. Risa sits watching me and laughs, "I'm not the best cook in the world but it's not poisoned."

"That's a lie," says the young man sat beside her, "she is the best cook in the world."

"Hear hear" cry the others whilst Risa just laughs and carries on dipping her bread into her stew. As the group begin chatting and laughing about the show I feel myself relax and start once again to eat. I have to admit that the stew is really good, very different to anything I have had at the palace, and as I look around at the strange company I find myself in, I realise that I am rather enjoying myself. As I sit and listen to this group of friends talking and joking I can't help but wish that I was a part of it. Wish that I could join in with the conversation and understand their inside jokes. Even though I can't contribute to their back and forth banter I can't remember the last time that I had felt so at home.

# Chapter 3

S unlight streams through an opening in the curtains temporarily blinding me as I open my eyes. Rolling over with a groan, I try to go back to sleep. I don't know what time it is but it definitely feels too early to be getting up. But as I roll over the bed suddenly disappears from beneath me and I fall onto a hard wooden floor with a thump. Realisation comes rushing back to me as I sit up and look around the cramped caravan. The events of last night had seemed like an extremely vivid dream but here was reality staring back at me from my position on the cold hard floor. Crap, my father was going to kill me. The caravan is empty and sounds from outside indicate that the travelling troop who had been my hosts last night were all already up and working. Glancing back towards the narrow bunk which had been my bed I sigh with relief when I see my cloak still bundled where it had been, with my tiara safely secured inside. There had been some raised eyebrows last night when I had removed my cloak to reveal my silk dress underneath. I could only imagine the reaction had they caught sight of my tiara.

Wrapping my cloak around me once more and ensuring that my tiara was well hidden I open the caravan door and slip out into the bright sunshine. It is clearly much later in the morning than I had originally thought. Sam, the boy who had first caught my attention in the square yesterday, is working with Luis, who I have discovered is Risa's husband, replacing some broken planks at the front of the stage. That must have been the banging I'd heard from inside the caravan. Pepe, the leader of the group, appears to be counting the takings from yesterday's show, whilst the two other men of the group Dav and Kinken, are nowhere to be seen. Risa, who had been so kind to me the night before, is making repairs to one of the costumes but she puts her work down as soon as she spots me and comes over with a smile on her face. "Good morning!"

"Good morning" I respond, automatically smiling back, "Sorry I overslept, I didn't realise how late it was."

"Nonsense, it's not that late, we're just all early risers, there's always stuff for us to do in between shows."

"Well I just wanted to say thank you again for last night."

"Oh you're welcome, anytime honey. To be honest it was lovely to have another girl around the table, I've lived with 5 boys for so long I'd forgotten what it was like" she laughs pulling me in for an unexpected hug. "I hope I'll see you again before we leave at the end of the week. Don't forget we're performing every night and there's always space at the table if you want to join us for dinner afterwards."

"Thank you, I'm not sure if that will be possible but I'll try. I can't tell you how nice last night was."

Giving Risa one last hug I turn and call goodbye to the other travellers who all briefly wave but then continue with their work.

Unsure what else to do, I turn and walk away. As I reach the edge of the square I glance back to see Sam stood watching me, although as soon as he realises that I've seen him he quickly turns back to Luis. Watching the travellers get on with their work a deep sense of regret that I can't explain washes over me. Part of me wants to go back to them. To pick up a hammer and help Sam and Luis, or a needle to help Risa, not that I know how to do either of those things but the thought feels right. But that is not reality. As nice as last night had been it was not my life, and like it or not, it is time to go back and face my father.

# Chapter 4

"A walk? You went for a walk? That's your only explanation for being gone for the last 18 hours. I had the entire guard out looking for you. The entire city searched and you stand there and say you went for a walk. Do you realise the danger you were in? The city is full of criminals and ruffians and convicts and crooks just waiting to attack. God only knows the diseases you could have contracted from the filth down there."

Resolutely keeping my mouth shut and head down I wait for my father's tirade to finish. My return to the palace has certainly been more dramatic than even I had expected. Apparently my disappearance had caused quite a stir. The look on the guards faces when I had simply walked up to the main gate had almost made me laugh, but I certainly wasn't laughing now.

Glancing to the guards stood to his left my father dismisses me with a wave of his hand, "Take Princess Elisa back to her room and make sure she stays there."

Curtseying quickly I follow the guards in silence until I can safely shut my bedroom door and finally breathe a sigh of relief. I can't remember ever seeing my father so mad but at least the worst was over with. My father was not one to hold grudges for long and once he had had the opportunity to rant he usually got over things quickly. Removing my grubby and wrinkled clothes I make my way towards the bathroom to wash away the final remains from my night in the city.

As I lie in the tub thinking back over my eighteen hour adventure I can't help but feel like I'm missing something. I remember the laughter and smiles on the people's faces, their cheers for the show. It was so different to how I had imagined. But then the guards had come and it had all changed. Why? Why had people been so afraid? What had Pepe meant when he said that people were being enslaved? Why was there a curfew in the city? None of it made any sense.

Dressing once more in a clean dress I wander back into my main room. Looking around the familiar setting I feel strangely detached from it all. My entire life had played out in the walls of this castle and not once had I thought to question it. I accepted what my tutors said, what my father said. And only now did it occur to me that maybe I should have been asking more questions. Well I was certainly going to start now. I wanted answers. But where to get them from? The obvious answer was my father but given the chastisement he'd just laid down that didn't seem like the best option. Besides he had made his views on the city and it's people quite clear.

As I pondered what my next move should be a small knock came from the door followed by a young maid entering with a tray. She places it on the central table and turns to me with a curtsey, "Your lunch, you're highness. Is there anything else I can get for you?"

As I look at the girl, only slightly older than me, but with very similar colour hair, an idea begins to form. Glancing back towards the open door I see two guards stationed outside. My father has banished me to my room for the day, no one will be expecting to see me. How often do opportunities like this come up? A whole day free with no-one watching me. Maybe there was a way to get some answers.

Casually closing the open door, I turn back towards the kitchen maid with a small smile, "Actually yes, there is something else you could do for me."

# Chapter 5

------------------------------------------------------------

It worked. I can't believe it actually worked. Walking through the castle gates out into the city the guards hadn't even glanced at me, dressed as I was in a set of Molly's spare clothes. She had certainly taken quite a bit of convincing but eventually Molly had agreed to cover for me and lend me a dress and cloak which made blending in much easier this time around. So long as Molly didn't betray me and ensured that she was the one to deliver my dinner tray later that evening then my absence shouldn't be noticed. I had the whole afternoon to explore the city. To find answers. To see the Gallavanties again. A smile lit my face at the thought of seeing Risa.

Turning down the same cobbled street which had led me to the Gallavanties before I couldn't help but feel at home. Strange how the city could seem so familiar and welcoming after only one visit. The streets were certainly busier than they had been the day before. For a moment I just stand and watch, absorbing everything around me. Many doorways stood open with people bustling in and out. Some carried baskets full of shopping whilst others strolled down the street empty handed. There was a woman sweeping leaves that had gathered in front of her door as a man opposite washed the windows of a shop which appeared to be a bakery, the smell of freshly baked bread wafting up the street. One woman hung washing from an upstairs window and another tended to a small box of flowers. They called to each other with a smile and wave. These people were so far removed from the thieves and cut throats my father had described I wondered where his low opinion of the city folk had come from.

Continuing down the street I notice an older woman sitting crossed legged on the ground, her hands held out in front of her. Is she praying, I wonder? Or meditating? But then realisation dawns as a young man walking past hands her an apple, her answering smile and call of thanks receives a small nod before the man moves off. As the lady takes a bite from the apple I watch as the man moves further down the street and produces another apple from his pocket. Following him curiously I spot another person sitting on the corner of a crossroads holding a sign begging for food, money or work. Again I watch as he is handed an apple by the kind man and gratitude lights up his face. It occurs to me how dire their situation must be if a mere apple can bring them such joy. Why is more not being done to help these people? To give them proper food? Guilt gnaws at my stomach when I think about the meals I get back at the palace. Perhaps next time I can sneak some food out with me to give to these people. Resolving to do what I can I continue down the road, but now with more awareness of those I see sat at street corners begging.

Finally reaching the square, I see an almost identical scene to the one I left just a few hours earlier. Luis is painting the now repaired planks at the front of the stage, Pepe's writing in a notebook and

Risa is sat at the same table as before, but this time peeling pota-toes. There's no sign of Sam or Dav though Kinken is here, lugging a large crate across the stage. As Risa spots me a welcoming smile lights up her face and I can't help but run into her opening arms for a hug.

"Well hey there, I wasn't expecting to see you again so soon."

"I escaped again" I respond with a giggle suddenly feeling so giddy at being with the Gallavanties again.

"Well I'm glad. You didn't get into any trouble when you got back did you?"

"No it was fine," I shrug my shoulders and glance away, not want-ing Risa to see my unease. I'd been very careful the night before not to talk about myself. After seeing my dress the Gallavanties guessed that I was from the palace but not exactly who I was. How could they? My sheltered life hadn't led to much interaction outside of the castle so being recognised was unlikely.

"You here for the show again kid?" Pepe asks as he wanders over still clutching his notebook.

"Yeah, you said it was something different every night and last night's was so great so I just thought..."

"Well you're a bit early, show's not for another couple of hours."

"Oh that's ok, I don't mind. I'm just enjoying being out in the city again."

"Hhmmm" Pepe murmurs as he turns away again, "nice dress by the way" he calls as he walks over to join Kinken.

Glancing down at my borrowed outfit Risa smiles.

"I thought it might help me blend in a bit better," I said by way of explanation.

Risa laughs, "I think you'd stand out whatever you wear but yes I suppose it helps. Come on you can help me sort out these costumes."

# Chapter 6

It was hard work. I'd never actually done any kind of manual labour and even lifting costumes made my arms ache. But this was what I had wanted last night when I had been sat at the table unable to join in with the banter of the Gallavanties. Helping to put away last night's costumes and getting the new ones prepared for tonight filled me with a purpose and sense of belonging. Chatting with Risa, discovering how she had first come to be a part of the Gallavanties touring group and hearing stories from her time on the road, meant the next hour passed in a blur. Risa had been with Pepe travelling the world ever since her and Luis had eloped, their parents having tried to prevent them from marrying back in their home town of Andrent in Toria, a country to the far south. This was her third visit to Carrard in as many years.

"Has Carrard always been like this?" I ask.

"How do you mean?"

"Like it was last night. With everyone running from guards and the curfew and everything. And there're so many people begging for food on the streets. Is there no-one to help them?"

"It seems to be getting worse. It's never been this bad before." Risa nods grimly, "Taxes keep going up, people lose their jobs because employers can't afford to keep them on, and then they can't afford to pay their rent so they end up on the streets with no job, no money, no food. Prices for everything keep rising to pay for the taxes and it's just a continuing downward spiral for many. People who can help do but most are just barely surviving themselves."

I nod in understanding, "And the curfew?"

"The first time I came here almost four years ago the curfew had not long started. Never really understood why it was needed in the first place to be honest. I asked around at the time but no one knew. There was no warning. The order just suddenly came down from the palace and that was that. I think some folk tried to fight against it at first but when they ended up either beaten or imprisoned everyone else just learnt to accept it I guess."

"Beaten? For breaking curfew?"

Risa fixes me with a serious expression, "The city guards can be brutal. With no one around to check their behaviour the power's gone to their heads. They can do what they want without repercussions. Promise me you'll be careful around the city Cara, and if you see guards you get out of there fast ok?"

"Ok."

Risa looks at me for a moment, making sure that I'm taking in the seriousness of her request, before nodding and accepting my response. "Come and help me finish getting dinner ready before the show. I'm making Luis' favourite, lamb and potato hotpot."

"I'm not sure I'll be much help, I've never cooked before." I confess as I follow her into the caravan.

"Don't worry, I'll teach you. You'll be a pro in no time," she grins.

Twenty minutes later and I'm carefully stirring a large pot of lamb and potato hotpot. Risa is chopping carrots next to me whilst telling me about the time Luis and Sam nearly set one of the caravans on fire.

"The caravan smelt of smoke for a week" she laughs, "and the chicken was so burnt that we couldn't eat any of it. Honestly, never let Luis cook for you. It's not worth the risk."

"Hey! I heard that!" Luis exclaims, entering the caravan door just as Risa is finishing her story, "and it wasn't entirely my fault, Sam was involved too."

"Pretty sure it was you who forgot to add more water. There's still hope for Sam." Risa teases.

"Honestly Cara, I don't think she'll ever let me live that one down. You try and do something nice for someone and I get nothing but criticism, mocked by my own wife." He shakes his head in faux disappointed but then can't keep the grin off his face. Wrapping his arms around Risa's waist he gives her a quick kiss on the cheek, "We're in much safer hands with you my love, thanks for cooking again, smells wonderful."

"Cara helped," Risa's quick to point out.

Luis turns to me, "Thanks for helping out Cara, you joining us for dinner again tonight?"

"Oh I really didn't do anything. I'm just in charge of stirring." I say, although there's a little part of me that's quite proud I've helped make something for the first time.

"Well stirring is a very important part of the process," Luis says with seriousness, "and you haven't set the place on fire so you're already doing better than me."

I grin at Luis and wish I could stay for dinner with the Gallavanties again, especially as I've contributed towards the cooking of it. "Unfortunately I can't stay for dinner tonight though. I need to get back straight after the show. I'm hoping no-one's noticed my absence but I don't really want to push it."

Risa looks disappointed, "Ah honey, that's a shame, after you worked so hard as well."

"Will you be alright getting back? Do you need me to go with you?" Luis offers looking concerned.

"No, no, I'll be fine. I know the way. If I leave as soon as the show ends then I should make it back before darkness falls."

Risa doesn't seem happy with my answer but lets it go. Putting the lids on top of the pots, she declares dinner is prepared. A rap on the door and Pepe's voice indicates that it's show time and Risa and Luis need to get into costume.

As we exit the caravan Risa pulls me in for a hug.

"I'm sorry you're not staying for dinner but I'll see you tomorrow right?" Risa asks.

"I hope so" I smile back already thinking about how I can get away again.

Risa tenderly strokes my hair and gives me a soft kiss on my forehead, "Take care of yourself sweetheart."

"Best go get yourself a good spot" Luis adds, "You're gonna want to be right at the front for this one."

And with one last smile and wave Risa and Luis disappear backstage.

"You came back then" Sam states, making me jump. I hadn't heard him come up behind me.

"Err yeah, hi. I wanted to see another show so managed to slip out whilst no one was looking. Even put on a disguise and everything" I say gesturing at my dress with a nervous laugh.

"By disguise you mean a normal dress?"

"Well yeah, I thought it was better than the one I was wearing yesterday. Less inconspicuous."

"Right." he says, drawing out the word sarcastically. "Where did you even get it?"

"Oh, I borrowed it from one of the kitchen girls."

"Kitchen girls? You don't even know her name."

I can't understand the hostile look in Sam's eye and I'm not sure how to respond, "Her name's Molly."

For a moment we just look at each other quizzically, trying to figure each other out but neither of us knowing what to say next.

Sam breaks the awkward silence stepping backwards as he say, "Well I'd better go get ready"

Quickly I step back too, "Yeah I need to ummm, I don't want to miss the start of the show." We both turn and head in different directions, though I'm still contemplating the look in his eyes and trying to figure out exactly what I said to upset him so much.

Word has clearly spread about the Gallavanties as the crowd is much larger than yesterday. I manage to manoeuvre myself to the front as the excitement builds. The audience are expectant. Where yesterday's was a pirate adventure full of dramatic sword fights, tonight's show is a comedy that has the audience literally crying with laughter. It's clear that I don't get all of the jokes and references but I still enjoy the show, feeding off the buzz around me and joining in with the laughter. With a huge grin on my face I give a wave to Risa and the others as they take their final bows, then slip away through the masses, making my way back towards the palace. I hadn't given much thought to how I was going to get back into the castle, after the ease of slipping out, but Lady Luck is with me and I manage to safely reach my room, meeting no more than a few servants who stare at me with quizzical faces but say nothing.

I collapse onto my bed and then let out an excited giggle. Today has been the most fun day I've ever had. The only question now is how I'm going to manage to get out again tomorrow. Today was only possible because of my father's banishment, meaning that I wouldn't be missed around court. But my father's temper is quick to fade and I know that tomorrow I'll be expected to return to normal, lessons with my tutor in the morning and courtly meetings in the afternoon. I'll have to come up with a plan but already I can feel today's events catching up with me and a huge yawn stretches across my face. Taking off Molly's dress and cloak I stash them in a trunk at the foot of my bed before going to clean up. As I lie in bed contemplating everything from the last few days my final thought before sleep claims me is of Sam's hostile face.

# Chapter 7

The following morning I'm woken as usual by Diane, my lady's maid, and told to prepare for lessons. When my breakfast is delivered by Molly, she gives me a small smile but with Diane there it's impossible to talk. Instead I smile back and give her a thumbs up. Diane runs through my schedule which includes two lessons this morning and a council meeting this afternoon. Truth be told, a fairly standard day in my life, but after two days of experiencing the world outside of my castle, it's a shock to get back to reality and I can't find any enthusiasm for the day ahead. Another knock at the door signals the arrival of Tutor Jenna. She strolls in with an armful of books, does an awkward curtsey and then moves over to the large table at the opposite end of the suite. As she begins setting up I grab my notebook and pen and head over. Grabbing a glass of water and settling into my chair I wait for Tutor Jenna to begin but then Joseph, Lord Fagan's son and an entitled arrogant asshole, suddenly strolls in. With a cocky smile he takes the seat next to me, "Alright Princess?"

I don't smile back, "What are you doing here?"

"What? Not happy to see me?" Joseph laughs.

Tutor Jenna explains, "With the arrival of Ambassador Dorn from Navas tomorrow, today's lesson is focused on our history with Navas, as well as their traditions and culture, so that you can make the best impression at the ball tomorrow. Master Joseph is here for the same reason. Lord Fagan has specifically requested that I give you all the information you need and that I make it absolutely clear to both of you how vital it is that tomorrow's meeting goes well. You will both be expected to represent the future of Aleti in a positive light and demonstrate our prosperity and therefore worthiness of an alliance to Ambassador Dorn. I cannot stress enough the importance of tomorrow."

She briefly fixes us both with a serious stare before sharply turning to the board behind her. For the next hour she talks non-stop, feeding us so much information I feel that my head is going to explode. Whilst I have been frantically taking notes, Joseph, sat beside me, has been nonchalantly staring out the window or doodling on his paper, seemingly not paying any attention. Unable to keep up I put my pen down to rub my aching wrist, and as Tutor Jenna's voice drones on I find my mind drifting back to the Gallavanties. I wonder what Risa is upto right now? Just as I'm starting to completely tune Tutor Jenna out the topic switches to the reason for the Ambassador's visit, the proposed trade deal between Navas and Aleti.

"The alliance will increase the availability of luxury goods such as silks, gold, silver and precious gems, which of course Navas is famous for. Lord Fagan has also negotiated promises from the King of Navas to support the development of our navy. Increased taxes and the introduction of gate tolls will pay for the south road improvements so that transportation of such goods is quicker and smoother. In return Aleti have agreed to cease our fruit trade with Cobback in recognition of our relationship with Navas being more important."

Suddenly shocked out of my daydream I cut her off in the middle of her speal, "Wait, what was that you just said?"

Tutor Jenna seems surprised at my abrupt interruption and sudden keen interest. "All fruit trade will cease upon the signing of the new agreement with Navas."

"Why? Why are we cutting off trade with Cobback to please Navas? We've had an open trade arrangement with Cobback for several decades. I don't understand."

"Whilst that is true, Lord Fagan believes that a deal with Navas is more beneficial and this is a condition that the King of Navas has insisted upon."

She turns once again to the board as if to restart her lesson but I argue back, "How is it more beneficial to the people of Aleti? Surely the open trade of food is more important than silks and gold and gems?"

"I'm sure that Lord Fagan has taken everything into consideration and done what is best."

"Best for whom? It doesn't make sense."

"It is not our place to question the decisions of those who know better. Now let's get back to..."

"But why not? We should question it! I want to question it. Who's to say that Lord Fagan knows better?"

Joseph has been silently watching our exchange but doesn't seem impressed with my continued argument, "What the devil's got into you? Since when have you cared about fruit so much? Just let her finish her lesson so we can get out of here."

"But it's not just the fruit. What were you saying about raising taxes, and gate tolls? Lord Fagan can't do that. The people are struggling enough. We don't need more silk or gold. We need to be helping our own people more, not making life harder for them by raising taxes and cutting off food trade."

Joseph stares at me like I've suddenly grown two heads. "Have you actually gone mad? What are you talking about? Why do we need to be helping the people?"

Standing up in a fit of passion I declare, "Because it's our responsibility. Our duty. Surely we should use our positions of power to do good. To improve things for those less fortunate than us. To help those in need and try to enhance the lives of everyone, not just ourselves."

For a moment Joseph just stares at me, and then he starts laughing. He laughs so hard that tears form in his eyes and he's banging the table with his fist. "That's hilarious. You're funny. Seriously. Help the people," he laughs again, "Wait till I tell my father you've suddenly become a passionate philanthropist and advocate for the poor."

"I'm not joking. Laugh all you want Joseph but my eyes have been opened to what is really going on in this city and now that they are I'm going to change it."

"You won't do anything. My father won't let you. He's in charge of pretty much everything and I can tell you now he won't give a rat's ass how horrible things are for the poor people."

"You really don't care, do you? You're as bad as your father. And I think you're forgetting that I am the Princess and future Queen of this country. Your father won't always be Lord Chancellor."

With a cold laugh and smug smile Joseph answers, "And I think you're forgetting that I'm the future King of this country. Your father's already agreed to the marriage match."

For a moment I stare at Joseph in surprise. I had heard rumours. I know there has been gossip around the castle surrounding myself and Joseph, and I knew that Lord Fagan had been pushing my father on the subject of my future husband, but that there is an actual agreement in place has shocked me to my core. Surely he's lying. Surely my father wouldn't force me into this marriage. He knows that I've never really liked Joseph, despite the pair of us being forced together throughout our childhood. But as I look at Joseph's confident smile I know that he isn't lying. My father really has agreed to this.

"Well wifey I think that's enough fun for today, don't you?" He chuckles at my still shocked face and turns to leave, "See you tomorrow at the ball darling," he calls as he walks out of the room without a backward glance.

Slowly I turn to look at Tutor Jenna but she is quickly gathering up her books without making eye contact. Sketching a small curtsey she flies out of the room so fast she almost stumbles into Tutor Michael who is entering the room for my next lesson. Sinking back down onto my chair I try to process my apparently impending marriage to Joseph Fagan. Totally unaware as to what has just happened Tutor Michael starts chattering away as he sets up but I'm not listening to a word. My mind is struggling to comprehend the idea of spending my entire life with Joseph. I need to talk to my father. He can't make me do this. Taking a deep breath I try to gather myself, to think calmly and find a solution.

After another hour of being talked at, and me not hearing a word of it, lessons are finally over for the day. After going over and over my predicament in my mind, and composing my anti-Joseph arguments I'm feeling much calmer about the proposed marriage situation. Marriage isn't possible until I'm 18 so I have at least 18 months before this nightmare becomes a reality. That's plenty of time to fix this, to change my father's mind. Molly enters with my lunch tray as Tutor Michael is packing up. Catching my eye Molly hovers by the table, pretending to fuss with the napkins and cutlery until he makes his exit. Sensing Molly wants to talk, I follow Tutor Michael to the door and casually shut it behind him. Instantly Molly races over, "I've been dying to know what happened. You got away ok? The disguise worked?"

"Yes and yes," I reply with a beaming smile. "It worked perfectly, no-one even glanced my way. Was everything alright here? You didn't have any problems?"

She shakes her head, "No problems here. Everyone had heard about the King's shouting at you and you being sent to your room, though no-one knew really why. I guess they wanted news of you disappearing kept hush hush. Anyway I delivered your evening tray as promised and no one questioned anything. I did meet Lord Fagan in the corridor as I was leaving. He asked how you were so I said you were tired after everything that had happened and were going to bed early."

"Perfect, thank you. Honestly yesterday was the most fun day I've ever had and it wouldn't have happened without your help."

Molly beams at me, "You're welcome, your highness, I'm happy to help. Are you going to try and sneak out again?"

I shake my head miserably, "I want to but it's just not possible. After yesterday's banishment I'm expected in court again this afternoon. I have to be there to hear the draft reading of the Navas treaty."

Molly pulls a face which makes me laugh. It's nice having someone to talk to and Molly is clearly desperate to know more, "Tell me about yesterday. Did you meet up with the Gallavanties like you wanted to?"

Bursting to talk with someone about everything I fill Molly in on the last few days. I tell her all about the Gallavanties, about helping Risa with the costumes and dinner. Then as I relay the show to her in every detail, it occurs to me that Molly might just have the answers to some of my questions.

"Molly, can I ask you something? You work here in the castle but live in the city, right?"

"Yeah with my mother and father, and two younger sisters."

"Do you know why the curfew is in place? And why the people are so scared of the city guards?"

"No-one knows for sure why the curfew was brought in. I remember asking my father about it. Supposedly it's to reduce crime but my father says that's not true. He reckons it's to stop people getting together and talking. After work in the evenings is when people used to meet with friends and groups and stuff."

"But why would you need to stop people talking to each other?"

"If you don't like what they're talking about." Molly says meaningfully. "People haven't been happy for a long while now. With the guards, the taxes, the harsh rules and excessive punishments. When people started being sold into slavery for the smallest of crimes, folk started to talk about doing something. Rising up, taking a stand. That's when the curfew came in and meeting in groups was banned. Anyone caught breaking it is imprisoned or enslaved and their property and possessions forfeited to the crown."

I stare at Molly in shock, "But that's awful. Someone needs to do something."

"Who? The order came from Lord Fagan. He's in charge of the city guards and who's gonna go up against him. Only the King is higher than Fagan, and Fagan won't let anyone else get close enough to the King."

"Well I'll talk to my father. I'm sure if I can just talk to him, explain. It shouldn't be like this. I'll make him listen, I promise."

Molly gives me a sad smile that doesn't truly reach her eyes, "I believe you'll try, but for now let's see what we can do to get you out of those boring court meetings."

"Really?"

"If the Gallavanties are only here for a few more days then you've got to make the most of it and take every chance you get."

# Chapter 8

Nervously entering the chamber I see that most of the Lords are already gathered and it seems that we are just waiting for my father and Lord Fagan to arrive. As I make my way to my seat a couple of the councillors are already giving me strange looks. Molly has lightly sprinkled flour onto my face in an effort to make me look paler. It's step one in her plan to get me out of the meeting and give me time to visit the Gallavanties again. The risk of trying to sneak out for a third day in a row is high but Molly's right. The Gallavanties are only here for a few more days and then they'll be gone and my life really will return to its normal boring pattern. Although whatever happens, I know that I will never forget what I've learnt about the city in the last two days, and I still intend to do what I can to change it.

I take my place at the top of the table, just to the left of where my father will sit at the head, and opposite Lord Fagan's seat to my father's right. A few moments go by with the Lords all engaging in murmured conversation with each other whilst I sit there in silence. Today's council meeting is focused first on the visit of Ambassador

Dorn and the agreement with Navas, followed by the usual other business including an update of the situation in Karhaner, an agriculture report from Vamanst and a finance report from the treasury department.

Still thinking about my lesson earlier I lean over to the Lord next to me, Lord Culton I think his name is, "This trade agreement with Navas, do you truly think it's the right thing for Aleti? The plans to increase taxes and introduce toll gates to raise money for the work on the highway. I checked and Navas aren't contributing anything towards the costs of improving the Southern road even though more than 60% of it is in Navas territory, not Aleti. That doesn't seem right. And the condition that we have to end all fruit trade with Cobback? We seem to be doing an awful lot to please Navas, more than we should. Is it really in our best interests?"

Lord Culton stares at me with a dumbfounded expression. "I err, I don't know. I haven't read the agreement."

Now it's my turn to look dumbfounded, "You haven't read the agreement? What do you mean you haven't read the agreement? Isn't that what we're all here to discuss?"

"Lord Fagan hasn't shared the details with the rest of us. He has worked on the deal alone. Today is the first time we're hearing what has actually been agreed."

I'm baffled by this. How can Lord Fagan have negotiated an entire trade agreement with Navas without consulting any of the other Lords? Before I can respond my father and Lord Fagan enter the room and everyone stands. Quickly joining them I watch as they round the table and take their seats before everyone else sits down too.

My father doesn't even look at me or the other lords before he turns to the right and gestures for Lord Fagan to begin. Lord Fagan nods and rises. In his hand he clearly holds the Navas agreement but I notice he doesn't have copies for anyone else. Instead he starts to read. Or at least I assume he is reading the document. He could easily be missing key information out. When he reaches the part about ending fruit trade with Cobback there is a surprised murmur around the room.

Lord Fagan ignores this and tries to continue but I jump in, "Why have we agreed to this? Cobback have been our allies and trade partners for decades. Our fruit trade with them is a huge part of our economy. Why would we sacrifice that? I don't like that the King of Navas is dictating such strict terms. An agreement should be about compromise. What are Navas compromising for us?"

Lord Fagan gives me a stare so deadly a chill runs down my spine. My father seems surprised at my outburst but Lord Culton beside me also speaks up, "I believe the Princess has a point. She also mentioned some discrepancies with the Southern road improvement costs."

Lord Fagan tries to hide his frustration but doesn't do a good job of it, "The southern road improvements are vital to ensuring that trade with Navas is as efficient as it can be. The benefits to improved access to the gold and silver markets are untold. I think the Princess is highly exaggerating the importance of fruit trade with Cobback. As the Princess points out we have been trading with Cobback for decades and look where we are. We shouldn't be focusing on the past. We should be looking to the future. The future lies with Navas, not Cobback. The deal in all its complexities can be difficult to understand coming from a position of ignorance" Lord Fagan says giving me a poignant look as he says the word ignorance, "but I can assure everyone that I have worked tirelessly on this deal and there is no need to be concerned about anything."

There is a moment of silence. Lord Fagan gives everyone a brief look as though daring any of the other Lords to challenge him. When no-one does and my father doesn't seem to disagree either, Lord Fagan moves on. He immediately ends the discussion on the Navas deal, presumably in an attempt to prevent further questions, and instead moves on to other business.

As he begins talking about wheat production and turnover in Vamnast I can already start to feel myself losing concentration. I know that I'm not going to get any further with my questions today. I need to speak to my father alone. I need to get him away from Lord Fagan and make him listen. The more I learn about this deal the more I'm concerned it's not right. I just can't see the benefits for Aleti, although there seem to be a lot of benefits for Navas. Looking around I can see the other Lords have switched off too. They're slumped back down in their chairs and any interest they had in proceedings is gone. It's time to implement Molly's plan and get out of here. Carefully reaching into my right pocket I pull out a pot of salt. Making sure that no one is looking, I pour the salt into my water. I wait a minute before taking a large gulp. Instantly the salty water makes me gag and causes a coughing fit so violent I almost truly make myself sick.

My father looks at me with something like concern whilst Lord Fagan merely seems annoyed at the interruption.

"Are you alright Elisa? Do you need a doctor?" My father asks.

Trying to breathe through the coughing I pretend to try and put a brave face on "No I'm alright father. I'm just feeling a little unwell. A little run down after a rather overwhelming morning."

The meeting resumes and I reach automatically for my water to ease my throat, forgetting that I've added salt to it, and causing another dramatic coughing fit. "Sorry" I murmur as the Lords stare at me again.

I wait ten minutes before moving onto part two of the plan. Everyone's attention is still on Lord Fagan and his agriculture report so I reach into my left pocket and get a pinch of the black pepper that Molly gave me. Quickly I shove the pepper up my nose. I immediately start to sneeze. Six huge sneezes interrupt the meeting. Quickly I grab my handkerchief as once again fifteen pairs of eyes turn to look at me.

Lord Fagan looks at me with such scornful disdain I wonder how no one else in the room can notice. Sarcastically he suggests, "Oh dear. It's probably as a result of breathing the dirty air of the city during your walk."

I defiantly return his stare but then another sneeze builds up and the impact of my defiance is rather lost as three quick sneezes have me reaching for my handkerchief again. Perhaps I overdid it on the pepper.

As Lord Fagan resumes the meeting and once again starts reading numbers from the agriculture report I glance at the clock. Almost 4 o'clock. Lord Fagan has been leading this meeting for nearly two hours now. I'm sure that he is deliberately making it as boring as possible so that none of the other Lords pay close attention to what he is saying, and just end up agreeing with him, purely to end the meeting and get out of here. I'm supposed to have another private meeting after this one with just Lord Fagan, Joseph and myself to discuss tomorrow further. I do not want to get stuck with Lord Fagan for any longer than necessary. I need to get out of here.

Time for the final trick. As casually as possible I reach into my dress pocket for the vial of red powder that Molly handed me earlier. Slipping the lid off the top I glance around once more before deciding to go for it. Pretending another cough I reach up a hand to cover my mouth and tip the contents onto my tongue. Furiously I chew and then quickly swallow the pepper pieces before I have the chance to chicken out. I don't have to wait long for the chilli to take effect. The burn quickly creeps up my throat and sets my mouth on fire. Within moments my whole body is consumed by a hot flush. I can already feel my face turning red and beads of sweat are running down my forehead.

As my eyes start to water the Lord next me finally notices my distress. "Goodness Princess Elisa, you really don't look well." He says as he leans as far away from me as possible so as not to catch whatever it is I apparently have.

"I think perhaps I need to go and lie down." I say meekly.

"Do you need a doctor?" My father asks looking genuinely concerned although he too is leaning away from me in alarm.

"No no" I say quickly. The last thing I want is people checking up on me. "I think I just need to rest. Undisturbed. Alone. To rest." I add again and emphasise the undisturbed part.

"Well you had better be alright for the Ambassador's visit tomorrow" Lord Fagan adds coldly.

"I'm sure I will be, if I can just rest without interruption for the evening, I'm sure I will have recovered sufficiently for tomorrow."

Father nods "Go then."

As I rise from my chair and head for the exit he is already turning back to Lord Fagan who has started his never ending spiel again. Slipping silently out the door I race around the corner and find Molly waiting for me in a small nook just down the corridor.

"I thought you were never getting out of there." She says with relief. "Here's a dress and cloak for you to change into."

Ignoring the outfit she is holding out to me I desperately clutch at my throat, "Water, I need water. What the hell was that you gave me?"

Molly laughs but does hand me a glass of water which I gulp down.

"Hottest chilli powder I could find in the kitchen. They normally only add a small pinch at a time."

"Why didn't you tell me that? I poured half the vial onto my tongue."

This just makes Molly laugh even more and I can't help but smile back. Now that the burning pain has gone and I've successfully escaped from the council meeting I can see the funny side a bit more.

"Come on. The nearest exit is on the east side and I've already checked the coast is clear. The only guard on duty is a friend of mine so he won't ask questions."

After swapping my silk dress for Molly's I follow her to the east exit. As we reach the castle gate Molly's guard friend raises his eyebrows in surprised recognition but doesn't say anything. I give Molly a quick hug, "Thank you for everything. I'll try not to be too late back. You're going to go to my room and make sure no one comes to check on me right?"

"Yes, don't worry. I've got you covered here. Have fun." She gives me one last squeeze and then I slip through the gate and out into the city once more.

# Chapter 9

By the time I'm able to get away it's late afternoon already. Exiting the castle from the east gate means entering the city at a different point to normal and it takes me a moment to orientate myself. Heading in what I think is the right direction I'm nearly knocked over by a young lad who is dodging through the crowd with a ball tucked under his arm. A young girl chases after the older lad but can't keep up and trips on the uneven stone. As she begins to sob, holding her grazed knee, her father appears beside her, scooping her up in one motion to dry her tears. The tender look in his eyes as he kisses her forehead before setting her back on her feet is a look that I don't ever remember seeing on my father's face. Certainly I've never felt the warmth of a fatherly hug or experienced a kiss on the forehead like that. Wait, that's not true. I have experienced exactly that, with Risa.

As I watch the girl and her father walk away I'm left with the awareness that there is so much I've missed out on living my luxurious life in the castle. Stuff I wasn't even aware I had been missing. Real friends, a real family. To think that just four days ago I had been blissfully ignorant as to how empty my life had been. How strange to think that one trip into the city would change that and open my eyes to so much.

As I contemplate this the sudden sight of Dav Creek interrupts my thoughts. He strolls down the street then turns left into a narrower alley. On impulse I follow. I reach the top of the alleyway just in time to see Dav make another left turn further ahead. Quickening my pace so as not to lose sight of him I follow him right, then left, left again, then up a set of stone steps, across a narrow wooden bridge and down another flight of steps, then right and left again. I try to keep track of the turns we are taking but it soon becomes too much and I've no idea the path we're now on, I just continue to follow. But soon the twisting lanes mean it becomes impossible to keep Dav in my sight line and I lose him. I keep going, glancing down each turning, trying to spot his familiar curly hair but I don't see Dav anywhere. He could've turned down any one of these alleys.

Deciding to give up I spin around to go back the way I came and instead slam straight into a chest that is as hard as a rock. I would have fallen were it not for the two strong arms that shoot out to catch me. I look up and breathe a sigh of relief. Dav Creek.

"Are you following me?" He says releasing my arms.

"Not intentionally." I try to bluff, "I was just exploring the city and saw you coming down here."

"Well I suggest you go back the way you came. This ain't a part of town you wanna explore. Only thing you'll find round here is trouble."

"Really?" I say looking back down the street with renewed interest.

"Oh no no, you're coming back with me." Dav takes my arm, although much more gently this time, and starts to lead me back up the road.

"Why? Is it really that dangerous?"

"It is for someone like you." he mutters.

"Someone like me?"

"Young, pretty, sweet, innocent. The people who spend time in this part of town would eat you alive."

"But you're spending time in this part of town and you wouldn't hurt me."

Dav stops so suddenly I almost run into him again. Deliberately looming over me, he raises one eyebrow and snarls at me, "What makes you so sure of that?"

I shrug, completely unfazed by his attempts to intimidate me, "I just am. I'm not saying you couldn't hurt me," I gesture towards him in a vague indication of his large bulk and muscles, "obviously you could, but I know that you won't. I feel safe when I'm with you."

Dav looks surprised at this statement and turns away to resume walking, but not before I see the beginning of a small smile. "Come on, let's get you back to the others."

As Dav marches me back through the streets I try to keep up whilst stealing glances at the large tattooed man beside me. He was probably the exact image my father would conjure in his mind were he to think of a dangerous criminal. Tall and muscular, an aura about him that made everyone in the street move out of his way. Yet despite his intimidating size I couldn't help but trust him. This was a man who underneath the hard exterior was kind and caring. Funny too. I remembered the way he had joked at dinner with the other Gallavanties. I couldn't explain why I had such trust in him but I did.

"Stop staring at me" he mutters.

"Just trying to figure you out," I say with a smile. "So how long have you been with the Gallavanties?"

"Since the beginning."

"You and Pepe must be pretty close."

"We have each other's back."

"It must be nice."

"What?"

"Having a best friend. Someone's who's got your back."

"You don't have a best friend?"

"I don't have any friends," I say matter of factly as we enter the square and spot the rest of the Gallavanties milling around the stage. "Except Risa. I think I can say Risa's my friend now," I add, smiling as Risa grins and waves at us both. Risa is always smiling and I can't help but always smile back. If there is a happier, more cheerful person in all the world than Risa then I'd like to meet them. "Where've you two been?" she calls, "The crowd's starting to gather."

"Just exploring the city" Dav says with a quick wink at me, "but we're back now. Let's costume up and get this show on the road."

"Glad you could make it." Risa says as she gives me a quick hug. "See you in a minute" she smiles as she follows the others backstage.

"Good luck," I shout back, before once more finding my place at the front of the stage for tonight's performance.

The Tragedy of Matilda is a love story so powerful and so wretched it has most of the audience crying at the end, including me. Risa and Luis play the besotted couple and as I watch the pair's struggles and then eventual success I can't help but wonder if the play is actually based on them. They certainly don't need to act their love overly much. That it is real is so blindingly obvious. It's what makes the whole play. When the characters finally marry and end with their happily ever after I feel a pang in my heart so deep I actually have to rub my chest to try and ease the ache I feel. Once again the audience are enraptured and coins flow for the Gallavanties. Leaving the buzzing audience behind I slip backstage. "That was incredible" I declare as I greet the Gallavanties coming off the stage.

Risa beams at me. "You really think so? It's a new show we only wrote a few weeks ago. That was actually our first real performance. It seems to have gone down well."

"Gone done well" I say in disbelief, "Did you not see the audience at the end? It was a triumph!"

Luis grabs Risa in a hug and swings her around as she squeals with delight. Pepe laughs while Dav gives Luis a pat on the back, "Congrats man, your first play and they loved it. We'll have to perform it everywhere we go."

I grin at Luis and the look of pride on his face.

"You staying for dinner tonight honey?" Risa asks me, "I made enough for you just in case."

"Yeah I think I will tonight" I say knowing it's a risk but not wanting to leave the Gallavanties so soon. I follow the group into Risa's caravan and take my place at the table.

After the incredible success of the show everyone is in high spirits. Even Sam doesn't seem as annoyed by my presence as usual. The conversation flows and I join in, sharing in their laughter and joy. I'm there for more than an hour. Even after dinner is finished, I sip my drink and can't bring myself to leave. But as I glance outside and notice that darkness has fallen I stand up suddenly.

"Crap I have to go." Risa tries to persuade me to stay but I know I have to get back. With everything that is happening tomorrow Diane will be there to wake me up early. Luis and Dav insist on walking me back. I try to argue with them, knowing that it's after curfew and if caught they could get into trouble, but they use the same argument to justify going with me. It's not a long walk though and Molly's friend is still on guard as he said he would be. He opens the gate without a word and I slip back in, silently waving goodbye.

Creeping through the castle it seems that most people have decided to retire early, probably because of the Ambassador's arrival tomorrow. However when I reach my room I immediately notice the guard stationed outside. Crap. How am I supposed to get back into my room with him stood there? Looking around I spot an old vase on a table. Hoping this works, I pick up the vase and throw it across the landing. It lands with a crash and shards shatter everywhere. The guard turns his head in puzzlement and heads over towards the sound. As quickly and silently as possible I run to the door and squeeze through, carefully closing it behind me. I breathe out and relax once more.

As I enter my bedroom I'm halted by the sight of Molly curled up in my bed asleep. I can only assume that Molly's stayed here all evening to protect my cover. Undressing quietly so as not to wake her I slip into the other side of the bed and fall asleep almost as soon as my head hits the pillow.

# Chapter 10

Something suddenly jolts me out of my sleep and I shoot up, looking around in panic.

"I'm so sorry, I didn't mean to wake you. I was trying to sneak out quietly. I never meant to actually fall asleep. Your lady's maid, Diane, came to check on you last night so I climbed into your bed with the covers pulled up to pretend to be you and it worked pretty well cos it was dark and we kind of have the same colour hair and then I don't know what happened, I must of drifted off and I'm so sorry Princess."

Rubbing the sleep from my eyes I look at Molly's worried face with confusion. "It's fine. I don't mind, you were helping me." I flop back down onto my pillow with a groan before sitting back up again as another thought occurs to me. "Your parents won't be mad at you will they? You've been gone all night, they'll be worried."

"Oh no it's fine. They know that sometimes duties can keep us here. It's not unusual."

"Oh ok, that's good. I don't want to cause you any trouble when you've been so great."

Molly smiles, "I'm enjoying helping you, your majesty."

"Cara, you can call me Cara."

"Cara?" She questions.

"It's what my friends call me" I say with a smile. A slow grin spreads across her face and she nods, "Ok Cara."

She turns to leave again but then halts when there's a sound from the living suite. We both stare at each other in horror as we hear Diane's voice issuing instructions.

"What do we do?" she mouths at me in panic.

Leaping out of bed I look around the room for somewhere Molly can hide but there's only my trunk and I'm not sure Molly will fit. "It's fine. We'll just go out like everything is perfectly normal. You can say you were checking up on me after my illness."

Both taking a deep breath I open the door and stroll out like I don't have a care in the world. Molly follows after me. Diane is stood there with a clipboard like always but she also has Crella and Jonathon, my hairdresser and stylist for special events, with her. Diane does a double take at the sight of Molly emerging from my bedroom and looks at me as though waiting for an explanation. When I don't answer she returns her gaze to Molly, "Can I help you? What were you doing in the Princess' bedroom?"

Molly keeps her eyes meekly downcast as she answers, "I was just checking up on her highness after her illness."

"Thanks Molly" I add, just to make it clear to Diane that Molly was welcome.

Molly gives a deep curtsey and then leaves the room, giving me a wink and smile just as she closes the door. Diane immediately launches into organising mode.

"We have 150 minutes until Ambassador Dorn arrives and we have much to do. First will be the official welcoming ceremony of course.

You remember your Navasian etiquette lessons from Tutor Jenna?" she asks, fixing me with a stare until I nod, "Good, then there will be a lunch in the great hall."

"Who exactly will be at this lunch?" I ask.

"The king of course, you, the ambassador and his deputy along with Lord Fagan and Joseph obviously, and all the Lords of Aleti who have traveled to Carrard for this momentous day." I fail to contain my groan at hearing the Fagan's will be there but although Diane glances at me she continues on with the schedule. "After the lunch Ambassador Dorn will be given a tour of the castle including the portrait gallery, great library and throne rooms. You and Joseph will escort him and you will put on a good show," she emphasises. "Then it's just a case of getting ready for the banquet and ball this evening." Diane slams her clipboard folder shut and turns to look at me expectantly. "Well why are you still standing there? Go and get in the bath so Crella can get on with doing your hair."

Not daring to disobey Diane in this mood I quickly head to the bathroom where a warm bath has already been prepared. I try to enjoy my soak in the tub but Crella is there washing my hair and scrubbing my body. When I return to the living suite my breakfast has been delivered, although there's no sign of Molly. I sit down and start to tuck in whilst Crella begins brushing the tangles from my hair. I spend the next hour and a half being waxed, groomed and styled to perfection. Wearing my ceremonial gown and with a gleaming tiara on my head, I make my way down to the main castle entrance. The courtyard is almost unrecognisable. Every cobble shines, the wood panels have been repainted and Aleti flags hang from every post. All of the Lords are gathered on the front steps. As I step into place Lord Fagan looks me up and down before giving a satisfied nod. Watching him closely I notice that he seems on edge. Not his usual arrogant calm self. Is he nervous? The last to arrive is my father, also dressed in his ceremonial robes, who walks down the front steps just as a Navasian carriage pulls into the courtyard.

Guards rush to open the carriage door and place some steps at its entrance. Everybody seems to hold their breath, for a moment nothing happens. Then a tanned man sticks his head out, looks around with a cold assessing expression, before finally stepping down from the carriage. Tall and slender with dark hair he approaches with a swagger. He is dressed in the finest and most elaborately decorated silk I've ever seen, and is dripping with jewellery, a ring on every finger. The man is clearly dressed to impress but to me it comes across as though he is trying too hard to emphasize his country's wealth. But glancing to my left at Lord Fagan's greedy eyes it is clearly having the desired effect on at least one person. My father steps forward as the man reaches the bottom of the steps and confidently dips into a bow. "Your Majesty, I am Ambassador Dorn, here on behalf of King James of Navas who extends the arms of friendship to you and your nation."

"Thank you Ambassador Dorn. We welcome you to Aleti and accept the arms of friendship that King James of Navas offers. May this be the beginning of a prosperous and unbreakable alliance."

The Ambassador bows again and everyone seems to relax now that the formal words of welcome are completed.

My father turns and gestures me forwards, "May I present my daughter, Princess Elisa Cara Paisley Regal."

"It is my greatest honor to meet you" he says with a charming smile and another extravagant bow. Instantly Lord Fagan steps forward too, eager to assert himself. "Ambassador Dorn, a pleasure to see you again. Welcome to Aleti."

The Ambassador nods, "Thank you Lord Fagan, I am glad to be here and to be agreeing this deal with Aleti."

Lord Fagan nods, "Shall we proceed to the Throne chamber and presentation?"

On his words everyone turns to re-enter the castle. My father and the Ambassador lead, closely followed by Lord Fagan. I fall into step behind him as do the Lords behind me. We file into the long narrow chamber reserved for ceremonial activities such as this. My father takes his seat on his raised throne and the ambassador takes his place to my father's left. Lord Fagan stands to his right whilst I seat myself on my own throne on the step below. We wait patiently for all of the Lords to file in afterwards and take their places on the lower chairs. It takes several minutes as it seems that every Lord in the country has travelled to the capital to be here for today. Finally everyone is seated and my father stands to begin the formal declaration.

"Lords of Aleti. I have gathered you here to declare my intent to enter into an alliance with the Kingdom of Navas. Today marks the beginning of formal negotiations and I hope the beginning of a friendship that will benefit both our countries for generations to come. If there is anybody present who believes my intent not to be true speak now."

There is an awkward pause as my father waits for any objections to his declaration. This is merely a part of the process, part of a written script that must be followed. No one ever does actually question the King's intent, although the question is always asked. For a moment I have an overwhelming urge to stand up and declare that I do not believe the intent of Navas to be true. But I am not a Lord and I am not allowed to speak. I hold my tongue.

"Then all Lords are in favor of my intent and the alliance shall proceed."

My father returns to his seat and Ambassador Dorn steps forward, gesturing to the back of the room. A younger Navasian man who I saw exit the carriage behind Ambassador Dorn earlier begins making his way up the central aisle carrying a large scroll before him.

"Your majesty, I present to you the proposed treaty documents for your approval."

My father nods and a guard steps forward to accept the scroll.

Lord Fagan once more takes over proceedings, announcing that the welcome ceremony and treaty presentation are complete. With the formal ceremonies done, the atmosphere relaxes and conversation flows more easily.

"Ambassador Dorn may I introduce you to my son Joseph Fagan."

"Ah yes, young Joseph, I have heard much about you from your father. You have a bright future ahead of you."

"Thank you sir" Joseph replies, bowing so low I think he might topple over.

Turning back to my father the Ambassador says, "You have a most beautiful country your majesty. I could not help but admire the landscape as we drove through it on our way here. Is the whole nation as beautiful as the south?"

My father beams with pride, "Indeed we are blessed with the most handsome countryside throughout the land although I would agree the south is the most pleasing."

Joseph adds, "The mountains to the north are also stunning. It is a shame you will not get the chance to see them, what with your visit being so short."

"Yes, a great shame but King James is most anxiously awaiting your visit to ratify our agreement."

I can't help but chip in, "A pity that King James could not travel to Aleti himself if he is so eager to complete the deal. Then it would save my father the bother of travelling so far to Mata himself."

The Ambassador glances at me in surprise at my boldness. Lord Fagan quickly steps in front of me with a laugh, "The Princess is quite the joker. Shall we proceed to the Great Hall for lunch Ambassador, I'm sure you must be quite famished after your journey."

As I move to follow them Joseph grabs my arm tightly and growls in my ear, "Comments like that will not be tolerated by my father. Play your part." Then he lets go and strolls past as though nothing has happened. I give my arm a rub before proceeding down the corridor to the immaculately presented Great Hall.

A huge table spans the full length to allow for all the Lords and Navasian guests to be seated. Flowers and candles form a central line and plates piled high with bread are already placed every few metres. Gold plates and cutlery indicate each place, though I notice that the Lords at the far end of the table have been given silver tableware, clearly we don't possess enough gold ones for the sheer number of people in attendance. My father's elaborate high backed chair is situated at the head of the table with the ambassador and Lord Fagan either side of him. I have been relegated to the position next to the ambassador and opposite Joseph. I am pleased to see that the Lord to my other side is none other than Lord Culton, the only member of the council who even attempted to question Lord

Fagan about the Navas deal. Perhaps I will get the opportunity to speak with him further. I could do with an ally. Once my father has taken his seat everyone else quickly finds their place and the waiters step forward to pour the wine. A fanfare announces the arrival of dinner as hundreds of dishes are brought in and placed before us. I have to admit it smells incredible, but then instantly my thoughts turn to the beggars I saw on the streets, and my mood sombers. We all wait for my father to be served and then everyone begins to tuck in like eager vultures. The amount and variety of food is almost overwhelming, some of which I've never seen before. Not wanting to miss out I reach for a small portion of everything I can see. Lord Culton beside me does the same and we share a small smile. Lord Fagan, my father and the ambassador are already engaged in conversation so I decide to take the opportunity. Leaning towards Lord Culton and lowering my voice, "Lord Culton, have you had time to look at the Navas deal in more detail. I would be interested to hear your thoughts."

The effect is instantaneous. His smile drops and he leans away. A cold mask falls into place and he says, "I'm sure Lord Fagan has got everything covered."

I look at him in surprise but then I see the look of almost panic in his eyes as he stares at me and then glances at Lord Fagan. Slowly I nod. Lord Fagan has got to him. I don't know what he said, threatened probably, but Lord Culton has been brought to Lord Fagan's side. I shake my head and turn away. For a moment gritting my teeth in anger. What a coward. Is everyone too afraid to stand up to Lord Fagan?

It's hard to enjoy the food so much after that. My head is full of depressing thoughts. How on earth can I take on Lord Fagan all alone? I pick at the delicious food in silence for most of the meal. The hall is a buzz with conversation and the more the wine flows the louder it becomes. Suddenly I hear my name being mentioned to my left and glance up.

"Such a shame you had no male heirs" the ambassador is saying. A comment which I can tell annoys my father though he doesn't say it. A sole living princess has always been a sore spot for my father who dreamed of having sons. "Still," the ambassador continues, "the future of Aleti is secured. They'll make a fine couple I'm sure."

Fine couple? Is he talking about me? Judging from the satisfying smile on Lord Fagan's face he's talking about me and Joseph. Why do I feel like everyone has suddenly decided that Joseph and I are inevitable. I feel like a decision has been made but I am in the dark. Next time I speak with my father I need to make my feelings absolutely clear. Lord Fagan may be in charge of a lot of things but he is not in charge of me. Surely I will have some say in my choice of future husband.

The dinner lasts for almost three hours. Each time I think it's finally going to end, another course is brought out. I seriously didn't know this much food existed in the city. I can't possibly eat any more. That doesn't stop those around me from diving on the cakes and pastries like starving hyenas, as though they haven't just eaten a ridiculous amount already. I can't help but wonder what happens to the food that doesn't get eaten. I must find out. If there is spare then perhaps I can arrange for it to be distributed to those who need it in the city. Eventually the continuous arrival of dishes stops and my father rises from his chair, signalling the end of the banquet. My father nods to Lord Fagan and Ambassador Dorn whilst everyone else simultaneously stands and bows as he takes his exit through his private door.

After my father leaves the rest of the lords begin to disperse too. Lord Fagan pulls the ambassador to one side where they have what looks like an intense whispered conversation. Joseph hovers nearby and at a nod from his father steps forward. "Ambassador Dorn, it would be my pleasure to give you a private tour of the palace if it pleases you."

"Well that sounds delightful." The ambassador says. Lord Fagan claps the ambassador on the back with a smile before giving me a meaningful look. Giving a deep sigh I approach Joseph and the ambassador, who looks up in surprise. "Will you be joining us princess?"

"Yes, I thought I would if that is alright, unless you would prefer to just tour with Joseph." I say in a desperate attempt to get out of it but the ambassador replies, "Not at all. Please lead the way."

We exit the great hall and make our way down the corridor to the throne room whilst Joseph starts giving the ambassador a history lesson about the castle. Joseph seems to be taking the role very seriously, probably on the orders of his father. From the way he drones on he sounds like he has been given a script to memorise and he is delivering it word for word. He points out details in the throne room that I've never even noticed before such as the carved angels above the fireplace and the gold embroidery on the drapes. As we leave the throne room he launches into a speech about Aleti's vineyards and is describing various Aleti wines in alarming detail, despite the fact that I know he doesn't even like wine. I can't help but roll my eyes as I follow after them.

"Joseph my boy," the Ambassador says putting his arm around Joseph's shoulder as they walk, "I'm very much looking forward to developing our future relationship now that our countries are set to become partners."

"Absolutely" Joseph replies like an eager puppy.

"I would be interested to discuss your thoughts on the future expansion of Aleti's army."

Joseph nods thoughtfully, "Absolutely, although I believe our primary focus should be on improvements to our navy. I would be keen to see how we can work with Navas's navy in securing the western waters. I understand you've recently commissioned a new type of battleship."

"Yes, although plans are in the early development stage and at this point are confidential you understand? Our nations may be considered friends now but we can't be sharing all our secrets." He laughs.

Unable to hold my tongue any longer I interrupt their conversation, "Mr Ambassador, forgive me, but I'm not sure why your questions seem to be directed at Joseph. As heir to the Aleti throne I believe I might have something to say about my country's future."

"Yes but I'm sure that once you are married and start a family, Joseph's role will become more substantial."

"And why is that? Family or not I will be the Queen of Aleti."

"Of course, of course, that title is yours by right but to be frank dear a woman's place is not to rule. Your strengths are far more suited to raising an heir, securing a strong and stable future for Aleti beyond yourself. Best to leave the actual governing of the country to men with the mind to do it."

Joseph pipes up again, "Absolutely Ambassador Dorn. I am my father's son after all and have had all the schooling necessary to prepare me for my future. And of course I will work to ensure that the bond between Aleti and Navas is even stronger and more prosperous than ever."

I stare after both men in shock as they begin to stroll away continuing their conversation, once again totalling dismissing me. Because I am a woman, evidently without a mind, who is good for nothing but having baby heirs apparently. I take a deep breath to try and calm myself but can still feel my blood boiling at the Ambassador's comments. Gritting my teeth I follow after them.

I reach the portrait gallery to find the pair of them stood admiring a painting of my great-great-great grandfather, King Philamus.

Joseph is clearly in the midst of telling the Ambassador the tale of the Battle at LeForth, "...complete bloodbath but King Philamus endured against all odds. His tactic of drawing the enemy down onto the left side of the river, opening them up to an arrow attack from the east, was what proved pivotal in our victory."

Stepping forward I interject, "Of course the battle would have been lost were it not for Queen Heta. She was the one to come up with the plan with the arrowmen. Otherwise the Aleti army would surely have been overrun."

Ambassador Dorn seems surprised by this fact but Joseph glares at me and states, "There is no evidence of that."

"King Philamus himself credited his wife the Queen with the victory. I don't think you can really argue with a man who was actually there."

There is a moment of awkward silence before I decide to continue. "And over here Ambassador, is Queen Shofia. Her husband died less than a year into her reign. She refused to marry again and so ruled the country entirely independently for the next 47 years. It was a great time in our country's history where our economy boomed and peace flourished. Many advancements were made during her reign due to her passionate support for industry, and she was very popular with the people because she introduced a number of welfare reforms aimed at supporting the less fortunate. An inspirational woman wouldn't you say?"

Both men stare at me. "I have recently become aware of the true plight of those outside the castle walls and I hope to follow her legacy when I am Queen. I intend to rid the city folk of the criminals who are suppressing them and plan to work on a future that is of benefit to all who live in Aleti, not just the rich. A worthwhile cause don't you think?"

I don't give them a chance to answer, instead turning to inspect the next painting. "Ah Queen Freya, married to King Edvald, who was quite mad of course, although that is not common knowledge. Most assumed that it was King Edvald conducting the council meetings but he was quite incapable so Queen Freya stepped up in his place. Remarkable woman. To do so much good and accept no credit, instead giving it all to your husband who barely left his bedchamber."

I move further down the hall, gesturing for the men to follow me, "Oh and look Ambassador, down here you can see Queen..."

"Please forgive me Princess Elisa, your grasp of Aleti history is incredible and I'm sure you have many more fascinating stories of your ancestors, but I'm afraid I have some work to attend to and really must return to my room. I thank you graciously for the tour."

"Oh well if you are sure Ambassador. Perhaps we can continue another day. You really must hear about the three Jennet Queens, sisters you know, who ruled together and..."

"Yes yes quite, perhaps another time." The Ambassador says quickly whilst simultaneously bowing and walking backwards away to escape. "Until this evening your majesty."

A small laugh escapes my lips as the Ambassador makes for the exit. Turning back Joseph is glaring at me once more but I smile sweetly and ask, "Do you want to hear more about the incredible independent Queens in Aleti's past Joseph?"

"What the hell do you think you're playing at?"

"Nothing" I say with a slight smirk.

"How dare you embarrass and upstage me in front of the Ambassador like that? And if you think for one moment that your story is going to turn out like any of these so called incredible past Queens you are sadly mistaken. So long as my father is around you will never truly rule this country, and all your dreams and wishes to help the poor will be nothing but dust."

I look Joseph straight in the eye as I say, "So long as your father is around."

Joseph's palm twitches and for one shocking second I think he's going to hit me but instead he turns on his heel and storms out. Letting out a breath I didn't even realise I was holding, I glance back up at Queen Freya's portrait and smile. I think I won that round.

# Chapter 11

W hen I return to my room I am once again greeted by Crella and Johnathon who immediately set to work on transforming me for the ball. 60 minutes later and with a new dress, tiara, make-up and hair style, I find myself leaving my room once more.

I enter the ballroom from the upper balcony and have to admit that I'm impressed. This is by far the most elaborate ball the castle has thrown, at least as long as I've been alive. It's clear that no expense has been spared. Every inch of the large hall has been decorated. Extravagant flower arrangements line the room and footmen stand every few metres with trays full of champagne. Silver chandeliers filled with burning bright candles illuminate the festivities and an orchestra plays from the balcony opposite.

As I make my way to the top of the grand staircase and wait to be announced Joseph sidles up to me. "You're looking delightful. Although it wouldn't kill you to smile. This is supposed to be a celebration."

"And what exactly are we celebrating?"

"My father's success of course, and Aleti's bright future."

"If you say so." I shrug. I'm not in the mood to engage with Joseph right now.

"Shall I escort you to the ball?" He says holding out his arm.

"No, I can escort myself." I say turning away. But suddenly Joseph grabs my arm and drags me back. Digging his nails deep into my arm he pulls me close and hisses into my face, "You ungrateful little bitch. You won't be above me in rank for much longer and I won't forget what an arrogant stuck up cow you're being. Any girl in the country would kill to be escorted by me."

"Then go and torment one of them" I say, pulling my arm free and getting away from Joseph as fast as I can. Glancing down at my arm I can see the marks and some blood where his nails dug into my flesh. I head to the bathroom to clean up the blood and regain my composure. I must find my father. Surely if I show him this he won't make me marry the brute. The more time I spend with Joseph the more I see his father in him and truth be told that scares me. There's a look in both of their eyes that says they would do anything to get to the top and no one should get in their way. And that's exactly what I'm doing, getting in their way.

Searching the ballroom is not an easy task. Every Lord and Lady and dignitary in the country is here. Every two steps I'm greeted by someone who I've never met before but who seems desperate to meet me. I nod and smile and greet them all, but then move on as quickly as possible. Circling around the edge of the room to try and avoid further introductions, I still can't see my father, or Lord Fagan for that matter. Suddenly I feel a cold breeze on the back of my neck and a whisper in my ear. "You need to dance with Joseph. It's expected."

"Lord Fagan, I'm afraid I'm not feeling well enough to dance, I'm still recovering from yesterday you understand. Have you seen my father?"

"Your father is extremely busy. You're not to disturb him. If you are unable to dance then you can keep the guests entertained with your charming conversation." He gives me a false smile and then walks sharply away, weaving through the crowd. I watch him exit the ballroom and am just about to continue my search for my father when I notice Ambassador Dorn slipping out the same exit. My curiosity instantly awakens and before I can think better of it I follow after them.

As I sneak into the corridor I'm just in time to see Ambassador Dorn turning the corner. Tiptoeing after him I peak around the wall edge but the corridor beyond is empty. Quickly moving further I race to the end of this hallway but still can't see either the Ambassador or Lord Fagan. Annoyed with myself for losing him, I turn to go back to the ballroom when I hear Lord Fagan's voice drifting out of the open door from a room on the left. Silently I creep closer.

"...shouldn't be a problem. The deal has been through the first council reading without objections."

"That's not what I heard, didn't the Princess raise some concerns?"

"The Princess is a sixteen year old girl. She spoke up but was swiftly dealt with, I can assure you."

"So long as there won't be any more issues. We don't want people looking into the agreement too closely do we?"

"I'll take care of it, and the second payment will come once the agreement has been signed?"

"Yes, as agreed, the King is pleased with your work."

"Excellent. I look forward to our future working together."

Sensing their conversation is coming to an end I quickly try to duck away. I shoot across the corridor and hide in the nearest open room. After hearing their footsteps echo away I wait a few more moments before slipping back out and setting off to return to the ballroom. But as I round the corner I see Lord Fagan. Although my steps falter I continue on my path trying to pretend like I have every right to be in this corridor at this particular time. Lord Fagan's eyes narrow at me as I approach but I keep my head up and avoid eye contact. Just as I think he's going to let me pass without saying anything he grabs my arm and digs his nails in, in exactly the same way that Joseph did not so long ago.

"What are you doing here?"

"Just getting some air. I'm heading back to the ball now" I try to say as calmly as possible.

He glances back the way I came before turning to me again. Slowly Lord Fagan backs me up against the wall, "Someone might start to think you're becoming a problem. You're not going to become a problem, are you Princess?"

When I don't answer he gives me a smile and then turns and walks away, but not before giving me one last warning, "Don't test me."

As he rounds the corner I breathe out a sigh of relief. Now I really need to find my father. I'm even more certain that Lord Fagan and the Ambassador are up to something, and whatever it is, is not good for Aleti.

Re-entering the ballroom, the dancing is in full flow and judging from the conversational hum most people are starting to feel the effects of the champagne. Luckily I almost immediately hear my father's booming voice above the din. I follow the sound to the sight of him surrounded by Lords and Ladies. I head over and interrupt the group with a deep curtsy and polite greeting. "Good Evening Father. I'm sorry to disturb you but I have an urgent matter to discuss with you if you please."

My father is shaking his head and waving his hand dismissively before I've even reached the end of my sentence. "Can't it wait girl. This is a party. I think we need more Champagne."

I try again, "Father, I'm afraid I must insist..."

"Ah there is Lord Fagan" My father says and starts to walk away. Not knowing what else to do I grab my father's arm and drag him into an alcove.

"What on earth do you think you are doing?" Father hisses, glancing around to see if anyone saw me literally pulling him away.

"Father please, I'm sorry, I really am, but this is important. The future of our country could depend on you listening to what I have to say."

My father finally seems to hear what I'm saying and stops looking around. Fixing his eyes on me and actually seeing me. "Please." I beg. "Hear me out."

"Alright, but not here, not now. I can't leave the ball, it would be an insult to Ambassador Dorn. I'm in meetings all day tomorrow but we can meet after dinner and then we can discuss whatever it is that's so urgent, ok?"

"Ok" I breathe a sigh of relief that I'll finally have my chance to talk to him, "Thank you. Just promise me one thing father. Don't agree anything with Ambassador Dorn until after we've spoken. Don't sign anything ok? Please. And don't tell Lord Fagan about this, trust me. I swear to you, you'll want to hear what I've found out."

My father stares at me in confusion, like he doesn't know who I am, but he gives me a nod before turning back to the ball. I watch as he re-enters the room and is instantly surrounded by Lords once more.

"It's rude to stare." I jump out of my skin and spin around only to find Joseph stood so close to me I have to take a step back.

"It's also rude to sneak up on people." I shoot back.

Joseph grins, "If we're going to be married you're going to have to get used to me being around."

"Well I don't want to get used to it. Go and be an asshole else-where."

"An asshole?" he laughs. "I'd watch your mouth if I were you. Once we're married and I am King, you're going to want to be nice to me. It would be terrible if something were to happen to you leaving me to rule on my own."

"Are you threatening me?" I stare at him incredulously.

Joseph pretends to be shocked at my question, "Threatening you? Of course not. Why would I threaten you dear future wife. I'm just saying, accidents can happen." He winks and then walks away with a swagger so pronounced it makes me want to vomit.

I can't handle returning to the ball after that. I know Lord Fagan will be furious at my absence but I don't care. I slip away to my room, avoiding everyone, and lock the doors securely behind me before climbing into bed early. Tomorrow I have the meeting with my father that I've so desperately been waiting for and I can finally try and change the dangerous path that my country is on.

# Chapter 12

The following day I don't even try to hide my visit to the city. I even go so far as to tell Diane, my lady's maid, that I'm going. She tries to stop me of course but I ignore her protests. When she reaches the gates she tries to get the guards to intervene, insisting that they at least escort me, but I disappear into the crowd so fast they can't keep up. I take a winding route, deliberately doubling back on myself several times and avoiding the route to the square, just in case anyone is following me. When I'm sure the coast is clear I get to the Gallavanties square as fast as possible. Just stepping into the familiar square feels like coming home. I immediately head over to the Gallavanties' set up in the corner, although I can only see Pepe and Sam around. When Sam sees me I give a wave but he simply gets up and goes into one of the caravans. I frown. He really doesn't like me and I really don't know why. I'm cheered up though when Pepe spots me and comes over with a smile. "Alright there Princess? Nice to see you again."

"Princess? I'm not a Princess." I say panicked. Does he know who I am? How did he figure it out?

But Pepe just laughs, "I know. It's a figure of speech. Guess you're not allowed to joke about Princesses up in the castle in case the actual Princess is around and gets offended right?"

"Oh right, yeah" I say, trying to laugh it off and hide my initial reaction, hoping Pepe didn't read too much into it.

"Risa isn't here right now. Her and Luis have gone off for the morning but you can hang with me if you want. I'm off to check on the three other members of the Gallavanties if you wanna join."

"Three other members? I didn't know there were more of you. How come they're not here?"

"They're not in the show and they prefer larger lodgings than we can provide in the city." He says as I fall into step beside him.

"What are their names? How come I've never heard you mention them before?"

"Whisper, Storm and Rain."

Pepe gives a booming laugh at the confused expression on my face, "Horses, they're three horses. We're going to the stables."

"Oh" I say, feeling like a complete idiot.

"How did you think we travelled? Did you think we pulled the caravans ourselves?" He continues to laugh.

"I guess I didn't really think about it. I love horses though."

"Ah they're beauts too. 'Specially Storm, he's mine and he's gorgeous." Pepe says with a look of such devotion on his face.

"I can't wait to meet him."

We walk in comfortable silence for a few minutes, enjoying the sunshine as we stroll through the city, until I break it, "Pepe, can I ask you something?"

Pepe looks at me with his trademark one eyebrow raise, "Go on then."

"If you wanted to improve things for the people of Carrard, for the people of Aleti generally, how would someone do that? What would you do? What would you change first?"

Pepe gives a wry laugh, "Well that's a mighty big question. Not sure there's an easy answer to that. I guess I would ask the people. You can't please everybody o'course but if you wanna know what the people want and how to fix it, seems to me the best place to start would be by talking to them."

I nod. That makes sense. Molly said that before the curfew people were gathering in groups and talking about changing things. They must have had ideas of what they wanted to do. I start to think about how to possibly pitch the idea of people' forums, and giving ordinary folk a voice in the castle, but again I come up against the same stumbling block. Lord Fagan.

Finally reaching the stables Pepe walks straight over to a large black stallion and starts stroking his nose and cooing, "Well hey there boy. How you doing today? You good? I missed you." The horse, which I presume is Storm, starts snuffling at Pepe's jacket causing him to laugh. "Yeah yeah alright. You're all about the treats ain't you? No love for me until I pay up" he says as he draws an apple from his pocket and gives it to the impatient horse. "There you go boy, happy now? Look Storm, brought a friend to meet you." He gestures me over and Storm turns his head to greet me. Stroking his nose and neck I can't help but agree with Pepe, "You're right. He is gorgeous."

Pepe smiles, "Seems like he likes you. He's not always so great with strangers. I always trust Storm's instincts. You must be a good egg."

I smile back, "So you gonna introduce me to Whisper and Rain?"

"Yeah come on then." Pepe gives Storm one last pat and leads me over to a brown mare and grey stallion in the next stalls.

As I greet each of them in turn a skinny man with ginger hair comes over to speak with Pepe. Pepe starts asking about the horses' welfare and the man who clearly runs the stable answers his questions. I tune out most of their conversation, too busy fussing over the horses, but when I hear the word Navas mentioned I tune back in.

"I dunno man, just rumours I've heard. Certainly noticed a lot more Navasians around of late. You've not heard anything on your travels? I figured a guy like you might've heard something."

"No, can't say I've heard anything."

"Alright, worth an ask. You hear anything in the next few days you let me know alright. A lot of people on edge about it. Anyway, your boys and gal are all good and should be ready for Monday no worries."

"Ta. I'd better get going. I'll see ya tomorrow Finn." Pepe shakes the man's hand and turns back to me. "You ready to head?"

"Yeah" I say, giving Storm, Whisper and Rain all a kiss on the nose and then following Pepe back onto the street.

Running to catch up, I ask, "What was that guy saying?"

"Finn? Not sure. Something about Navas. Rumours going around the city that a trade deal is being agreed with Navas. A lot of people just wondering what it means. Most people rely on trade with Cobback so guess folk are just trying to work out if this deal with Navas is gonna be good or bad for them." Pepe gives me an inquiring look, "You know anything about it? You must hear more about this sort of thing up at the castle."

Suddenly my throat goes dry and I struggle to swallow. I don't know how to answer but I don't want to lie to Pepe either. "I've heard stuff. Not good stuff. I don't think the deal is a good one for the Aleti people."

Pepe raises an eyebrow, "Really? Why are we doing it then?"

"That's a good question." I answer, "A really good question."

Pepe nods his head thoughtfully but then turns and continues walking. We return to the square in thoughtful silence, both lost in our own thoughts.

When we arrive back Pepe gives me a small smile and then disappears into his caravan.

I see Luis has returned and is stood with a clipboard surrounded by a pile of boxes, "Hey, what are you doing?"

"Hey" he smiles. "I'm just doing an inventory of supplies. Making sure we've got everything." That's right. The Galavanties are preparing for their next journey. They leave the day after next and I'm already dreading the moment I have to say goodbye.

"Risa's in the caravan if you're looking for her."

"Oh ok, thanks," I start to leave but then turn back, "Unless you need any help?"

"Really? That would actually be great. Usually Dav helps and it goes so much quicker with two people. I'll look through the boxes and you tick it off on the list." Luis says handing me the clipboard.

As we work I spot Kinken sat in a chair outside his caravan just watching everyone around the square.

"He doesn't speak much does he?"

"Who?" Luis questions looking up and following my gaze, "Kinken? Nah prefers to listen. When he does speak I've learnt it's worth paying mind to though. Cleverest guy I ever met him. Knows everything, reckon that's what comes from listening all the time. See him talking with Pepe sometimes, and Dav. They're an odd trio but thick as thieves. Been together a long time. Spose they know each other so well they probably don't need to talk much, sometimes I reckon they can read each other's thoughts." Luis laughs. "Best guys you'll ever meet though. Don't know where me n Risa would be without them."

I smile, "Risa told me how you and her ran away to be together, hiding in Pepe's caravan when they were leaving Andrent."

"Yeah, it wasn't the most thought out plan to be honest. Thought Pepe would kill us when he found us hiding there, but he didn't."

"Instead he took you in."

Luis nods, "Instead he took us in. Gave us jobs, and a home, and a family. No questions asked, just straight up offered." Luis shakes his head with a rueful smile, "Still can't believe how lucky we got sometimes."

"I keep thinking the same thing. How lucky I was to walk into this exact square at that exact moment Sam was starting the show. If I'd walked down a different street on a different day then I never would've met any of you."

"Maybe it ain't luck. Maybe it's what's meant to happen. Risa believes in all that stuff. Things happening for a reason."

"She does?"

"Yeah. Ya know she said you'd back. That first day, when you left, said you'd be back again. And she was right weren't she. Right fond of you she is, ya know? Cares about you a lot. You know she had me follow you, when you left straight after the show the other day to get back, she was worried and wanted me to make sure you were safe, make sure nothing happened to ya. Said it's like having a little sister she wants to look out for."

A warmth spreads through me at his words, "A sister?" I ask in wonderment. "She really thinks that? I've always wanted a sister."

Luis laughs, "So's she. See told ya. Meant to be!"

# Chapter 13

---

As Luis goes to load the boxes of supplies onto one of the caravans I spot a group of guards entering the square. Instantly I'm on high alert. Watching them carefully to ensure they're not heading in my direction I track their approach to several market stalls at the north end of the courtyard.

The guards pause in front of the fruit stall run by the Rivelli family. I've spoken with Peter Rivelli and his wife Susan a couple of times in visits to the square, they usually come over to watch the show, and they're nice people. The stall is their livelihood. I remember them talking about how tough it could be to make ends meet when they jokingly thanked the Gallavanties for setting up camp in this square and driving up trade for them over the last few days. I watch as one of the guards picks up several oranges and begins to try and juggle, performing for the others who cheer him on. When another guard tries to snatch one out of the air all of the oranges fall to the floor. The group simply laugh and kick them away. Grabbing several pieces of fruit each, they start to walk away when Peter's son Patrick tries to stop them. I can see from here that he is indicated the guards need to pay for the fruit, including the smashed oranges on the floor.

In the blink of an eye the soldier has drawn his sword and is holding it against Patrick's neck. Holding my breath I wait paralised. Surely he's not going to do anything in the middle of the market with everyone watching. For a tense moment everything is frozen but then Peter comes running out to intervene, pulling Patrick away. The guards laugh and walk away, eating their stolen fruit without a care in the world. Inside I'm seething and wish I could go over and reprimand the guards. Tell them who I am and demand they pay for the fruit they've just taken, but I know that I can't. Instead I add the incident to my mental list of things to discuss with my father. I watch as Peter sends Patrick back inside and then goes to pick up the now ruined oranges. Tomorrow I'll make sure I bring some extra coins with me and visit the Rivelli family to buy as much fruit as I can.

With the guards now gone, the square returns to its bustling self and I look around for something to do. Spotting Sam making further repairs to a piece of scenery I wander over.

"Can I help?"

Sam stares at me with a raised eyebrow, "You want to help?"

"Yeah why not?" I say feeling slightly offended by his hostility.

"Hand me that hacksaw then" he gestures. Turning around I see a table full of various tools and I have no idea which one is a hacksaw.

"Errr which one's the hacksaw?" I ask feeling stupid.

"Seriously?" he scoffs before pushing past me and picking up what is evidently the hacksaw.

"Sorry, I haven't really had much experience with tools before."

"Obviously not, why would you?" he mutters.

Ok now his attitude is starting to irritate me, "What is your problem? I'm only trying to help."

"Well I don't need your help so just go back to your castle and leave the rest of us alone."

"What's that supposed to mean?"

"You heard me. Some of us have to work hard for things in life, we don't get everything handed to us on a gold plate."

"You don't know anything about me or my life. Just because I live in the castle doesn't mean my life is some perfect fairytale."

"Yeah right. Your life must be so tough. Standing up there in your ivory tower judging everyone below you. You have no idea what life is really like down here in the real world."

Hurt by his clearly low opinion of me I can't help but snap back, "I'm not the one making judgements here. You took one look at me and decided you knew me. I didn't do that to you. I wanted to get to know you but I guess that was a stupid idea. Clearly I'm not good enough for you to talk to, I'm just a spoilt girl from the castle who isn't worth your time. I'm sorry for bothering you."

Turning on my heel I stomp away absolutely fuming. How dare he talk to me like that? How dare he say that I'm the one judging people? Maybe I have lived a spoiled life in the palace, and maybe I don't know what life is really like for most people, but I'm trying to alter that. I'm learning. I'm even attempting to talk to my father, to change things and make life better for the people, though not very successfully yet. I've been nothing but nice to Sam since the moment I met him. I just don't understand his hostility. The way he spoke wasn't just dislike, it was like he truly hates me.

As I repeat all of this to Risa, pacing backwards and forwards across the caravan in fury, she merely sits and listens, letting me get all my anger out of my system. "He doesn't hate you, he just doesn't know you yet. Sam's had a tough life. He's had to fight tooth and nail for everything and he doesn't trust people easily." A slow secretive smile then spreads across her face, "Truthfully I think he likes you and that's the real problem for him. He likes you but feels like he shouldn't. He's at war with himself."

"Likes me? Are you joking? Have you not heard a word of what I just said?"

She laughs, "I heard you."

A knock on the door interrupts our conversation as Luis sticks his head in, "Everything alright in here? I heard raised voices."

Taking a deep breath to calm myself I reply, "Everything's fine."

"Hhmmm" Luis doesn't seem convinced by my response, "So the fact that Sam's out here with a face like thunder, hacking away at a piece of wood doesn't have anything to do with anything."

Risa laughs while I try to maintain a somewhat dignified expression, "I don't know what his problem is, but whatever it is, it's his problem, not mine" and with that I turn, pick up a potato peeler and start peeling potatoes ready for dinner. I can sense a silent conversation going on between Luis and Risa behind me but I keep my back ramrod straight and focus all my attention on my task.

I spend the rest of the afternoon helping Risa and Luis whilst avoiding Sam at all costs. He appears to be doing the same so it works quite well. Eventually though I run out of things to do so decide the best option is just to head back to the castle. I have to attend dinner with the Ambassador and then comes my meeting with my father so I can't stay for the show anyway, and I should probably prepare exactly what it is I'm going to say. I hug Risa and Luis and ask them to say goodbye to Pepe, Dav and Kinken for me. "Not Sam?" asks Luis with a smile. I roll my eyes at him, "Sam doesn't deserve a goodbye."

Risa and Luis just laugh, clearly not taking me seriously although I was actually being quite serious. I'm still upset over Sam's words. I turn and head off with one final wave. Confidently strolling up to the castle gates I walk past the bemused guards and head straight for my room. Before I can reach them however I run into Lord Fagan. Why do I always seem to be running into Lord Fagan of late. Is he following me?

"Enjoy your walk?"

I try to ignore his question and step around him but he moves into my path. "Why the sudden interest in walks in the city? Where exactly is it that you go?"

I stare back with a passive expression, determined not to show him how much he scares me. He leans forward so close that his breath fans across my face, "Don't think I've forgotten you're interruptions in the council meeting. You need to learn your place Princess."

"And you need to learn yours" I declare before finally pushing past him and escaping once more to the safety of my room.

# Chapter 14

A knock at the door interrupts my pacing and Diane enters with Johnathon and Crella. She bustles over without saying a word, clearly still angry about my trip to the city this morning. Crella and Johnathon begin sifting through a selection of dresses which have been brought up and discussing hair styles. Diane comes and stands beside me without making eye contact. I think she might be waiting for me to say something but if she wants an apology she is not going to get one. Both of us stand watching the dress selection process letting the tension between us build. At the exact moment Diane turns to me and opens her mouth to speak Molly enters the room. Instantly I race over to her. "Molly, excellent I err need your help with something" I say as I practically drag her into my bedroom and shut the door. "Sorry, just needed to get away from Diane."

"Is everything alright?"

"Yes, well, I mean yes it is. It's just that I'm meeting with my father later and I'm going to talk to him about what's happening in the city, the curfew and the guard's brutality, and I'm just panicking that I'm going to mess it up. What should I say?"

"Oh Cara," Molly says, pulling me in for a hug. "You won't mess it up. Just the fact that you're trying is everything. Just speak from your heart."

Taking a deep breath I give Molly a small smile, "Thank you. I just feel this weight on my shoulders, like the fate of the entire city and country depends on me."

Molly shakes her head, "You'll do what you can, but it's not up to you to save the whole world."

"Oh" I suddenly remember, "Can you do something for me? I know I'm always asking for favours but this is the last time I promise." I rush to my trunk and dig to the bottom to find my purse. Pulling out a silk green coin bag filled with golden haltos I press it into Molly's hand. "On your way home tonight can you take this to the Rivellis."

"The Rivellis?"

"They're the family who own the fruit stall in the west square where the Gallavanties are."

"I know them," Molly nods.

"Great. Don't say who it's from, just tell them it's a gift."

"Ok"

"Thank you, you're the best," I say, hugging her just as the door opens and Diane enters. We spring apart but Diane clearly saw as she stares at us in surprise and horror.

Molly curtseys and squeezes past her to exit the room as quickly as she can.

Diane returns her gaze to me, "Care to explain? First walks in the city and now hugging the servants."

"I don't have to explain anything to you" I say brushing past her. Crella and Johnathon are both stood waiting and ready to prepare me for the dinner with the ambassador and my father. Once again

I'm styled up and dressed in another elaborate gown. Although the dinner is not the all out extravagance of yesterday's banquet, my father's private dining parlour has still been lavishly decorated. I enter the room just moments before Lord Fagan and Ambassador Dorn who are deep in whispered conversation, though they stop when they see me.

"Princess Elisa," the ambassador comes over and sweeps into a low bow whilst also taking and kissing my hand, "you are a vision of beauty."

"Thank you" I murmur, feeling slightly creeped out.

But then my father enters the room and the ambassador releases his hold on my hand to greet him. We take our seats and dinner is just about to be served when Joseph rushes in.

"A thousand apologies, your majesty, ambassador." He says bowing and out of breath. Lord Fagan stares daggers at his son as he takes his seat and Joseph sheepishly avoids his gaze. Instead he turns back to the king and ambassador and starts a conversation with them about the upcoming journey to Mata, the capital of Navas, where my father and King James of Navas will sign the agreed treaty. We are all supposed to leave the day after tomorrow.

Suddenly the Ambassador turns to include me in the conversation, "I heard you went out into the city today Princess Elisa?"

Lord Fagan freezes with his fork halfway to his mouth, waiting to see how I will answer.

"Yes, I did. I'm enjoying finding out about my city and its people. It's very interesting." I say looking rather pointedly back at Lord Fagan.

"Hmmm, not something a Princess should really be doing though is it? Mixing with the common folk."

I open my mouth to respond but Joseph jumps in, "I quite agree Ambassador. You certainly wouldn't catch me associating with the riff raff." I glare at Joseph across the table but he's too busy looking at the ambassador to notice. "Now I've heard Ambassador Dorn that you like to hunt? Rumour has it that you are rather talented with a bow and arrow." I roll my eyes at the clear attempt to change the conversation and over the top flattery from Joseph but no-one seems to notice.

The Ambassador chuckles, "Well I don't want to boast but it has been said."

Lord Fagan picks up the conversation again, "We must arrange for a hunt during our journey to Mata. The Forest of Talor has excellent game."

"That would be wonderful, my thanks Lord Fagan."

"Of course Ambassador, the king also enjoys a hunt. I'm sure it will be a pleasing diversion on the journey."

"Certainly" my father agrees, "Make sure it is arranged."

Lord Fagan nods as the ambassador and my father begin sharing hunting stories. The Ambassador doesn't try to talk to me again so I spend the rest of the dinner in silence, half listening to the conversation around me and half going over my speech in my mind. Finally the ambassador throws his napkin down on his plate and starts to rise, "If you will excuse me, it has been a busy day and I think I shall retire to my chambers now."

"Of course I shall escort you." says Lord Fagan, also standing.

The ambassador and Lord Fagan bow to my father before leaving the room together. Almost immediately my father also stands and makes to leave. Quickly I follow after him. "Father, you remember we are to meet now? I have important information I need to share with you. You said yesterday at the ball that now was the best time."

"Oh right yes, alright. Out with it then, what is it that's so urgent the fate of our nation depends on it." Firmly shutting the door to my father's private lounge behind me to ensure we are truly alone I begin my prepared speech.

"Well father it's really two things I need to discuss. The first is this agreement with Navas. I do not believe it is the best interest of our country to sign this deal. I've read the document thoroughly and I can't see any true benefits for us. The only benefits seem to be for Navas. The insistence that we give up fruit trade with Cobback will be a disaster for our economy and cause untold hardships for people who rely on that trade for their livelihoods. The costs of improvements to the southern road are placed squarely on us and not on Navas at all. Father I think..."

My father shakes his head, "Lord Fagan has personally written this agreement alongside the Ambassador and he is very complimentary about it. He thinks that an alliance with Navas is the right move for our future and with all his experience and knowledge I'm sure he knows better than you."

"But father have you read the deal? And I don't mean listened to Lord Fagan read it or seen summary notes I mean actually read it. The proper deal, all of it, even the small print? There are clauses in there which include giving up land if we fail to meet certain targets. There's even a sentence which suggests the King of Navas can have control of our army and navy if he so desires."

This news does cause my father to pause for a moment, "That must be a mistake, you must have misinterpreted it."

"Father, I haven't misinterpreted it. What's more, I've been watching Lord Fagan and Ambassador Dorn since his arrival and I think there is more to their relationship than they are letting on. I overheard a private chat between them in which I heard them mention money and the King of Navas and Lord Fagan's service to him. Father please listen, what if Lord Fagan is actually working for the benefit of Navas, what if they're paying him off?"

Now my father scoffs and turns away, "Now you really are being ridiculous Elisa. Lord Fagan has been a dedicated servant to the crown for over a decade. He's never put a foot wrong. To suggest he is a traitor is ludicrous."

"But father, that was the other thing I wanted to discuss with you. The way Lord Fagan is running the city. It's terrible. The city guards are bullies who steal and beat innocent people. Lord Fagan doesn't check their behaviour and the power has gone to their heads. There's a curfew in place for no good reason and the punishments for the smallest indiscretions are cruel. The punishments don't fit the crime. Torture, imprisonment, being sold into slavery, father how are you allowing this to happen?"

"Honestly Elisa, two visits into the city and you think you know everything. I've heard Lord Fagan's reports. Crime is rife and punishments must be harsh to keep people in line. It's the only thing these violent ignorant people understand and respond to."

"But that's a lie father. The city folk aren't all violent criminals. I've met them. They're ordinary people, they're innocent, they're kind and hardworking, talented and friendly. I'm not saying there aren't some bad people, there will always be some bad people in the world, but the majority aren't and they don't deserve to be treated so cruelly. Please father. These are our people. It's our duty and responsibility to do what's right for them. Perhaps if you were to go out into the city and see for yourself you would understand."

My father looks at me as though I've grown a second head, "Go out into the city? Are you insane?"

"Or they could come here. Not all of them of course. The city folk could choose some representatives and you could meet with them and just listen to what they have to say."

"Where on earth have you got these ridiculous notions from Elisa? Kings don't mix with the people. It's bad enough that you've been into the city twice, and don't think that'll be happening again by the way. Lord Fagan is Mayor of Carrard and Commander of the city guards, speak to him if you care about the people so much."

"But father please, you're not listening to me. Lord Fagan is..." but suddenly the door opens and Lord Fagan enters.

"Ah excellent," he says as he strolls in. "I assume you've shared the good news with the Princess."

"Lord Fagan this is a private meeting between my father and I."

Lord Fagan merely raises an eyebrow and looks to the king.

"Our discussion is over with Elisa." My father says firmly.

"But..."

"Now let us move on to far more pleasant topics. Your marriage." My father beams at me like he's said the most wonderful thing.

I stare at him in shock. Please no, please let this not be what I think it is. My father doesn't seem fazed by my horrified reaction and continues, "Tomorrow your engagement to Joseph Fagan will become official. We will make the announcement to show Ambassador Dorn and the King of Navas how stable and bright our future is. Although the wedding won't take place until you are eighteen of course."

I turn to look at Lord Fagan who gives me the most self-satisfying smile. How have things gone so drastically wrong? I came in here hoping to convince my father of Lord Fagan's duplicity and instead he has dismissed everything I've said, and I'm stood here listening to him tell me I'm to marry Joseph.

Trying to stay calm I turn back to my father and firmly say, "Father, I'm sorry but I cannot marry Joseph. I understand that it is what you want but I can't do it. I do not love Joseph. I don't even like him."

"Love? Don't be silly girl. Marriage isn't about love and I'm sure you'll grow to have some affection with him once you are married."

"No, I'm quite sure I won't." My father's expression goes from mildly annoyed to angry in a heartbeat and I know this is a battle I'm losing. Desperately I roll up my sleeve to show him the marks on my arm, "Look. He did this to me. Joseph did this to me, yesterday at the ball. He's violent and he threatened me, you don't know what he's really like. Please," I beg. Tears filling my eyes, I get down on my knees and clutch my father's hands in mine. "Please don't make me marry him. I am begging you father, if you love me at all. If you have even the smallest amount of affection for me, don't do this." For a moment I think I see it. Compassion, maybe even love. But then he looks up towards Lord Fagan and I see the emotional shutter go down again. His face returns to its usual cold impassive expression. He pulls his hands from mine and rises to stand next to Lord Fagan. "You're being ridiculous Elisa. This is over dramatic teenage non-sense. Joseph is a good boy and will make a fine husband. He is the son of the most respected man in the country. The announcement will be made at dinner tomorrow and I'll hear no more about it."

As I stare at my father standing beside Lord Fagan I know that there is nothing more that I can say or do. With a sob I flee the room. Tears streaming down my face I stumble along the corridor.

When I finally reach my room to find Joseph lounging on a sofa I nearly lose it, "Get out" I yell at him.

My outburst seems to take him by surprise. "What's wrong with you?"

"I said get out of my room. You have no right to be in here!"

"I was told to be here. My father said we need to run through the plans for the engagement announcement tomorrow."

"There's not going to be an announcement. I'm not getting engaged to you. Not tomorrow, not the next day, not next year, not ever. God I am so sick of people trying to dictate my life to me. Listen to me very carefully Joseph Fagan. I WILL NOT MARRY YOU. I hate you. You're just like your father. I think you're a horrible person and you'll be a horrible husband and a horrible king."

As he listens to my rant I can see his face growing red and his teeth gritting together, his hands curling into fists until he can contain his anger no longer and shouts back, "You have no choice. It's already agreed. It's been agreed since we were babies. Everyone knows it. I'm the future King and nothing you can say will stop it. Your father won't listen to you. The only person he listens to is my father. My father, commander of the city guards and royal household. My father, who's in charge of the treasury and Lord chancellor of the privy council. My father who controls everything inside and outside of this castle. My father who whispers in your father's ear and can get him to do anything he wants."

"I don't care what my father says. I won't do it. I won't allow you and your father to take over this kingdom and do to the rest of the country what you've already done to this city."

"You spoilt bitch." With a speed I didn't know he possessed, his arm swings and his fist meets my face with a resounding crunch, my head snapping backwards with the force. For a moment I'm stunned. Holding my face where my cheek is already beginning to swell, I hiss back at him, "I'll never marry you."

Instantly another punch comes my way, knocking me to the floor. Suddenly the door flies open and Lord Fagan enters the room. He takes one look at the scene and shuts the door firmly behind him, as I get to my feet.

Joseph immediately looks sheepish and starts to plead with his father, "Father, I had to. She's gone mad. She says she won't marry me. Tell her..."

"I heard what she said." he interrupts, "For God's sake Joseph use your brain, she's the princess. You can't just punch her in the face. Look at her eye. How are you going to cover that up? If you need to teach her a lesson then hit her where no one can see."

And with that Lord Fagan swiftly turns and punches me in the gut before I can react. I hear a crack as I go down and black spots dance before my eyes. Gasping for breath, it takes me a moment to recover enough to pull precious air into my lungs once more. I feel a trickle on the side of my face and when I reach up my fingers come away with blood on them. I realise I must have hit my head on the table. I try to stand but a sharp pain in my side stops me. Clutching my ribs with a groan I start to crawl towards the door.

"Oh no you don't. We can't have anyone asking questions about that face." Lord Fagan sneers as he grabs my ankle and sharply pulls me back. "Such a stupid girl. Why couldn't you just keep your mouth shut and do as you were told?" Striding over to the door he opens it and calls to the guards outside. The guard glances at me lying on the floor but snaps his attention back to Lord Fagan. "You lock this door and no-one except me goes in or out. You got it? Anyone asks, the princess is ill."

I stare at the guard helplessly. I'm the princess, surely he can't just ignore the state I'm in. He must realise what has happened. But the guard simply nods, "Yes sir." And without a backwards glance Lord Fagan and then his son stroll out the room. The guard closes the door and I hear the ominous sound of a key turning in the lock. For a moment I just stare at the shut door in bewilderment. I can't believe what's just happened.

# Chapter 15

S lowly I climb to my feet. My only thought escape. I can't stay here. Remembering the impassive look in the guard's eyes I know that there is no help there and no way out through the door. That only leaves the windows. Gingerly holding my arm across my throbbing ribs I walk out onto the balcony to assess my options. I have a large stone balcony which runs the entire length of my room. It's also incredibly high up. There's no way down. But maybe I don't need to go down.

Looking across I can see the balcony for the next room about 10 metres away.  If I can get across to that balcony then I can escape through the guest room, which I know is not in use at the moment. All the Lords are either being housed in the north wing or in the city. There's a small ledge that runs between the two balconies. It doesn't look that far. But then I look down at the sheer drop which awaits me should I slip. Suddenly it seems a lot further. I cast my gaze around again but I really can't find an alternative way out. I think about the guard again. Is there a way past him? But I know that he won't be alone and from the way he snapped to attention for Lord Fagan I can only assume that other guards will do the same. My choice is simple, I sit in my room and wait for either Joseph or Lord Fagan to return, or I get out of here. I don't want to sit and do nothing. Giving up feels like letting Lord Fagan win and I'm not about to let that happen.

I look at the gap between the balconies again. I could make it, I reason. I will make it. Glancing back at the locked door I climb up onto the balcony wall. Ignoring the pain in my side I swing my legs over and reach to get one foot on the ledge. Pausing, deep breath, there's nothing else for it. With a quick push I manage to get both feet onto the ledge and press myself into the wall. Trying desperately not to think about how high up I am, I begin to edge my way along. Inch by inch I make slow progress. The ledge is much narrower than I had first thought. I hardly dare to breathe for fear the movement will make me fall. Twice I almost lose my footing before I finally reach the other balcony. With both sweat and blood dripping down my face I grab onto the stone rail and haul myself over, collapsing onto the floor with relief.

The pain in my side has worsened and every breath is a struggle. Pulling myself up on shaky legs I stumble towards the balcony doors. I grab the handles and pull but nothing happens. Locked. I almost break down in tears of despair but I know I need to keep it together. I wasn't giving up now. Without thought I smash my elbow into the glass pane, shattering it. A sharp sting and more blood tells me I've cut myself but I don't stop to check. Reaching through the now broken pane I'm able to unlock the door and get into the empty room.

Knowing the royal guards are all under Lord Fagan's command has me on edge as soon as I step from the room into the corridor.

If any of them spot me then I'm done for. I manage to make it from one side of the left wing to the other, and down two flights of stairs without much difficulty. I've almost reached the ballroom without encountering anyone when I hear voices approaching. I dodge into an open doorway just in time to avoid Lord Fagan and my father. As they pass my hiding place I catch a snippet of their conversation.

"Sixteen year olds often go through a rebellious stage. I think some time alone will do her good. Her behaviour shouldn't be rewarded with trips abroad."

"As you suggest Lord Fagan, whatever you think is best."

"I'm sure by the time you return from your visit to Mata she will be much improved."

As they move further down the hallway I fail to hear my father's reply but I've heard enough. There's no doubt they were discussing me and it appears that Lord Fagan has explained my future absence from the tour to Navas easily enough, my father accepting whatever he says. Knowing this reinforces my decision to escape and I swiftly move on. Finally reaching the lower level, normally reserved for servants, I make my way to the kitchens. Moving as quietly as I can I sneak past the open doorway.

Turning the corner and spotting the exit I race down the corridor. But as I reach for the door handle, I notice the blood on my hand. Looking down at my clothes I'm shocked by the amount of red I see. There's no way I'm not going to be noticed if I go out onto the street looking like this. Glancing back up the corridor I recall a bunch of hooks on the wall filled with cloaks, presumably the kitchen staff's, which I've just run past. Hoping one of them won't mind too much I grab one and wrap it around myself. Lifting the hood to provide cover for my bloodied head, I slip out the door and into the courtyard. Pausing for a moment to allow a group of guards to disappear on the other side of the yard, I race across to the stable.

Heart pounding, I peer out towards the gate. Two guards are stood at the exit chatting. Looking around I wonder how I'm going to get them to move when the answer literally sticks it's head out of a stall. "Hey there old boy." Quietly opening the stable door I whisper reassurances to the large black stallion stamping his feet. Gently leading him out I check the guards are still in the same place and no one else is around. Then with a shout and sharp smack on his rump, I send the horse flying out the stable and into the open courtyard. Startled, the guards race to try and catch the spooked horse and I take my opportunity, slipping through the gates and out into the city. Keeping my head down, I take the now familiar path, not pausing for anything, until I reach the Gallavanties' square.

Looking up I see Sam sat on the front of the stage reading and a sense of relief flows through me. I made it. After the adrenaline rush of successfully escaping, the shock and loss of blood suddenly catches up with me and I start to sway on the spot. With my vision blurring I stumble over to him, "Sam, I need your help."

Sam glances up at me and then does a double take. Grimacing, I remove my hood to reveal the true extent of my injuries and Sam looks at me in horror, "Cara, what happened? Are you alright?"

Numbly I shake my head.

Jumping up from the stage, he gently puts his arm around my shoulders and leads me backstage, calling as he does so, "Pepe, Risa."

Seconds later they both appear along with Luis, Dav and Kinken. They all take one look at me and their horrified expressions are enough for me to know that I'm in a bad way.

With a sob I run into Risa's arms and before I can stop myself I'm hysterically crying on to her shoulder. Stroking my hair she murmurs reassurances into my ear, "Shhhh, it's alright sweetheart, you're ok. You're safe now, I've got you. It's alright, it's alright." She says the words over and over again until finally the shaking and tears begin to subside. Gulping in deep breathes in an effort to calm down I wince as the sharp pain in my side stabs again. Without a word she leads me into her caravan and gently sits me down on the small sofa. First she inspects my face. I can still feel the blood oozing down the right side of my face, though not as fast as it was. My left eye is already swollen shut and as she tenderly feels along my cheekbone I can't help but let out a groan. Pursing her lips she mutters "just bruised I think, and this cut is going to need stitches. Let me see your ribs," she instructs as she carefully helps me to lift my shirt. A hiss escapes her mouth as she views the damage done by Lord Fagan, a large purple patch covering most of my left side. She repeats her careful examination here too and I try to let her but the pain is excruciating. "Some bruised ribs too I think, not broken which is good."

"Who the hell did this to you?" asks Sam, a furious look in his eye as he stares at my battered ribs.

Risa sighs "I told you it wasn't safe to explore the city on your own."

"You tell me who it was kid and I'll deal with them." adds Dav looking deadly.

I shake my head. "It happened in the palace. There's nothing you can do."

"In the palace?" Sam asks with surprise.

I nod. My response doesn't affect the murderous glint in Dav's eye. Noticing the blood on my arm, Risa peels back my sleeve to look at my elbow, "more stitches" is her assessment.

Pepe is seething, "I'm gonna kill this bastard."

"Actually that one was me." I admit.

Pepe raises a single eyebrow in question.

"I had to break a window to escape," I explain.

Dav steps forward and kneels to look into my eyes, or atleast the one eye which isn't swollen shut, "I don't care where it happened or who this guy is. Just give me his name sweetheart and he'll pay."

I shake my head, "You don't understand. The man who did this, he's a very powerful man with a very powerful father. I didn't realise how powerful until now. He controls all the city guards, all the royal guards, he even controls the king. There's nothing you can do." The overwhelming truth of this hits me and tears begin to fill my eyes.

Then Sam says the most ridiculous thing, "Then leave. Come with us."

I almost laugh at the absurdity of his suggestion, "I can't. I can't just leave. They'll never let me just leave."

"Of course you can. You already left. You don't have to go back. You don't have to do anything you don't want to do. It's your life, it's your choice."

His statement, said so passionately and matter of factly, shocks me into silence. I glance around at the rest of the group who are all staring at me with worry etched on their faces. Kinken gives me a small nod.

"I think that's the first time anyone's ever said that to me" I reply and as I stare into Sam's earnest eyes I believe him. This is my life. This is my choice. I don't have to marry Joseph. I don't have to go back. I can choose, and looking around at the Gallavanties, these people who have come to mean so much to me in so little time, there really is no choice to be made. "Please" whispers Risa. That single word tips me over the edge. Slowly I give a small nod, "Ok."

# Chapter 16

Awareness slowly returns as I feel someone gently stroking my forehead. The soothing motion is comforting and makes me smile. Opening my bleary eyes with a groan I'm surprised it's Sam's concerned face which greets me, not Risa's. Instantly the stroking stops though Sam's hand still rests on the side of my face. For a moment we just look at each other. Then Sam seems to realise where his hand is and quickly draws it away, leaning back with an embarrassed cough. "How are you feeling?"

"Everywhere hurts," is my quiet response.

Sam nods, "Your eye looks a little better at least. And the stitches in your head are still in place. Here, have some water." He says as he lifts a glass to my lips. I take a small sip without taking my eyes off Sam's. It's so strange that he is the one here taking care of me. He seems nervous, nibbling his lip, "Can I get you anything else?"

I shake my head then wince as pain shoots through my head.

"I'll get Risa, she'll want to know that you're awake."

Sam rises and leaves the caravan giving me time to reassess the damage done yesterday. Lifting my shirt to look at my ribs I see only the same purple patch from last night. So long as I only take shallow breaths the pain isn't too bad. Manageable at least. My elbow hurts when I bend it but the cut here turned out not to be as deep as first feared. The worst injuries seem to be concentrated on my head which throbs incessantly. Gently prodding at my face I sense the swelling has gone down, though I still can't open my left eye fully. As I tenderly feel the stitches along my hairline the caravan door opens and Risa comes in, a relieved look on her face.

"Oh Cara, you had us worried there," she says as she takes Sam's place on the wooden stool beside me.

"How long have I been out for?"

"It's 4 o'clock in the afternoon, you've been unconscious a good 20 hours."

"20 hours?" I say in alarm. "That long? What happened? Is everything ok? Has there been any word from the castle? Has anyone come looking for me?" I panic.

"It's alright," Risa tries to soothe, "This sometimes happens with head injuries. After everything you went through your body just needed some recovery time. And there's not been anything unusual up at the castle. Pepe, Kinken and Dav all went up there this morning, chatting to the guards and stable boys to see if there were any rumours about a missing girl. Seems there is a lot going on at the palace at the moment with visitors from all over, so one young girl not where she should be might not be so noticeable. In any case they heard nothing so I think you're undiscovered so far at least. With luck we'll get you away before those evil men who did this realise you're gone and come searching for you. Now my dear, let me get you some broth. You haven't eaten and you'll need to keep your strength up if you're to heal properly." Risa says as she bustles over to the kitchen.

Something doesn't feel right. It seems strange to think that I've been gone for that long and no one is looking for me. When I think back to that first time I ran away the guards came searching after a couple of hours. But then remembering the events of last night I recall the conversation I overheard between Lord Fagan and my father, it was clear that Lord Fagan was readying excuses for my disappearance. Telling the guards to spread rumours about my being ill and telling my father that I needed time alone, to be punished for my behaviour. If the guards had done their jobs and not let anyone enter my room then the only people who would discover I was not in my room would be Joseph or Lord Fagan. Would they want to raise the alarm, to tell people that I'm missing? Would they want people to find me given the state they left me in? Perhaps not. Which means they can't send the guards out in dramatic fashion like they did before. It would alert the whole castle. They might still be looking for me but discreetly. That could only be of benefit to me.

Risa comes over with a warmed bowl of soup and settles onto the stool once more. She patiently helps me to sit up and then spoons me each mouthful. I feel like I'm a small child again but it's nice being fussed over by someone so caring. A creak signals the opening of the caravan door. Luis and Pepe enter and both smile when they see me sitting up and eating.

"Alright there sunshine."

"You're looking better already."

I grimace, "You don't have to lie to me I know I must look awful."

Luis grins, "Yeah you do to be fair."

Risa goes to wash up the empty bowl and Pepe comes to sit beside me on the bed. "You wanna tell us the names of the scumbags who did this to you yet?"

I sigh, "I really love that you want to go after them but I can't let you. They really are too powerful."

Pepe seems disappointed with my answer but accepts it. "Well I think it's best you keep hidden for today. Final show in a few hours and then we'll be packing up and leaving first thing in the morning. Quicker we can get yous far away from these cretin the better."

I spend the rest of the day drifting in and out of sleep. Risa checks my stitches and changes my bandages, and the Gallavanties seem to take it in turns to sit with me, except for when they are performing the last show in Carrard. As Pepe suggested I don't leave the caravan so have to make do with listening to the performance and cheers from the audience through the small open window. After a restless night in which I'm plagued with nightmares of guards bursting into the caravan and dragging me back to the castle, the first rays of dawn are a welcome relief. The Gallavanties are all up early and making final preparations. I'm still bed bound and staying hidden so feel rather useless. It's not long though until Sam sticks his head in to tell me we're all ready to go.

As I feel the caravan start to move there's an anxious flutter in my stomach. I can't believe I'm doing this. I'm actually leaving Carrard with the Gallavanties. Peeling back the curtains I peek out the window as we approach the city's north gate. The guards stop the procession of caravans and call up to Dav who is driving the first, though I can't hear what they are saying. Please let us pass, I silently pray. Please don't check inside the caravans, I beg. After what seems like the longest agonising wait the guards step back and we begin to move again. Breathing out again I can't stop the beaming smile that spreads across my face. I'm free. I'm actually free. A giddy laugh escapes me but the pain in my ribs quickly makes me stop. Suddenly, after the bleakness of the last few days, I'm looking forward to the future. I'm excited. Briefly I think of the life I've left behind. But it's not my father or Joseph who fills my head. I think of Molly. I hope she's ok. Will she be worried about me? I resolve to send a letter to her as soon as I get the chance. I'll try to explain what happened. I promised her that I would make a difference, that I would help change the fate of this country and I failed. I underestimated the hold that Lord Fagan has over my father and know now that there was never any chance of breaking that really.

We travel for several hours without stopping, heading along the north road. I'm grateful our journey isn't taking us south where we would've had to avoid my father and Lord Fagan who will soon be making their way to Mata to meet King James. Eventually we stop for lunch and to give the horses a much needed break. Sam's the one to come into the caravan and help me to slowly stand. With one arm around me and the other holding my hand he gently supports me as I climb down the steps. It's nice to step outside again and, putting my face into the breeze, I breathe in the fresh country air. Sam eases me into a chair and then rushes to bring me a cup of water and some food, a selection of ham, cheese, bread, an apple and an orange. "I didn't know what you wanted so brought you a bit of everything."

"Thanks Sam, that's great" I smile and he smiles back. It's odd to be getting along with Sam after the animosity in Carrard. The other Gallavanties come over to join us then and I ask how far we've come "about 12 miles" is Pepe's answer, "We'll probably do another nine or ten this afternoon."

"And how far away is Ameve?"

"Just over 200 miles"

All the Gallavanties laugh at my shocked expression, "Yeah it'll take us at least two weeks to get there assuming the weather stays good."

"I didn't realise it was that far." I say feeling silly again.

"Well you could do it quicker," Luis explains, "If you changed horses or we didn't stop for shows but there ain't really no rush. We get there when we get there."

I smile, "And there's no chance of Pepe leaving Storm behind."

Pepe grins, "Never."

We let the horses roam free for an hour before reconnecting them to the caravans and setting off once again. As I rest the rocking motion of the caravan soon sends me to sleep. I wake to the sound of Sam's voice as he gently shakes me. "Sorry" he murmurs, "Need you to get out for a minute. There's a real narrow bridge we gotta cross and it's best you're not in the caravan just in case it goes over."

Sam helps me out of the caravan and guides me to the other side of a thin wooden bridge that runs over a small stream. The bridge is only just wide enough to take the caravans and its wheels are perilously close to the edge on both sides. The drop from the bridge is not high at all, only a couple of feet, but enough to do serious damage to the caravan if it goes. Dav carefully guides Rain over the bridge, moving painfully slowly whilst the others watch the wheels and shout if they're not going straight.

When the first caravan and Rain are safely across, they repeat the process for the second caravan, with Pepe leading Storm, and then the third. Luis is so focused on watching the wheels of the caravan as he urges Whisper slowly forwards that he's not paying attention to his own footing. One moment he's walking calmly backwards and the next he steps too far to the left. It seems to happen in slow motion, arms whirling like windmills he tries to right himself but can't and falls on his backside, off the bridge and into the shallow stream. Soaked to the bone with a look of utter shock on his face the rest of us burst into hysterical laughter at the sight. Meanwhile Whisper nonchalantly carries straight on and makes it across the narrow bridge without any guidance, which only serves to make me and Risa laugh even more.

We travel for a few more hours before stopping to set up camp for the night. A warm fire is built and everyone relaxes after a long day.

"How you doing Cara?" asks Luis.

"Getting better" I answer honestly, "Definitely less pain now than this morning."

"Well you take it easy. You can't rush healing from injuries like that." Risa says seriously. "You'll only do yourself more damage if you try and get better too fast." I nod and smile at Risa's concern.

"No regrets about coming with us?" asks Pepe.

"None at all. I can't thank you enough for letting me come with you."

"Don't be daft sweetheart" Risa says at the same time as Sam says, "You had to come with us." and Dav insists, "We sure as hell weren't gonna let you go back to those monsters. Ain't letting them anywhere near yous again."

The other Gallavanties nod in agreement. The serious conversation is darkening the atmosphere and I don't want my bad past to carry into my future so I quickly change the subject. We chat late into the evening and at some point Dav gets his guitar out and starts singing some old folk songs. I don't know the words but clap along and watch as Luis twirls Risa around in a dance. Sam sits beside me and tries to explain some of the songs, the stories and people they refer to. Eventually Pepe insists that everyone retires as there's another early start in the morning. Kinken kills the fire and a chorus of good nights echo around as we each climb into our own caravans to sleep. I'm sharing with Luis and Risa, who insists on tucking me in. With a gentle kiss on my forehead she whispers, "I'm so glad you're here with us." And as I drift off to sleep I think exactly the same thing. I'm so glad to be here.

# Chapter 17

The following day we've finally stopped after travelling for another fifteen miles, and I'm sat propped up against a tree watching Pepe and Dav give the horses a bath.

"Hey!"

I look up to see Sam standing in front of me, hands deep in his pockets and giving me a sheepish smile as he kicks at the ground, scuffing his boots.

"I wanted to say sorry."

"Sorry? For what?"

"For the way I acted back in Carrard when we first met. You were right, I made a snap judgement about you and it was wrong."

"It's ok." I say automatically.

"No, it wasn't ok. It wasn't fair, you didn't deserve it and I'm sorry. You were nothing but nice to me and I didn't treat you the same way."

"Well thanks." I say surprised and taken aback by his apology.

Sam nods and starts to walk away until I continue, "You know you weren't entirely wrong." Sam stops and looks back. "I was a spoilt girl from the castle who didn't understand the real world. But I don't want to be that girl any more."

Sam smiles, "You're not that girl. I heard what you did for the Rivelli's before we left. Even battered and bruised you were still thinking of others."

"Oh, well it was the guards. I saw them stealing from the market stall the day before and I know how hard the Rivellis work and I just wanted to pay them back."

"But you didn't steal from them. You're not responsible for the guards actions and yet you chose to go out of your way to help someone else. Made me realise maybe you're not such a bad person after all. Even if you did grow up in the palace" he says with a cheeky smile so that I know he's joking. As he starts to walk away again he calls back over his shoulder,

"One of the caravans has got a leak in the roof, wanna help me fix it?"

"Really?" I ask, surprised at his offer, wryly I add, "you know I don't know anything about tools?"

"I know" he smiles. He has a dimple in one cheek. I've never noticed that before. "Come on, I'll teach you."

Sam is an incredibly patient teacher as he shows me all of the tools, telling me their names and explaining what they're used for. He doesn't make fun of me for my lack of knowledge or get cross when I keep mixing things up. As he talks he ends up sharing stories of various disasters, including the time the stage collapsed mid-performance and he had to crawl under it to fix the broken support whilst they improvised a whole new section on stage. He keeps making me laugh which hurts my ribs but I don't protest too much. I'm actually having fun and the afternoon passes quickly. By the time dinner is ready Sam's finished the roof and we all gather around the fire. Sat out in the open countryside surrounded by people who I care about and who care about me I feel so at peace. Looking up at the sky, it's amazing to see so many stars. With the bright lights of the city, the sky is never clear enough to get a good view.

Each day it is much the same, we travel for most of the day before stopping to set up a temporary camp each night. Sometimes we stop in a village or hamlet and the Gallavanties perform smaller versions of the city shows for the inhabitants. They don't get much money from these shows but the audience's enjoyment and gratefulness is never ending. Thankfully each day also sees the ache in my head and pain in my ribs ease too. The bruises have faded to yellow and the cuts on my head and elbow are healing quickly thanks to Risa's tender care. When I'm deemed well enough Dav insists on teaching me some self-defense moves. He even tries to persuade me to carry a pocket knife in my boot but when I nearly slice my own foot open I decide against it. Surprisingly I spend most of my time with Sam who seems to have completely changed attitudes since we left Carrard. Or maybe more accurately since I was beaten by the Fagans. We often sit together at lunch time and dinner time, and once I'm recovered enough to sit up top on the caravan it's usually Sam who I sit beside.

Just two days from Ameve we're halted by bad weather as a storm hits and we're forced to stop early and shelter in Pepe's caravan whilst we wait for it to pass. Despite the wind and rain everyone is in high spirits knowing we're not far from our destination. I know I'm looking forward to not needing to travel every day and to see Ameve, a place I've never visited before. As we sit listening to the raging storm outside Dav and Pepe are doing impressions of each other's characters that they play on stage.

"I do not sound like that" insists Luis whilst the rest of us howl with laughter at Dav's dramatised version of when Luis plays Prince John.

"You do," I giggle, "You really do, you go all high pitched when you try to be posh."

"Well go on then show us how it's done."

"Alright," I say standing up and thinking of Tutor Zelda who used to lead my elocution and etiquette lessons and had the most ridiculously posh accent which I now copy, "To be truly royal you must pronounce every t in every word. It is of paramount importance to enunciate. One must always be clear and concise and ensure that the one with whom one is speaking understands every word."

The Gallavanties all roar with laughter as I grin and sit back down.

"Alright well that's cheatin, you bleedin grew up in a palace" says Luis still miffed, "Bet you couldn't do an impression of us as good as I can do one of you."

Instantly copying Luis' accent I say, "Course I could, yous are dead easy, jus gotta drop me t's n say everyfin all in one big mad long sentence dun I?"

This makes the Gallavantis laugh even more and even has Luis chuckling, "Yeah alrigh' that were pretty good" he admits.

"That were better than good," Sam says, "You're a natural. You should be up on the stage with us. Don't ya reckon Pepe? We could write a part in for her, couldn't we?"

"Yeah I'm sure we can. Or maybe you could take over from Luis."

"Hey" Luis laughs, throwing a pillow at Pepe.

"Could I really have a part in a show?"

"Yeah if you want one. We always look to change and mix things up, keep the shows fresh you know. Give me a bit o' time to write you a part, and it'll take a few rehearsals mind, but we'll have you up on that stage before you know it."

I grin at Pepe while Risa gives me a sideways hug and Dav claps me on the back. Sam smiles at me from across the table whilst I have to admit I'm giddy with excitement. The idea of going on stage and performing gives me a kind of thrill and I can't wait.

I'm up early the next day and helping Pepe brush the horses down when I have to ask him, "How come you took me in? I mean right from the beginning when you didn't even know me and I kept coming and hanging around, you were so totally open to me."

"I just knew."

"Knew what?"

"That you needed us. That you were lost and alone and looking for a family. I know that feeling. For a long time I was looking for a family and now that I'm lucky enough to have a pretty awesome one I don't take it for granted. Plus as weird as it sounds you just fitted right in. Like it was meant to be."

"You sound like Risa."

"Aye I do," he laughs, "Guess that's what happens with families, you kinda all become one."

"I like being part of this family." I smile. "Thanks for letting me in."

"No problem kiddo" he says, slinging his arm around my shoulders for a one armed hug. "There's no turning back now, you're one of us."

"One of us" I echo looking around at my new family. Nothing has ever sounded nicer than those three words.

# Chapter 18

After more than two weeks on the road it's a relief to finally arrive in Ameve and set up a more permanent camp in the southern market square. Sam and I are sent off to cover the city with posters and spread the word that the Gallavanties are in town. We work for over an hour posting leaflets and adverts on every street corner. We don't talk much but remain within sight of each other just as Pepe insisted. I follow Sam's lead as he knows the city well. I found out from Luis that Sam was born here and grew up on the streets until he was picked up by Pepe and Dav when he was nine years old. I try to engage Sam in conversation by asking him about it but it's clear he doesn't want to discuss his childhood. As I'm pasting a large poster to the wall I'm approached by a group of young lads about my age who look at the advert with interest, "What's this then?"

"Oh it's the Gallavanties touring show. They're incredible, you don't want to miss it. Adventure, romance, comedy, even magic. You should come along, bring your friends. You won't regret it."

As one casually leans against the wall beside me, another asks with a smile, "Will you be there?"

"Well yes but I'm not in the show. Seriously though, they're amazing. We're here for the next week and there's a different show every night."

"Well maybe we'll see you there."

"You definitely should, and remember to bring your friends and family" I add enthusiastically.

Suddenly Sam grabs my arm and is dragging me away without a word. He is clearly fuming.

"Sam, what are you doing? What's wrong?"

Suddenly he releases my arm and spins around to face me, "What the hell are you doing? Why are you talking to those guys? Are you trying to sell yourself? They were all over you."

"I was just..."

"I know what you were doing. Do you flirt with every man you see?"

"I wasn't flirting..."

"Didn't look like it to me. Looked like you were enjoying the attention. Well if that's the sort of guy you like then fine. Far be it for me to question your taste in men, you're welcome to them."

And with that Sam turns and storms away whilst I stand there in shock wondering what on earth just happened. It's only as I watch Sam's retreating back that it suddenly occurs to me that I don't know my way back to the caravans. Calling after Sam urgently I try to chase him but I've already lost sight of his curly brown hair. Reaching the end of the street I look left and then right but can't see Sam anywhere. Damn him. What the hell was wrong with him? I think we came from the left so I turn and start to follow the street, hoping that I'll recognise the next street to turn down when I see it.

As I take another turning and still recognise nothing I'm really starting to get concerned now. Where I was in a fairly busy part of town the area I'm in now looks more ramshackled and there aren't many people walking these streets. I'm totally lost in a city that I've never been in before. A city that both Pepe and Dav specifically told me not to get lost in.

Cursing Sam once more for leaving me, I try to stay calm, desperately searching for anything that seems vaguely familiar. I stop suddenly when up ahead two men stumble out of an alehouse. Quickly I turn around and take a different path but as I walk down this new alley I know I've made a mistake. The sound of heavy footsteps behind has me quickening my pace. A trickle of fear runs down my back and all my senses are heightened as instinct tells me that danger is near. Nearly running now I race down the twisting narrow streets, hoping against hope that I'm heading in the right direction. I scream as a sudden jerk on my arm swings me round and I find myself facing a tanned ugly looking man with a bald head and bushy beard. Two more men approach from behind him as I slowly back myself up against the wall. Looking around at the three large men now surrounding me I know that I'm in real trouble. These men are not like Dav Creek. These are no gentle giants.

As the men step closer wearing menacing smiles, I try to remember some of the self-defense techniques that Dav showed me, but my mind has gone totally blank with panic. Then suddenly, like I conjured him from my mind with my thoughts, Dav appears out of nowhere. He's floored two of the guys before they even realise what's happening. The third takes one look at him and turns and runs back down the alleyway. It's then that I realise Sam is there too, as he leaps in front of me. His panicked eyes inspect me, whilst his hands are everywhere, stroking my face, my arms, my hair, asking me urgently, "Are you alright? Did they touch you? Are you hurt?"

Still in shock I answer automatically, "I'm fine. I'm alright."

"God damn lucky is what you are." Growls Dav Creek. "Come on, let's get you back before trouble finds you again."

As we follow Dav back down the streets Sam walks alongside me continually giving me apologetic glances.

"I'm really glad you're ok." He says.

"No thanks to you!" I mutter, still mad at him for abandoning me. "Why did you just run off like that? One second everything's fine and then you're yelling at me and storming off. I don't understand why you got so mad at me for talking to those guys. We were just talking. I was telling them about the show. Trying to get them to spread the word and come along. And then you just grabbed me, dragging me away like I'd done something wrong."

Sam interrupts, "I was jealous, ok? I know you didn't do anything and it was all in my stupid head but I just saw you with those guys and I could tell that they were flirting with you and I just got mad and lost it. I'm sorry."

"Jealous? You were jealous?"

For a moment Sam just looks at me and then he seems to make a decision. With a sigh and a shy glance away he admits, "Yes, I was jealous. I like you and the thought that you might like someone else made me jealous."

"You like me?" I repeat, aware that I sound like an idiot just repeating his own words back at him but I don't know what else to say. I'm dumbfounded. He likes me? Likes me likes me?

He nods.

"Wow." I breathe. "You know I really wasn't flirting with those guys."

"I know. I'm so sorry I left you."

"It's ok."

"No it's not." He says adamantly, "I promise I won't ever leave you again."

"Ok."

We start to walk once more but the silence is deafening, and everything he's just said is reverberating around my head. I have to ask, "Since when?"

"Since when what?"

"Since when have you liked me?"

"Since the beginning."

"The beginning?"

"Since the moment I laid eyes on you."

"You mean when you dragged me into the caravan?"

"No, I saw you before then. I saw you the moment you came over to the stage, when I was doing my introduction. I saw you and I couldn't take my eyes off you. I thought you were the prettiest girl I'd ever seen. I watched you through the whole show. The way your whole face lit up. You had this sparkle in your eye, I couldn't look away." He laughs, "That sounds really creepy. Sorry. That's why I was so close to you when the guards showed up and everyone was running to hide. I was coming to talk to you. Then the guards came and it was all chaos. Even then my instinct was telling me to take you with me so I pulled you into the caravan. I just felt this overwhelming sense of... I don't know what. I just knew it's what I had to do."

"I thought you hated me at the beginning. You were always so distant whenever I visited in Carrard. It always seemed like you didn't want me around."

"I didn't want you around." He says matter of factly.

I look at him puzzled. Everything he says is so contradictory.

"You were so pretty, I wanted to know you more, but the moment I learnt you were from the palace I thought we could never be friends. Never be anything. So I pushed you away. Couldn't believe it when you kept coming back." He shakes his head with a wry smile, "Figured I just had to keep you at arms length until we left Carrard and then I'd never see you again."

I laugh, "And then I decide to run away and now you're stuck with me."

"Yeah" he laughs, "now I'm stuck with you." He hesitates and then adds, "I'm really glad I'm stuck with you."

We smile at each other and it seems like something has shifted between us. There's an electric current running between us that wasn't there before.

"Did you really think I was the prettiest girl you'd ever seen?"

He nods and then whispers, "I still think that."

For a moment we just look at each other, and then, ever so slowly, he leans forward and presses his lips against mine in the softest kiss. It only lasts for a moment. He leans back and looks at me cautiously. When a slow smile starts to spread across my face, his eyes light up and he leans in again. My eyes flutter closed and I surrender to his kiss. As he ends the kiss and gently rests his forehead against mine, looking deep into my eyes, I try to memorise everything about this moment. My heart is pounding, my stomach is doing somersaults and I'm so giddy I have the uncontrollable urge to laugh. We both just stand there like idiots, grinning at each other, until a shout from Dav ahead of us indicates that we need to keep moving. Sam takes my hand firmly in his and we walk back to the caravans together.

# Chapter 19

- - - - - - - - - - - - - - - - - - - - - - - - - - - - - - - - - - - - - - - - - - - - - - - - - -

Turns out the rest of the Gallavanties are not in such a forgiving mood. In fact they're all pretty angry. Not at me but at Sam. He has to endure heated lectures from Pepe, Dav and Risa about how much danger he put me in. Risa swears she's never letting me out of her sight again after Dav tells her what almost happened. I try to imply she might be overreacting but then she points out that I've only just recovered from a pretty serious beating and I don't really have a comeback for that, so end up just listening whilst giving Sam sympathetic glances. I mean technically what they're saying is true. He did abandon me in the middle of a city that I don't know, and I did almost get attacked by three pretty scary guys but I can't help feeling a little sorry for the grilling he's taking. Especially when Pepe starts listing the extra chores he's now going to have to do as punishment. Sam stands there silently, seeming to accept everything they say. Eventually Sam's sent to get started on his now seemingly endless list of chores whilst Risa asks for my help to prepare tonight's dinner. Now that we're on the coast Risa's making the most of it and seems to be planning fresh fish into every meal. I don't see Sam again until everyone is gathering for the first show. We give each other a secret smile but don't say anything as Dav launches into his usual pre-show pep talk he likes to give to get everyone 'in the zone' as he says.

The crowd isn't as big as previous city shows but I suppose word hasn't had much time to spread throughout the city yet. Luis says the crowds always grow each day and that the shows at the end of the week are always the busiest. Still the performance is greeted enthusiastically and there seems to be a fair amount of coin thrown into the hats. The biggest difference I notice comes after the show. There's no curfew here in Ameve and no city guards terrifying the citizens, so when the performance ends the audience don't leave. They stay in the square chatting with each other. An alehouse just opposite us is overflowing with patrons as people enjoy their evening together. This is what it should be like in Carrard I can't help thinking.

When the Gallavanties appear they're approached by tons of people who want to shake their hands and congratulate them on the show. By the time they're done and make their excuses to return to the caravans it's much later than usual. We take our now familiar places around Risa's table tucking into the fish stew we prepared earlier. I comment on the differences between Ameve and Carrard that I've already noticed and Pepe nods in agreement. As the Gallavanties start discussing similarities and differences between all the places they've visited, comparing their favourites, unbeknownst to them all Sam has taken my hand underneath the table. We eat our dinner hand in hand, occasionally catching each other's eyes with a smile but trying not to let everyone else see us. When I look up and catch Risa watching she simply raises her eyebrows at me. Maybe someone has noticed. I give her a small smile but say nothing. As everyone stands to leave, returning to their own caravans to sleep, Risa leans over and whispers in my ear, "I think you and I need to have a little chat in the morning." Sam sees the interaction and gives me a quizzical look but I just shake my head, not able to say anything in the moment, and then Risa's shooing them all out the caravan declaring that she's tired. I'm not sure what Risa will think of me and Sam. I hope she's ok with it.

Just as I'm starting to drift off I hear a quiet tap on the window next to my bunk. At first I ignore it but then it becomes slightly louder and more persistent. Peeking out from behind the curtain it's Sam's smiling face which greets me. Glancing towards Risa and Luis' bedroom I quietly open the window as much as is allowed. "What are you doing?" I whisper.

"Saying good night" he replies with a cheeky grin, then he leans in and gives me a quick kiss, "See you tomorrow beautiful." I laugh at his cheesy line but can't help lying awake for hours afterwards thinking about his kiss. A huge smile all over my face.

The next morning I can feel Risa's eyes watching me and Sam like a hawk all through breakfast. After we've eaten she sends Sam off on an errand, insisting that he head to the fish market in the northern quarter for a specific type of shrimp. Sam tries to take me with him but Risa lies, telling him that she needs my help with some costumes. As soon as she's practically pushed him out of the door she turns to me, raises her eyebrows and says, "Go on then spill. When did this happen?"

"When did what happen?"

"Cara" she pouts, "Come on girl, this is your big sis you're talking to you."

With a sigh and then a smile I can't contain, I tell her everything. How we've been getting closer and closer over the last few weeks. How he left me yesterday because he was jealous but then admitted his feelings for me and that we kissed. I even tell her about the hand holding under the table and him sneaking back to say good night. I tell her how giddy he makes me feel and how happy I am just being around him. By the end I've turned pink with embarrassment and my cheeks are hurting from my constant grin. And Risa is smiling too, "Oh honey, it's so good to see you happy like this. I could tell last night something had happened from the way you kept looking at each other. I just wanted to make sure that you were both in it for the right reasons and not just just because you're the same age and around each other a lot. But the way you talk about him I know it's more than that. You're both such special people to me. I love you both so much and don't want either of you to get hurt or rush into something you're not sure about. I know Sam and he doesn't usually open up to people much. If he's letting you in he really must care about you a lot."

"I really care about him too."

She nods, "I know. I don't think either of you would ever intentionally hurt one another but sometimes when it comes to young love things can be tricky."

"But you and Luis made it."

Risa laughs, "Yes we did, but trust me we had our fair share of ups and downs and moments of doubt. Love is rarely smooth sailing but if you're with the right person then you get through it and can survive anything."

Standing up I go and pull Risa into a tight hug, "I love you Risa. You're the best big sister a girl could ever ask for."

"Right back at you sweetie."

Luis interrupts our sisterly bonding moment and so we set about the morning tasks we need to get done. A grumpy Sam arrives back several hours later having been unable to find the specific shrimp that Risa requested, which the fishmongers said he'd never heard of. "Oh maybe I got the name wrong, never mind" Risa says brushing it off. Sam's huff of annoyance only makes me laugh, then we both just stand there grinning at each other like idiots. Luis looks between us with a puzzled expression, "You two alright?"

"Yeah fine" Sam answers, "Hey Cara, wanna look round the city a bit more? I could give you a proper tour."

"That would be great," I say leaping at the chance to go off together again.

"Just don't abandon her again," jokes Luis. Sam takes my hand and gives it a squeeze, "I won't" he says looking me straight in the eye.

We spend the whole afternoon exploring the city. Sam takes me all the way to the docks where the place is alive with ships loading and unloading. Dockworkers running everywhere and fishermen coming in with their afternoon catches. The place reeks with fish but there's so much interesting stuff going on I don't mind. I'm fascinated by the fish gutters who work with such speed, I can't understand how they don't cut themselves. We reach the end of the harbour and I stare out to sea in wonder. I've never been to the seaside before. My father never cared for it and so when we went on summer tours we always stayed inland. The open ocean seems so vast as I gaze at the horizon and wonder how far it goes. "Have you ever been on a ship?" I ask Sam. He shakes his head, "Not really, I did some work on a fishing vessel a bit when I was younger but that really mostly stays in the harbour, close to shore. I've never sailed on a proper ship out to sea."

"Imagine how exciting it must be. To set sail into that. Not knowing where you're going, what you're going to find."

"Or what weather you're gonna have to deal with. Got caught in a minor storm once n I can tell ya you'd never catch me sailing out into the openness with no destination in mind. No help out there if you get in trouble."

"That's a good point, and I can't swim so maybe it's not a very good idea. Should probably stick to land."

"Really? You can't swim?"

I put on the voice of Tutor Zelda, "It's not an activity for a young lady of proper birth."

Sam laughs, "Maybe I'll have to teach you if we ever get the chance, come on we'd best get back and make sure everything's set for the show." As we make our way back I can't help but feel a little disappointed. I loved Sam's tour of his hometown but I was hoping he would share a little bit more about his life here, but other than the fact he once worked on a boat he's said nothing. I guess he'll tell me when he's ready.

The shows in Ameve follow the same pattern as those in Carrard and as the week progresses I get stuck in with helping to sort props, costumes and scenery each day. Pepe has told me he's already working on writing in characters for me and I can't wait to be able to get on stage and perform too but for now I do what I can backstage. By the penultimate night the square is absolutely rammed for the performance and on the last day people start arriving three hours before the show just to get a good spot. The Gallavanties say Ameve is always a successful stop on the tour but I think even they are taken aback by the amount we make during our stay. On closing night the cheers go on for so long that the Gallavanties end up performing a little encore sketch and taking eight curtain bows. The atmosphere is so different to Carrard and I love it.

After a week of nightly performances in Ameve we have a couple of days off before our next journey and Luis, Risa, Sam and I take a trip to the beach. As we walk along the sand, eating ice cream cones and collecting shells it feels like a proper family day out. I insist on trying out every beach active that I can think of, including skimming stones, building a sandcastle, chasing seagulls and wave jumping. Sam tries to teach me to swim in the sea but given that I'm too scared to go where I can't reach the bottom he's not very successful and we end up just splashing around. By the end of the day I've decided that Ameve is my new favourite place and, desperate for a memento of the day, I manage to persuade Luis to lend me some coin so that we can get a caricature done from one of the beach artists set up on the pier. He draws the four of us all standing in front of the beach with our arms around each other. As we all look at the picture and the others joke about what the artist has done, "My nose isn't that big" insists Luis whilst Sam exclaims that his ears are sticking out far too much, my eyes almost well up. Looking at the picture fills me with such happiness. I carefully roll it up to take home with us. Home, I smile. A real home with a real family. Just what I've always wanted.

# Chapter 20

------------------------------------------------------------

The following day we are once again on the road, travelling through small towns and villages, performing at each stop on the way to our next major city, Leforth to the far north of the country, our final Aleti destination before we go across the border into Karhaner.

It takes ten days to travel from Ameve to LeForth and I think they may well be the happiest ten days of my life. I'm no longer an outsider but a true member of the group. I don't need to ask what to do each day as I seamlessly fit into the routine of packing up, travelling, caring for the horses, setting up camp again, cooking and working backstage whenever we get the chance to do shows. Pepe even lets me drive the wagons for a bit though only on straight easy roads. I feel like I've been with the Gallavanties forever rather than just six short weeks.

I spend every moment that I can with Sam and though we have to put up with endless teasing from the others, I don't really mind and find it easy to join in with the banter, giving back as good as I get. Pepe has written two characters for me and although at the moment they are only small parts, I insist on practising everyday, learning my lines and perfecting every moment so I'm ready for my debut in Leforth. Risa has already made my costumes and I can't help but keep trying them on in excitement.

Dav continues to teach me self-defense and when I manage to knock Sam off his feet and pin him to the floor I leap up and down cheering, whilst all of the Gallavanties applaud. When I lie awake at night I'm constantly amazed by my luck in finding this family. This is my life now and I love it. I don't ever want it to change.

The day before we reach Leforth we can't help but notice how busy the roads appear with people heading in the opposite direction. Most are young men, carrying packs and travelling in groups. When Dav returns from chatting with one such group he says that they're soldiers from the Leforth garrison who are being transferred to Albeck.

For a moment I question this action. Why would soldiers be needed in Albeck which borders Cobback? Is there trouble brewing between ourselves and our old allies who we've just abandoned in our deal with Navas. I can't believe that there would be. But I've not been in court for weeks and don't know how the landscape has changed since the deal with Navas was signed. I've heard nothing about it since leaving Carrard and whilst I assume it has gone ahead as Lord Fagan planned I hope that our friendship with Cobback has not been totally lost. I try not to think about it too much, telling myself there is nothing I can do, but the issue still bothers me and I'm still thinking about it later that night as we eat our final dinner outside Leforth. We will reach the city in the morning.

As the other's drift off to bed eventually it's just me and Sam, snuggled under a blanket together, staring at the dying embers of the fire, in comfortable silence.

"You know you asked me about my childhood? Back in Ameve."

"Yeah" I say suddenly much more awake.

"It's not that I'm embarrassed about where I come from or anything. It's not a secret, I just don't like talking about it and especially with you. I don't want you to think less of me when you know everything."

"Sam..."

"I know, I know. Stupid, you're not like that."

"You don't have to tell me anything Sam."

"I know, but see when I'm talking to you I wanna know everything there is to know about you, but how can I ask that if I don't do the same. Ain't fair. And anyhow I trust you. I want to tell you."

Snuggling closer so Sam knows that I'm there no matter what he tells me I wait for him to begin.

"So you already know I was born in Ameve. Never knew who my parents were. I was abandoned on the steps of St Martin's church same day I was born. Got sent to St Martin's orphanage, then the Ameve youth hospice when St Martin's closed down, think I was about four. Stayed there a couple years but it was horrible. So many kids that I usually ended up sleeping on the floor. The older kids bullied us, stole our food, beat us and the staff did nothing. They didn't care so long as they got paid. Survival of the fittest is what they always said. Life's tough so you might as well get used to it. They sent us out to work down at the fish markets, gutting fish for 3 spens a day, but we never got to keep any of it. That's when I started doing my own thing. I'll be honest it weren't exactly legal. Pickpocketing and stealing. I used to steal bottles of wine from the docks, then I'd water them down and sell 'em on. Sometimes I'd get enough to buy some food but if I didn't then I'd steal that too. I did whatever to survive. I'm not proud of it but that's the truth and at the time I just didn't wanna go back to the orphanage. Then one day I picked the wrong pocket, or right pocket as it turns out. Guess who?" Sam turns to me with a smile.

I laugh, "Pepe."

"Pepe" he nods and grins, "Even now I don't know how he got me. He moved so fast. Not to brag but I was a pretty good pickpocket, most people never noticed, but Pepe grabbed my wrist before I realised what was happening. Gave me a right grilling at first but then I think he looked at me. A scared little nine year old boy starving to death and instead of handing me in to the authorities he took me back to his caravan and fed me. I kept going back after that and everyday he fed me no questions asked."

"Kind of like how I kept coming back."

"Yeah I suppose it was like you, didn't really think about that. Eventually I just started hanging around the Gallavanties all the time, helping out with jobs and stuff and then when it was time to leave, well Pepe just turned to me n said 'Come on then, up ya get.' And that was it, I climbed in the box seat next to him and off we went."

"Pepe sure does have a way of picking up strays, doesn't he?"

"Yeah but he always picks the right strays for the family."

"I asked him about it once and he said that he knows what it's like not to have a family so now that he has got one he looks out for others who don't."

"That sounds like Pepe."

For a moment I sit and contemplate everything Sam's just told me, trying to imagine the little boy that he had been.

"Go on then, your turn," Sam says, nudging me with his elbow.

I hesitate. Sam's just opened up and told me about his childhood but I don't feel ready to do the same. I don't know what Sam's reaction would be to finding out who I really am so I try to tell the truth without telling the whole truth, "I don't really know what to say. My life up until I met you wasn't very exciting. Born and raised in the castle, never even setting foot in the city that's right outside. I never had to worry about food or clothes or where I was going to sleep. If I wanted something, a new dress or a book or toy, I just had to ask. Just a spoiled little rich girl. I know I have nothing to complain about, I know that I was incredibly lucky with the hand I was dealt in life."

"If I've learnt anything recently it's that everyone has problems. No-one's life is perfect, even people who live in a castle." Sam nods for me to continue, "Go on, what was it really like? I don't want the short version you think I wanna hear, I wanna hear the truth."

I pause but then decide that Sam's right, if I want to know about him then he has the right to know about me, even the stuff that I think he won't like. Knowing that Sam won't judge me, I open up. "Truth be told it was lonely. I've had tutors and lady's maids my whole life but not one of them cared about me. They were following orders and making sure that I followed orders. Everyday was the same, lessons in the morning, court duties in the afternoon. A strict schedule to obey. My mother died when I was a baby and my father was always busy so it never really felt like a family, and even though I was surrounded by people all the time I always felt alone. I think that's why I was always asking for new stuff, I was searching for something that would fill the void and make me happy. Maybe this dress will make me happy, maybe these shoes or this doll will make me happy. Turns out I just needed to step outside the palace and find you guys."

"What about the people who beat you? You said they were powerful men?"

"Yeah. Lord Fagan, you've heard of him?"

"Oh yeah I've heard of him" Sam says with a scowl.

"It was him, and his son Joseph. I'd just found out that I was expected to marry him for some sort of alliance or something."

Sam sits up outraged, "What? But you're only sixteen? And surely they can't make you marry someone you don't want to marry?"

"That's what I said. Told them I wasn't going to do it, and that's when the fists started flying and well, you saw the end result."

Sam shakes his head, gritting his teeth but turns to me in surprise when I say, "Suppose I should really thank them next time I see them."

"What?"

"Well if they hadn't done what they did I probably wouldn't have run away and I wouldn't be here now with you, would I? If you think about it I actually owe the Fagan's a lot." I say with an ironic smile.

Sam laughs, "I think a thank you might be taking it a bit far but I get your point." He continues to look at me thoughtfully for a moment, "Can I ask you something? How come you were in the square that first show? You said you'd never gone into the city before so what made you leave the castle that day?"

I laugh wryly, "Seems so long ago now. It was silly. I was angry at my father." I try to brush it off but Sam just looks at me waiting, urging me to talk, so with a small sigh I do. "It was my birthday, a few days before that Monday. Usually it's the one day of the year where my father actually pays me some attention, we always have lunch together, just the two of us. One afternoon in a whole year that was mine without interruption. But this year my father didn't come. He sent a message that he had been detained with Lord Fagan. Said that we would have dinner instead. But then dinner time came and he still didn't show. Then he promised, promised that he would spend the whole afternoon with me on that Monday. I don't know why I believed him. As if his promises to me ever mattered. He probably just said it to shut me up but anyway, needless to say, Monday came and my father once again said he didn't have time for me. So I went to his room and we got into an argument and then I ran away. Well I say I ran away, truth be told I wasn't really running away. I was being dramatic and acting like a spoilt brat, trying to get a reaction from my father. I thought if I told my father I was going he would chase after me. But he didn't. I felt like such an idiot standing there outside the castle gates for like an hour. When no-one came looking I realised no-one cared. And then I turned around and there was the city, laid out before me just waiting to be explored. And it was exciting. To do something that I knew I shouldn't be doing. So I just started walking and it was completely amazing and then I found you guys." I smile, "As Risa says, maybe everything happens for a reason."

Sam nods, "Yeah I think it does."

"Oh God, here's me complaining that my father never had time for me and you didn't even have a father. I'm sorry."

"Don't be sorry. I never knew me dad so I don't know what he was like so can't really miss him, but it must've really sucked growing up with a dad who was there but not there, not really much of a dad.

N it mighta been tough for a few years but then I found Pepe n he's taken care of me ever since."

"So when you joined Pepe, who else was there? Obviously Dav and Kinken but not Luis and Risa?" I ask trying to piece everything that I know about the Gallavanties together.

"Yeah but there was also Joana and Jack and Roddy then."

I snuggle up closer and say, "Tell me about them."

"Joana and Jack were brother and sister, twins. Jack was one of the funniest guys I've ever met, always making me laugh, never took anything too seriously. I think he sometimes took it too far and annoyed Pepe and Dav but as a kid I loved it. Joana was the total opposite, she almost took life too seriously. I think because Jack was always so care-free she maybe felt like she had to be the responsible one and take care of him. She used to tutor me, taught me to read and write, which a lot of kids like me don't get so I'll always be grateful to her, though I don't think I really appreciated it at the time. I was far more interested in following after Jack and getting into mischief."

I grin, "I can imagine that. What happened to them? Where are they now?"

"Joana fell in love. Took us all totally by surprise, never saw it coming. She just announced it at dinner one day, she was in love with this guy Flynn and she was staying with him. To be fair when we met him the next day we all saw it straight away, how in love they were. They're married now with two kids."

"And Jack?"

"Decided to stay in Estor with his sister. Last I heard he was working as a carpenter."

"What about Ruddy?"

"Roddy. Quiet man, a bit older than Pepe. Huge beard. Always nice to me but I don't think he really liked kids so I didn't spend a lot of time with him. He stayed with us longer but then just decided he'd had enough of the travelling life and wanted to settle. He lives in Shofia. I think him and Pepe still write letters to each other when they can."

"That's nice" I say but our conversation is interrupted by Risa appearing, "Come on you two, it's late enough."

We smile at each other and stand. Sam glances quickly at Risa to see if she's watching before giving me a swift kiss, "Good night."

"Good night" I murmur as I slowly start walking backwards towards the caravan, not wanting to look away from the twinkle in Sam's eye. As he goes to climb into his own caravan he grins and blows me another kiss. Lying awake that night trying to get to sleep I can't stop smiling. I think about the way Risa and Luis are with each other and how I feel about Sam, and I start to wonder, is this what falling in love feels like?

# Chapter 21

When we reach Leforth the evidence of soldier departures is
even more pronounced. As we enter through the city's western gate the courtyard to our left is filled with groups of armed men
clearly preparing to move out. I stare at them as we pass, unable to
shake the sense of foreboding that creeps over me. Why are all the
guards leaving? Is something happening in Albeck? After we reach
our base location in one of the larger northern market squares and
set up camp I head over to Dav to ask him for a favour. After years of
travelling Dav has friends in every city and I'm wondering if he knows
anyone who might be able to shed some light on what's happening
with the Leforth soldiers. I can't get rid of this nagging feeling and
need to find out what's going on. At first he's pretty sceptical about
why this is something I need to know but eventually agrees to help
and sends a note to arrange a meeting with a friend who works in
the Leforth garrison.

That night is my theatrical debut and although I'm nervous as
anything I somehow manage to get through the show without any
mistakes. My role only appears in a couple of scenes as a Princess

who is captured by the pirates and then rescued by Sam's character, so it's not exactly a character stretch for me but still, I remember all my lines and actions, and the indescribable buzz I feel when taking my final bows is electric. Afterwards I can't stop jumping about backstage, filled with adrenaline as I am. I can now totally understand why the Gallavanties love performing so much and can't wait to get back out there. The others all act as though I've accomplished some great feat with their congratulations and hugs. Sam even presents me with flowers which he must have bought in secret. With all the excitement I almost forget about my earlier request but then Dav tells me that he's had a reply and a meeting is set up for the following day.

The next morning Sam wants to accompany us to the pub where we are meeting Dav's friend Gini but Kinken insists that he needs his help reshoeing the horses so it's just Dav and I who set off. As we enter the public house, which is surprisingly busy for a midweek lunchtime, a tall skinny man with long ginger hair tied back in a ponytail immediately pulls Dav into a bear hug. When Dav introduces me Gini sweeps into a low elegant bow and kisses my hand which has me giggling because it's so out of place. Gini gives me a wink and then insists on buying the drinks while we settle into our chairs. When he joins us again Dav gets straight to the point. "Cara here's got some questions for ya." He gives me a nod and so I lean forward and start to question Gini quietly. I don't know why I feel the need to keep my voice down but it feels necessary.

"It's about the soldiers. We've seen they're leaving Leforth and heading for Albeck, or so we were told. Do you know why? Is something going on with Cobback?"

Gini shakes his head and leans forward, lowering his voice in the same way that I did. "That's just it. No-one knows. I've asked around and as far as I can tell no-one has heard anything about trouble between us and Cobback. We've been allies for years and there's tons of trades people who go back and forward to Albeck and Cobback all the time, and they know nothing. It's strange that troops are suddenly being sent there, and not in small numbers either. Three quarters of the Leforth garrison are set to move to Albeck by the end of the month."

"But why?" I ask again but Gini just shrugs his shoulders. "Dunno, that's everything I know I'm afraid kiddo. Worrying though. Leaves us pretty short for defenses up here and I wouldn't be trusting what I'm hearing from Karhaner."

"What do you mean? What's happening with Karhaner?"

"Nothing really. Kinda the point. Ever since that coup of there's years ago, trade has gone down hill between us and them. Got a fair few refugees telling horror stories of tha' general of there's, came 'ere escaping it, but not many people crossing the border nowadays and just recently, last few months, it's been even quieter than normal, which is saying something mind. Can't put me finger on it exactly but I don't like not hearing anything. Used to have friends in Karhaner who I ain't heard nothing from of late. Silence is worrying in my book. But maybe the higher ups know more than me given they're sending our troops in the opposite direction. You'll be travelling into Karhaner when you're done here won't ya?"

Dav answers with a slightly worried expression, "yeah three days here n then onto Otraf."

"Maybe you'll find out more n let me know when you pass back this way. Could be nothin' o'course, just a silly paranoid ex-army bloke but still."

Dav nods and agrees to call in on some of Gini's old friends in Otraf. Eventually the topic of the soldiers is exhausted and Dav and Gini start catching up on other news so I decide to leave them to it.

As I come out of the pub and begin the walk back to the square a young man leaning against the wall calls out as he steps in front of me, "Hey gorgeous. I recognise you. Look lads, it's the girl from the show." He says as his friends appear from a narrow alley beside us that I hadn't spotted. I try to stay polite but the hairs on the back of my neck are standing up and I can sense these boys are up to something. I give them a bland smile and then try to step around them but the ringleader steps once again in my way. "Actually darlin' we could do with your help. See we're havin' a bit of a competition. Tryna decide who's the best kisser. Jonny 'ere reckons he is but I know it's me. Thing is we need an independent judge as it were. To give us all a quick snog and then declare a winner. You'd be up for that wouldn't you sweetcheeks?" "No" is my immediate and firm answer. With the gang still blocking my way I turn and start to stride back up the street towards the pub where I know Dav still is. But the ringleader easily catches up to me, "Oh come on. Won't take two minutes."

"Unless you want it to take longer" shouts one of the others causing all his mates to chuckle. The lads are all grinning and egging each other on as they gather around me. As one of the lads steps forward I try to kick out at him but miss, causing all of the boys to laugh. "Calm down sweetheart, tis only a bit of fun. Don't you wanna have some fun with us?" he asks, grabbing my arm and pulling me in close. In one swift motion I bring my knee up between his legs as hard as I can. As he doubles over in pain I thrust the palm of my hand up into his nose, causing blood to instantly start pouring. As one of his friends steps forward and tries to grab me again I swing around with my other elbow, catching him on the side of the head and sending him stumbling backwards. Reaching down I grab the knife which Dav gave me and I've kept concealed in my boot. None of the lads are laughing now and with hostile glances they mumble something about it not being worth it and run off back up the street, their incapacated friend hobbling after them. "You can clear off and all." I say to a drunken man who's stopped to stare. He grunts, takes a swig from his bottle and then turns to continue on his way. Suddenly I hear the start of a slow clap from behind me and I see Dav emerge from the shadows with a beaming smile on his face, "That's my girl."

I grin back at him, "I think your lessons have really started to pay off."

"Good bloody job too. I've never known a girl get into so much trouble. Everywhere we go, seems you're like a bloody magnet. Three different cities n three attacks."

"I don't think you can count the one at the palace, that was different, and I don't ask for it." I insist as I put my knife away. "And I thought this wasn't a dodgy part of town."

"It isn't." Dav says with a shake of his head, "Don't matter where ya are though, seems a pretty face will make people lose their heads."

"Did you find out anything else?" I ask as we set off together back towards camp.

"Nah, not much more than what ya heard. Confusion about Cobback and the soldiers being sent to Albeck but people don't question much, just do as they're told."

"I don't like it. The whole situation doesn't feel right."

"I'd just leave it kid. If the higher powers wanna move their soldiers around then let them. What can you do about it?"

I nod. He's right. I don't understand it but it's not my place to understand it any more. My thoughts don't matter and there's nothing I can do.

As we sit at dinner that evening I struggle to listen to the others and join in with the conversation. No matter how much I try and tell myself to leave it alone I just can't. My gut is telling me that something is wrong. Sam gives my hand a squeeze and asks if I'm ok. I try to smile and nod but I think he can tell that I'm preoccupied. As I wallow with my inner thoughts swirling around in circles it suddenly occurs to me that Dav isn't the only one with contacts in the city. Unlike Ameve I have travelled to Leforth several times and know Lord Francis and his family. I spent quite a bit of time with his daughter Emily. Though I've not seen her for a couple of years we always got on well. Would she have answers? Is there a way to talk to her? Would she recognise me? More importantly would she expose my secret and turn me in? I think about the girl I knew and think not but it's still a risk.

I spend all night making a pros and cons list about trying to meet with Emily. One moment I'm convinced it's worth the risk and have to do it, and the next I'm remembering Dav's words and telling myself not to get involved and jeopardise everything I now have with the Gallavanties. If my identity gets exposed and I'm carted back off to Carrard then I'll likely never see Sam and the Gallavanties again. But after tossing and turning throughout a restless night I know that I have to follow my instincts. I can't ignore it just because it might be better for me. Not if something big is happening which could affect the whole country. The sobering thought of war with Cobback convinces me.

I rise much earlier than normal when only Luis is up and tell him that I'm going to visit the horses. He doesn't question me at all, just nodding and waving me on my way. Leaving the square in the direction of the stables I make a quick visit just so I can tell myself that I haven't really lied to Luis. I make sure that the stablemaster sees me so if the Gallavanties come looking he can verify I was here and then I double back on myself, instead heading east towards the Leforth Lord Manor House. Reaching the familiar main gateway I turn left until I find the smaller servants entrance. Taking a deep breath I remind myself confidence is key. That's what Pepe always says. If I act like I belong then people will assume that I do. Pushing open the door I keep my head up and take long strides across the courtyard and into the kitchen. Walking with purpose as though on an important errand I ignore everyone and walk straight through the throng of people. I catch a couple of puzzled glances but don't look back at anyone and make it across the room and out into the corridor without being stopped. Taking a moment to quickly get my bearings I pray that Emily is still in the same bedroom. Quickly climbing the servants stairs I exit onto the main upstairs landing. Luck is with me and no-one is about. Making my way down the corridor I think I've found the right room. Carefully twisting the handle and opening the door a fraction so as to peak in I catch sight of a sleeping girl in a large four poster bed. Emily.

Sneaking into the room and quietly closing the door behind me I turn the lock to ensure no others can follow and catch me in here. Emily looks much the same as I remember though several years have passed. Taking a deep breath and hoping I'm not about to make a huge mistake, I approach the bed and gently shake her shoulders calling her name. "Emily, Emily. Wake up, it's me Cara, I mean Elisa." Saying the name Elisa again after so long feels odd.

She groans and rolls over but doesn't open her eyes. "Emily," I try again, "Emily"

Suddenly she opens her bleary eyes and moans, "What? What is it?" I raise my eyebrows at her and watch as realisation dawns on her face. "Oh my God, Elisa. What are you doing here?" She sits up quickly and stares at me, "And what on earth are you wearing? Are you dressed like a servant?"

I laugh at her concern over my outfit rather than the fact I've snuck into her room at six o'clock in the morning. "It's nice to see you too. And no I'm not dressed up, these are my clothes now. I ran away from the palace over a month ago and have been travelling with some friends."

"Travelling with friends? I thought you were in Talor house being punished because you had some big argument with your father."

"Talor house?" I ask in confusion, "Where did you hear that?"

"My father told me, I'm sure he heard it from Lord Fagan."

"Oh" I say realisation now dawning on me. "I guess that's what Lord Fagan is telling everyone to hide my disappearance. I did wonder why I hadn't heard any rumours of the Princess running away. I wonder if my father even knows the truth or if Lord Fagan's told him the same lies." Pondering this for a moment I realise I'm getting off track but Emily still has more questions.

"So hold on a moment, you ran away from the palace? Why?"

"Because Lord Fagan and my father were trying to make me marry Joseph and when I refused Lord Fagan and Joseph beat me." Emily stares at me in shock, mouth hanging open and wide eyes disbelieving, but I continue. "So I escaped the palace and left the city. I've been on the road with the Gallavanties, this group of travelling showmen, and honestly Emily it's been amazing and they've become like my family and I've even got a part in the show now, and there's this boy Sam, oh I wish you could meet him, he's the cutest and we're kind of a couple now and..." Suddenly I pause for breath and realise I've completely got carried away with my story. Emily still hasn't said a word and seems to be looking at me as though I've gone mad. "But Emily, you can't tell anyone any of this. You have to promise, please. Despite his lies I'm sure Lord Fagan is still looking for me, and if he finds out where I am he'll take me back to Carrard. Please Emily, I came here because I thought I could trust you."

There's a moment of tense silence between us before slowly Emily starts to nod and I breathe out a sigh of relief. "I never did like Lord Fagan, or Joseph for that matter, he was always so arrogant."

"He's even worse now trust me."

"I can't believe they beat you. And then you ran away. We always talked about having exciting adventures when we were children and now here you are, actually living one, you're so brave."

I grin at Emily, "I was pretty scared at first but it's the best thing I've ever done."

"So what are you doing here in Leforth?"

"Well like I mentioned I'm travelling with the Gallavanties and we're here as part of our tour, only for a few days and then we head to Otraf, but I needed to speak to you. Do you know what's going on with the soldiers of Leforth? They're all being sent to Albeck and no-one seems to know why."

Emily immediately sits up straighter. "No-one here knows either. The order came from Lord Fagan about a week ago and I overheard my father arguing about it with the man he sent to deliver the decree. There was no explanation with the order and my father wanted to refuse it but he was told it wasn't a request. I know my father is as confused about the need for soldiers in Albeck as anyone. He's sent inquiries into Cobback to see what is going on but as far as he can tell there isn't anything wrong."

I shake my head, "It doesn't make sense. I suppose I shouldn't really be surprised that Lord Fagan is behind it but why would he want soldiers in Albeck if there's no threat from Cobback?"

Emily grimaces and shrugs, "Your guess is as good as mine."

"A friend I spoke to yesterday was more worried about Karhaner, have you heard anything from your father about the north?"

Emily shakes her head, "Not specifically no, but ever since the military coup I know my father's spent a lot of time and money bolstering the city's defenses to the north just in case. I've heard him talk numerous times about how untrustworthy General Srumthro is and I know he's sent letters to the King in the past about his fears."

"We're supposed to be travelling into Karhaner the day after next but the more I hear about it the less I want to go. I remember learning about the uprising when it happened and I definitely remember the moment my father was told King Sala had been murdered, but after that everything seemed to just go quiet. I don't think I've heard much at all about what happened after General Srumthro came to power. It's like we just ignored it."

"Understandable. They probably don't want to encourage talk about revolts against Kings, better to sweep it under the carpet like it never happened."

I think back to all those conversations I had with Molly about the curfew in Carrard and this explanation slots into place. I think

Molly's father may well have been right. A knock at the door jolts me out of the thoughts. A voice calls through, "My lady, are you awake? The door is locked."

"Oh, ah yes, just a minute" Emily quickly calls back. Jumping out of bed she frantically gestures for me to hide so I drop to the floor and crawl underneath her bed just as Emily opens the door. "Sorry about that Jane, I must've locked it last night without realising. I'd like to have breakfast in my room today if you don't mind and I'm extremely hungry so if you could bring two of everything that would be wonderful." Jane seems slightly taken aback by this odd request but agrees none the less and sends word to the kitchen. When she then glides past Emily to open the curtains I fear the bright sunlight is going to expose my precarious heading place. "Actually Jane I don't need your assistance today. I'm err, well you see, I'm err going to write some poetry. Yes that's it, I'm feeling quite inspired this morning and have all these ideas floating around my head and I need to get them down on paper before I forget them. I need complete time alone so I'm not distracted." A knock at the door signals the arrival of two maids carrying Emily's large breakfast. "Ahh excellent, thank you, if you could just leave it on the table and then yes if everyone would leave and I'll get on with my poetry in peace and I'll let you know when I'm finished. Thank you so much, wonderful, goodbye." she insists as she practically pushes them all out of the door, closing and locking it behind them. As I crawl out from under the bed I can't help but laugh, "Great cover story Emily, you do realise you're going to have to actually write some poetry though or Jane will get suspicious."

"Oh I hadn't thought about that." Emily grimaces, "Well you'll have to help me. Come on let's tuck in to these pastries. I'll come up with the ideas and you'll have to help me with the rhyming, I'm terrible at rhyming."

Joining her at the table I spend the morning, far longer than I had originally planned, eating food, drinking tea and writing poetry. And as much as I love my new life I have to admit that it's fun temporarily returning to a taste of my old life.

When I eventually make it back to the Gallavanties camp I find everyone gathered in Risa's caravan. As I open the door and step in they all turn to stare at me in shock. "What?" I say. Sam's the first to react, pulling me into a hug, "Are you alright?"

"Where the hell have you been?" Risa asks, hands on hips.

"We thought you'd gone and got yourself inta trouble again girl." Dav says before Pepe asks, "What were ya thinkin' just wondering off without telling no-one?"

"I'm fine. I went to see the horses. I told Luis where I was going."

"That was hours ago."

"Well I just went for a walk, exploring the city, you know. Nothing happened, I was perfectly safe."

"Told you she was alright" says Luis. "I knew you were over reacting."

Pepe rolls his eyes, "Well we was about ta send a search party out. Given your habit o' getting yourself caught up in stuff ya can forgive us fa being a bit concerned. Anyway ya back now, no harm done."

"Sorry, I really didn't realise how long I'd been gone. I didn't mean to make you worry."

Risa smiles, "That's what families do hun, they worry about each other. But Pepe's right you're back now. Just try not to disappear again, alright? Now I've been making some alterations for your costume tonight, I thought the hem was a bit too long now that we've added that climbing part in and I don't want you tripping over but I need you to try it on again to check." Risa leads me back out of the caravan as she talks and the rest of the Gallavanties disperse to get on with the usual pre-show jobs, though I can still feel Sam's eyes on me. I try to give him a reassuring smile but I can tell that he wants to talk more. I don't think he's accepting my 'I went for a walk' explanation. There's a huge part of me that wants to tell Sam the truth about where I've been but that also means revealing who I am and I'm not ready for that. No matter how much I tell myself that it won't change anything, in my heart I know it will. They might've handled the idea that I'm a rich girl from the palace but being the princess is a whole other step up and the risk of losing my new family if they don't accept me is too much.

"You're not listening to a word I'm saying are you?" Risa huffs as I suddenly realise that she has still been speaking to me for several minutes. She follows my gaze to where Sam is.

"You're good together you two."

I look at Risa in surprise, "You think?"

"Yeah." She smiles, "He's different around you. I've not seen Sam this happy in the whole time I've known him. He's not one to open up or let people get close to him. I think because of his childhood, there's been that fear of being rejected, not being wanted. I think the only person he truly trusts is Pepe. But seeing him with you, he seems relaxed, open, hopefully. You've changed too. You laugh and smile more. You're more confident, more sure of yourself."

"And happier than I've ever been." I chime in, "And only partly because of Sam. It's you too, and Luis. It's all of you. Having a family, a real proper family whom I love and care about and who I know care about me. I don't ever want to lose this."

"Why would you lose us honey?" Risa queries but I don't answer. I shake my head and brush it off, "Never mind, I'm just being silly. Let's try this costume on again then. I'm excited for my second show."

When Sam corners me later and asks what's bothering me I decide to go with half the truth. That I'm worried about the situation with Leforth's soldiers. I tell him that I walked to the garrison house to find out more information and overheard some talk about orders from Lord Fagan. He believes me and agrees that Lord Fagan's involvement is worrying, but like Dav thinks it's not really our concern. The evening's show goes ahead without a hitch and I do truly enjoy my second performance just as much as my first, but honestly I'm quite relieved when we start packing things up, preparing to leave for Otraf the next morning. I think until I've satisfied myself that there is no threat from Karhaner and the soldiers leaving Leforth is not a problem, I won't be able to shake this gnawing feeling in my stomach.

# Chapter 22

Over the next two days we cross the border and travel to Otraf. I swear the moment we crossed the border a dark shiver went down my spine. Nothing has felt right ever since. The road is empty. I can count the number of people we have seen on one hand. We go through several abandoned villages and pass countless farms which no one appears to be attending. The whole country feels deserted. All the Gallavanties feel it too. Even Luis is quieter than normal. I can tell that Pepe and Dav are on edge about it though they say nothing. The only one who seems unaffected is Kinken who maintains his outwardly calm demeanor. Finally as we draw closer to Otraf signs of life begin to emerge. Tents and ramshackled huts start to line the road. As we approach the city walls it appears as though this is where the people of Karhaner have come to. The population must have grown so much so that the inhabitants are spilling beyond the city walls and extending out into the surrounding countryside, although these makeshift homes have clearly been put up in a hurry.

Entering through the southern gate at first everything gives the appearance of a normal busy city on a midweek day. The streets are crowded and we pass a packed market square, but on closer inspection there don't appear to be many open stalls, and a lot of the people in the street are sat huddled under blankets. As we slowly negotiate the narrow lanes we attract many stares. Pale blank faces track our progress. At a nod from Pepe Sam starts to attempt to drum up business, handing out leaflets and shouting out that the Gallavanties touring show is in town. And whilst people take the leaflets and watch us cautiously, their faces remain cold and impassive. There's no buzz of excitement like in the other places we've been to. Not even from the children. They seem overwhelmingly wary of us. Pepe leads us to a large open space near the centre of the city and dismounts. "Things sure have changed a bit 'ere" is the only comment he makes about our lukewarm welcome. I catch Dav's eye and raise my eyebrows in question. He gives a nod to signal he understands what I'm saying. We need to investigate the worries we heard in Leforth and I can tell Dav is keen to try and find Gini's friends as promised. Whilst the others are already beginning to set up the stage Dav comes over to conspire. "Don't like this. Tis like Gini said, can't quite put me finger on what's troublin' but ya can feel it." I nod in agreement. "Ya ta stay 'ere kid. And that ain't a request" he says as I open my mouth to protest. "I don't like how quiet and suspicious the people were. Ya stay 'ere with everyone else, no wonderin' off ya hear? I'm ta look for Gini's friends and see what I can hear n I'll be back as soon as." Without another word he turns back to Pepe, mumbles something in his ear and then strolls off.

Annoyed at being left behind but knowing that he's right, I do as he says and stay in camp. We set up the stage and prepare for our first show and Dav still isn't back. I try to suggest to Pepe that Sam and I go and put posters up around the city like we did in Ameve but he says no. I think Dav's parting words may well have been about keeping me in sight. With all our preparations done and not being allowed to leave camp, Sam, Luis, Risa and I sit down to play a game of cards. Sam is trying to teach me the rules of a game I've not played before but I'm easily distracted, looking up at every sound, and Risa and Luis are comfortably winning.

Finally catching sight of Dav strolling back into the square I race over to him to see what he has discovered. But his grim expression and the shake of his head tells me it isn't good news. "Couldn't find them. Went to the address Gini gave me but it's all bordered up. Tried asking the neighbours but no-one would talk. Literally slammed the door in me face. Figured an alehouse would be a better bet, people always talk more freely when they got some drink in 'em, but the place was virtually empty. And the few people who were in there kept their lips tight. Started talking to one bloke but soon as I started asking questions he practically ran out the place without even finishing his pint."

Pepe presses his lips into a thin line at Dav's recount, clearly not liking what he's heard any more than I do. Then he seems to snap out of it because he claps Dav on the back and commands that we get on with the show.

Only a small crowd make their way to the square for our first performance that night. In fact it's the smallest audience we've had, even taking into account the village shows we've done. And whilst those who are here appear to enjoy the play, almost everyone leaves as soon as it finishes and there's barely any coin collected. I ask Pepe if there's a curfew in place here like in Carrard but he shakes his head, "I think it's more than that. It's been a few years since I was last in Otraf and the whole place feels different. After the King died n the General took over power things changed a bit but not like this. I never would've imagined this. Otraf used to be one of me favourite places to come. This is like a ghost town."

We're all feeling a little deflated and despite Luis' attempts to remain positive, insisting that word hasn't got out yet and it'll be better tomorrow, the mood is subdued. As I help to put away tonight's costumes and props I almost collide with a tall man who suddenly appears next to the costume rack. Stumbling backwards with a yelp, he puts out a hand to stop me from falling, "Forgive me miss, I didn't mean to startle ya. Excellent show tonight."

Swallowing my fear and trying to calm down my frantically beating heart I try to be polite, "Thank you. Please tell your friends about us, there'll be another show tomorrow."

"You're from Aleti aren't ya?"

"Errr yes, we've just come from Leforth."

"Why are ya here?"

"Errr" I stumble over my words, unsure how to answer his question, "we're a touring show, we go everywhere."

"We don't get visitors from Aleti no more. Odd timing, to be here now."

"Why?" I ask, but just as I do Sam appears. He looks at the man with suspicion and comes to stand by my side, "You alright?"

Before I can reply the man gives Sam a nod and then turns and disappears without a word. "Who was that? What was he doing back here?"

"I don't know. He started off friendly. Said he enjoyed the show but then I kind of got the impression he was saying we shouldn't be here."

"Shouldn't be here? Why?"

"He didn't say."

After putting the final costumes away I seek out Dav to share what the stranger had said.

"Odd timing? Those were his exact words?"

"Yes, odd timing to be here now. That's what he said. What do you think he meant?"

Dav seems to think about it for a moment and then calls a meeting with everyone. After sharing the man's strange attitude and discussing our less than friendly welcome, and with everyone feeling the same unease, it's decided we won't stay in Otraf as long as we originally planned. Pepe makes the final call, "We'll do tomorrow's show and then leave the day after." When I try to argue that we need to find out what's really going on the idea is quickly shot down, but Dav says he'll give it one last try reaching out to some old contacts from years ago. This time I insist on going with him and Sam insists on going with me so it's early the next morning when the three of us leave camp to get answers. Trying not to draw attention to ourselves we make our way through the streets of Otraf, following Dav to a warehouse on the western side. As we keep our heads down and move quickly we are mostly ignored but at the same time I have an overwhelming feeling that we are being watched. I keep finding myself turning around to check that no one is following us. One such time I spin around so quickly and suddenly I think I catch sight of a man ducking into the alley we just passed. He seems somewhat familiar though I can't think where from. Sam takes my hand, "What's wrong?"

"I could've sworn I saw..." I shake my head, "Never mind, probably just my imagination."

Trying to ignore my feelings of paranoia we reach our destination and at Dav's instruction wait just outside the large loading doors whilst he checks it out first. I nervously continue to search around us, checking again for the man who I thought I recognised in the street. Sam seems on edge too, still holding my hand his thumb rhythmically strokes up and down the back of mine. After a few moments Dav reappears and beckons us inside. The warehouse is almost empty except for a few stacks of large crates and a muscled man stood next to one such pile. His arms folded over his burly chest he looks us up and down before glancing at Dav, "They're kids."

"They're with me" is Dav's only answer.

The man seems to hesitate but then shrugs his shoulders. "What do you wanna know?"

Questions burst out of me, "What's going on in the city? What's happening to the people? Why is everyone so afraid to talk?"

The man laughs, "Ain't nothing new. Been like this for years. Ever since the General took control life ain't been so peachy here in Karhaner. Trade with Aleti stopped almost over night and after a couple of bad harvests and even worse winters the people are starving and desperate. Unless you're living in the castle, you're living in poverty now. And as fa why they don't wanna talk to ya, well you're the enemy far as a lot of people are concerned. The General's been telling everyone all their problems are Aleti's fault for cutting us off. A lot of anger and resentment towards anyone coming from that part of the world. He's convinced the whole country you lot are out to get us. 'Cause everyone seems to have forgotten it all started with the General's coup in the first place. Didn't have these problems before then, did we? Mind, easier to blame foreigners and outsiders than look at your own leaders, aint it?"

Dav nods but the man continues, "Listen if I was you I'd get out of here, quick as ya can. And I wouldn't be staying long in Aleti either. I'd go to Cobback and..."

Cutting in I ask, "Why shouldn't we stay in Aleti?"

The man seems annoyed at my interruption. He looks at me carefully, scrutinising my face, and when it seems like he's not going to say anything more in front of me, I back away. "I'll just wait over here." I say dragging Sam with me and giving Dav a meaningful look to gain the answers we need. We wait anxiously by the door whilst Dav and the man continue a mumbled conversation. When they're done Dav reaches out to shake his hand and then strides back over to us. "Let's go." He says continuing out the door and back on to the bustling streets, leaving Sam and I to chase after him. "Well, what did he say? Why isn't Aleti safe?"

"Not here" Dav growls at us without breaking his stride. Sam and I look at each other in concern but follow after him in silence.

As soon as we're back at camp Dav gives a whistle and signals for everyone to gather in the caravan again. Once the door is shut I can't contain my questions any longer. "What is it Dav? What did your friend say?"

"We need to leave. Head to Cobback. A lot more going on in this city than we thought. Seems the General has been extremely busy of late and a recent order has called up every able bodied man to join the Karhaner army."

My blood runs cold as what he's saying sinks in and connects with everything else we've heard. A single look from Dav confirms my worst suspicions. "They're going to attack Aleti."

Slowly Dav nods, "They're going to attack Aleti."

# Chapter 23

-----------------------------------------------------------------

Walking up and down the caravan in agitation I plead with the Gallavanties, "We have to go back. We have to do something. They're about to invade my country. We need to warn them."

Pepe shakes his head, "What can we do? No-one of any importance is gonna listen to us."

I barely pause in my pacing, already planning ahead exactly what we need to do, "We need to get to Carrard, as fast as we can, and tell my father what we know. We warn the people in Leforth on the way and send word to the soldiers who have already travelled to Albeck. We need to call them back to Leforth immediately. If we go to Lord Francis, he can start the defense preparations while we continue our journey. If we reach my father in time then reinforcements from Carrard shouldn't take too long to organise. If Leforth's walls can just last until then. And the alliance we've just signed with Navas, if my father sends word they'll have to help. With their army and ours we should be able to do it."

Luis interrupts my frantic planning, "Cara who exactly is your father in the castle that he's gonna be able to just order all of that? Surely we need to somehow get to the king?"

"My father is the king" I say without thinking through the impact of my words, still pacing and mentally calculating distances and travel times in my mind.

Risa waves her hand and pulls me to a stop, "The King is your father?"

Sam stares at me in shock, "Wait you're a princess."

Luis is also looking at me in total surprise, "Not a princess, the princess."

I look around at the Gallavanties who are watching me with wide eyes, like they don't know who I am. In a quiet voice I admit it all, "Yes. I'm the Princess." When no one makes a sound I try to explain. "My full name is Princess Elisa Cara Paisley Regal. I'm sorry I lied to you. I didn't mean to deceive you. I thought you would treat me differently if you knew who I was. And I'm not even that person any more, I'm Cara. I'm still just Cara. Only knowing that Aleti is in danger. We can't ignore what we know. Please we have to go back and warn them. If we don't, thousands could die and the whole country be destroyed. Please, I'm so sorry I lied, but please help me."

There's a bang from outside which all makes us jump and for a moment a stunned silence is all that fills the caravan. I try to catch Sam's eye but he won't look at me.

Pepe is the one to finally break the silence, "I don't like liars Cara. We're supposed to be family and that's a pretty big thing to hide."

"I know."

"But I kinda get it. And regardless of your secret, you're right. A war is about to start and innocent people are gonna get hurt. If we can do something to prevent it we should. We'll leave for Aleti first thing in the morning. We'll get ya back to Carrard and then the rest is down to you. Ain't gonna pretend I'm not still angry at ya though kid, but family sticks together even when one of us makes a mistake."

I let out a breath I didn't realise I'd been holding, "Thank you". But just as I start to relax Sam looks up, "So we're just gonna help her even though she's been stringing us all along with a pack of lies for weeks."

"Sam..." Risa starts to say.

"No," he says, pushing past me to get to the caravan door. "If you wanna help her then that's your choice but I ain't sticking around to be mugged over again." The most awkward silence descends as Sam looks at the Gallavanties and I look at Sam. The anger rolling off Sam's taut shoulders is palpable. When no one answers he shakes his head and glares at us all, "So much for trust and family loyalty." He flings open the door with a crash and storms out of the caravan.

"Sam please" I call after him as he walks away. Not knowing what else to do I chase him up the street, grabbing hold of his arm "I'm sorry. Please, don't leave, just come back with us. I'm sorry, I'm so so sorry."

"Get off me. I don't even know who you bloody are. You lied to me. Right from the beginning ya lied to me. Maybe I could've forgiven ya at first but what about the last few weeks. Have they meant nothing? I thought we was close, I've told you stuff about me I've never told anyone and you ain't even told me your real name." He shakes his head, "Go back to the caravan. I don't wanna see you right now, I don't wanna talk. I just... I can't believe I thought... I thought you and me... I need to go." Ripping his arm out of my grip he turns and storms away.

Falling to my knees with tears flowing down my face I try to call after him again but know it's no use. He's gone. I stay like that for I don't know how long but eventually I know that I have to get up. I have to get back to the Gallavanties. We have to leave for Aleti and warn them of the upcoming attack. I may have just lost the most important person in my life but thousands of my countrymen will likely die if I don't pull myself together. Standing slowly on shaky legs I take one last look down the empty street where Sam disappeared, wiping my eyes, I whisper a goodbye, then turn back to where I need to go.

# Chapter 24

As I exit the street and reach the square someone from behind suddenly wraps their arms around me, picking me up and trying to carry me away. I scream and throw my head backwards like Dav taught me, catching the person off guard he drops me with a curse. Not stopping to see who the assailant was, I make to sprint towards the Gallavanties caravans but another man comes from the side and tackles me to the ground and then another dives on top to help him. It's then that I see these are not ordinary men taking a chance on a random girl. These are Karhaner soldiers and true fear now sets in. These soldiers are here with a purpose. They are not here to kidnap any ordinary girl, they are here to get a Princess. There is no doubt in my mind, these men know who I am.

I scream and fight, kicking my legs and trying to hit anything within range, but it's no use. Not with four of them now holding me down. They manage to catch my flailing legs and bind my ankles to stop me kicking any more. Then they do the same with my hands as I still desperately scream out until someone stuffs a rag in my mouth, silencing my protests. Just when I think all is lost the Gallavanties suddenly appear. As they race towards me, Risa calling my name, for a moment I think rescue is coming, but then at least twenty armed guards flow into the square from all sides, surrounding us all, and I know there's no hope of the Gallavanties coming to my aid. Instead the soldiers insist that they are to come with us too. In contrast to my battle the Gallavanties allow the soldiers to lead them without protest. I stare at Pepe and Dav who appear to be furiously thinking and sharing a hurried whispered conversation. Looking at Risa I see my own fear reflected back in her eyes too. What is happening? What are they going to do with us? This is all my fault. The Gallavanties are only in this danger because of me. I try to tell Risa and Luis how sorry I am with my eyes but I'm not sure they understand my message. With my legs bound the soldiers practically drag me down the twisting streets. People come out of their houses to watch the procession in an eerie silence. We reach the castle walls and enter, the thick barred portcullis closing swiftly behind us. They march us up the entrance steps and through a wide corridor which seems vaguely familiar from my one and only previous visit here when I was a child. I'm sure there used to be royal portraits hung all the way along here but now the walls are plain.

We arrive into a large great hall, not unlike the one back in Carrard. The guards lead us down the central aisle until I'm pushed to my knees in front of a man wearing military uniform and sat on a large throne raised above me. General Srumthro I assume. The Gallavanties remain standing somewhere behind me. "Well well well, this is an interesting development." The General stands and approaches, looking at me intensely. Slowly he nods, "Yes, I see it now, once you ignore the grub and the clothes, you look exactly like the girl in the portrait. A little more grown up perhaps.

Princess Elisa. The only daughter of King Rafael and heir to the Aleti throne here in my Great Hall. A most unexpected though not unwelcome surprise I must admit. How on earth did you end up in Otraf, Karhaner of all places? Last I heard you had been banished by Lord Fagan to some palace in the countryside?"

I shake my head at the cover story which Lord Fagan has spread, "I ran away from Carrard and Lord Fagan a long time ago."

"But now you plan to return and inform them of my plans, yes? Well I must disappoint you. Those in the city are extremely loyal you see." Glancing to his left I follow his gaze to see a man I recognise from the square. The one who was hanging around backstage and was always watching us from across the yard. He twists his hat in his hands and refuses to meet my eyes. "Yes, you see. Like a faithful dog. You will be rewarded." The General tells the man.

"Thank you sir," he bows.

The General waves his arm, "The Princess and her friends can be locked up. I will speak more with her later."

As the guards move to surround us once more Pepe suddenly pipes up, "We ain't friends."

The General looks up, appraising Pepe, "What did you say?"

"We ain't her friends. She ain't one of us. We've only known her a few weeks. Asked us for a ride outta Carrard and we said alright in return for payment, din't ask questions. We only found out who she was just before your men came bursting in. If your informant is any good he would've told ya that. She bloody lied to us, kept us in the dark for weeks bout who she really were."

General Srumthro glances at the thin man who is still hovering off to the side, "Err yes sir, I think that's true. They certainly weren't treating her like a Princess. They were calling her Cara when I first overheard them. The princess only revealed her true identity when she said she needed to get back to Aleti and warn them of our plans to attack. They all did seem rather shocked by it."

He seems to consider this whilst I try to catch Pepe's eye. What is he doing?

"And now that you do know who she is, what do you intend to do?"

"Well if we'd known there was a reward for her we would've turned her right over to you ourselves. Seems to me like we should get a share of the reward anyhow. We were the ones who brought her here to Otraf in the first place."

General Srumthro nods slowly at this, "Well clearly you're not close associates with the Princess here so I've no further use for you. A scrawny bunch of travelling showmen are worth nothing to me. They'll be no reward but you're not being thrown in jail so count yourselves lucky."

Pepe smiles and nods, "Thank you very much kind sir. Are we still permitted to perform our show for the good people of Otraf tonight before we move on?" he asks. The General waves a dismissive hand, "Yes yes, perform your show then continue on your merry way." Pepe then bows in response. He actually bows at him. Then the General calls out to his guards and he stands to leave the room, "Take the Princess away, lock her in the dungeons."

I stare at Pepe in shock. He can't mean what he's just said. But before I can say anything two guards grab my arms on either side and start to drag me from the room. I see Risa take a step forward but Pepe's arm shoots out to stop her and then Luis tugs her back. Tears fill my eyes. They truly are abandoning me. Tears splashing down my face as I wallow in my despair allowing the guards to take me down a flight of stairs without protest. They lead me down a mazy corridor and another flight of stairs before we reach what is clearly the prison dungeon. They open a heavy metal door and shove me inside. My eyes slowly adjust to the darkness to reveal a plain square room containing only a bucket and wooden pallet. I pull my cloak tightly around me as coldness seeps in and slowly sink to the floor. Unable to control my tears I let out a sob, and then another one follows. Once I start I can't seem to stop and just let everything pour out of me. The upset and sense of betrayal mixing with my fear.

Eventually my tears do dry up and I simply lie there curled up on my side on the cold hard floor, reliving that moment in the great hall over and over again. How could they do this to me? The more I think about it the more I just can't believe it. I know what I saw and heard with my own ears and eyes but the Gallavanties are my family. I trust them with my life. They wouldn't betray me like this. I know they wouldn't. Even after I lied to them about who I was they still forgave me and were willing to help. Suddenly I sit up. That's it. They promised to help Aleti, to warn them of the impending attack. That must be what they are doing. The General was going to lock us all up and then there would have been no-one free to travel south to get word to Aleti.

Pepe must've known there was no chance of the General letting me go, but there was a chance of him releasing the Gallavanties, leaving them free to fulfill their promise and alert Aleti. It makes such sense. It was a choice between sticking with me or protecting an entire country. And though I don't doubt it would have been tough for Pepe to make the decision, he always makes the right one. I breathe a sigh of relief that I've figured out what Pepe was doing. The more I think about it , the more I know in my heart that this is true. That the Gallavanties didn't betray me and abandon me, they made a choice to fulfill a promise. I send up a silent prayer of thanks to the Gallavanties. I try to send a message through the universe to tell them that I understand and support their decision and I wish with everything I have that they make it in time. Exhausted and with a pounding headache I finally drift off to sleep.

# Chapter 25

I'm woken by the rough arms of a soldier shaking me and dragging me to my feet. I'm removed from my cell, led down the corridor to another plain windowless room and sat on a chair. My ankles are secured to the chair legs and my hands tied forcefully behind my back with rope. The guard then leaves, closing the door behind him. I wait for something to happen. When nothing does I try to tug at the bindings on my wrists but only succeed in rubbing my arms raw from the rough rope, and not actually making the ties any looser. I wait and I wait and I wait. I think I even drift back to sleep at one point when suddenly the door opens and the most imposing man I've ever seen walks in. As I stare up at the giant of a man two other guards enter and stand behind me. The man stands in front of me and speaks in a deep gruff voice. "Here's how this is gonna go Princess. I'm gonna ask you questions and you're gonna answer. If you answer them properly then it's all good. But if you don't answer, or I don't like your answer, or I think you're lying then myself and my friends here are gonna hurt you. And we'll keep hurting you until you give us the answer we want or you're dead. Understand?"

I stare at him saying nothing. The man raises his eyebrows then slaps me across the face so hard and fast that the whole chair tips over and I hit my head on the floor. Immediately a guard rights the chair again. Pain radiates across my face, a thousand times worse than the hits I took from Joseph or Lord Fagan, this man is not messing around. He looks at me again, "Do you understand?"

"Yes" I answer.

"Good. First question, how many men make up the Aleti army?"

General Srumthro must already know the answer to this question, this isn't a closely guarded secret so it must be a test. I answer honestly, "about 25,000."

The man nods. "Where are they stationed?"

"I don't know."

"Don't like that answer." The man nods at the guards behind me and one of them swings a metal pole into my stomach, knocking the air out of my lungs.

"But I don't know. I haven't been at council meetings in Carrard for months. Last I heard some were stationed at Vamanst and there's always a garrison permanently in Carrard."

"What about Leforth?"

"Yes there's a large garrison stationed at Leforth." I don't mention the soldier movement I learnt about when we were there but this is clearly a mistake. Another blow from the metal pipe comes my way.

"Lying again, Princess. Soldiers are being sent from Leforth to Albeck, you know this. What plans are in place in the event of an attack or invasion? What emergency resources does Aleti have?"

"I don't know" I say, shaking my head with a sob.

Another gesture from my interrogator sees the two guards behind me leave the room. They return moments later carrying a large tub of water. Placing it in front of me they unceremoniously grab my head and plunge it into the water. I struggle as much as I can and try to keep my mouth closed. My head is yanked back and I gasp for air.

"What plans are in place in the event of an attack or invasion? What emergency resources does Aleti have?"

Keeping my mouth shut I refuse to answer. Pushed down again, this time for longer, I can't hold my breath and end up opening my mouth, water rushing in. They release me a moment later and I'm able to cough up the water and breathe again.

"Perhaps the princess needs some thinking space. Perhaps some time alone will jog her memory." The guards untie me and drag me back to my cell, throwing me to the floor. Soaking wet and shivering uncontrollable I crawl over to my 'bed'.

Hours pass in the murky darkness though it's difficult to really tell how long goes by, the only source of light coming from a lantern which burns in the corridor outside and filters through the small barred window set into the heavy locked door. I drift in and out of sleep, my dreams filled with horrific images. Leforth burnt to the ground, innocent people slaughtered. The harsh faces of the guards coming to torture me again. The giant man approaching me with a knife. The Gallavanties also murdered before my eyes. And Sam. Sam's face when he found out who I really was and left. That almost haunts me more than anything. Because whilst I can convince my-self that everything else is a nightmare, not reality, this one image I know to be true. At some point the door opens and a cold bowl of stew, chunk of bread and cup of water are shoved through. Clearly they don't intend to starve me to death. After that I'm left alone again in the endless gloom. Occasionally I hear footsteps or the guards mumbling from further down the corridor but no-one comes to get me, no-one speaks to me. This abandonment goes on for so long that I think I'm going to lose my mind and I almost wish that the guards would return for me. Just so I can hear another human being's voice again, just so I can get out of this cell, even for just a few moments. But when I do hear the tread of heavy footsteps heading my way I can't help but cower in the corner again. The door opens and two guards enter. Silently they walk over and haul me up, roughly pushing me out of the cell where two more guards wait. I follow them down the dingy corridor, two soldiers in front, and two behind. They take me to the same room as before and I can't help but hesitate on the threshold as I stare once again at the small wooden chair in the centre. One of the guards grabs my arm and forces me into the chair. Again my arms are tied tightly behind my back. Before they even say or do anything I can feel the fear trickling up my back as they stand staring at me and tears start to fill my eyes. I close my eyes and try to breathe, chanting to myself 'Stay strong, stay strong, stay strong' over and over again in the hopes that I can convince myself. It's not really working. The silence drags on and my fear continues to build as the soldiers do nothing.

Finally the door opens and I get a shock when General Srumthro himself enters with a swagger. "Good morning my dear, how are you? I hope the accommodation is to your liking." He says as some-one carries a large cushioned chair in and places it opposite me. The General takes his seat before holding out his hand and being given a cup of tea. He sits there drinking it with a smug smile on his face. "I would offer you a cup but unfortunately my guards here tell me that you're not exactly being cooperative with answering their questions, and unhelpful guests don't get luxuries like cups of tea or proper beds. Of course were you to provide us with some useful information, that could all change and your stay with us could be made much more comfortable for you."

I say nothing, staring at him with open contempt.

"Never mind. It really doesn't matter. Your country will be invaded and crushed regardless of you holding your tongue or not."

"Why? Why are you doing this? Aleti hasn't done anything against you."

"Well now that's not technically true, you did offer support to King Sala when I initially deposed him. Tried to help him back on the throne until I had his head cut off."

"That was nearly seven years ago" I try to argue.

"Yes, it's taken slightly longer than I anticipated to squash out some little resistance but now that control is absolute in Karhaner I've become a little bored. Everyone does exactly what I say here. So I've decided it's time to expand my empire. Ruling one country just isn't enough any more, I want to rule the world." He says with a mad glint. And as I look him in the eyes I realise that is exactly what he is. Insane. Mad with power. There's no reasoning with this man. He will invade Aleti and probably more countries after that.

Defiantly I say, "You won't win. They'll stop you. My father and his army will stop you."

"Oh really?" The General chuckles, "Oh I do like a girl with some fighting spirit. I think I'll keep you when I'm done destroying your country. It's always fun to have a fiery minx around to entertain me and you're quite a pretty little thing."

"You really think it's going to be that easy to invade Aleti? They're allies with Navas now. You're biting off more than you can chew."

The General tips back his head and roars with laughter at this. "Oh you are such a stupid naive girl, you think Navas will come to Aleti's aid? I know King James. He won't do anything. Why would he? He doesn't care about Aleti. Your father's an idiot for trying to do a deal with him. And in the process he gets rid of an ally who might have actually helped in Cobback." The General is grinning at me like a psychotic hyena. "You father's a moron, weak and spineless, and soon he'll discover exactly what his actions have lost. And you my dear will be there to witness it all."

Turning to the guards he says, "Make sure a prisoner's transport cage is made ready for our departure next week, the Princess will be accompanying us to the front line."

# Chapter 26

Finally, once the General has clearly had enough of taunting me with his future plans, I am returned to my cell. Lying on the wooden pallet which is my bed I try to count back the hours for how long I've been here since the Gallavanties left. It's hard to tell in the cell with no window but it must be at the very least two days. If they left straight away they could even be nearing Leforth right now. They could make it to Carrard by the end of the week if they pushed it. Is that enough time to get there and warn them? How will they even get into the palace to talk to my father? Will he even listen to them if they do make it? Probably not is my honest answer. I doubt very much that he will even see them, but maybe they can at least alert the residents of Leforth so they can prepare and are not taken totally by surprise.

As I contemplate the future awaiting my country and it's people I hear the sound of a key entering the lock and turning. I can't help but groan. Has the General returned to torment me again? Or worse the giant man who enjoys torture so much. I look towards the door expecting to see Karhan soldiers but instead find myself staring in shock at the sight of Sam. He rushes over to me with a bunch of keys in his hand, "You alright?" he asks, quickly looking me up and down but then not waiting for an answer. "Wait a second" he instructs before returning to the corridor. He re-enters the cell dragging the body of a guard, "Just knocked out" he reassures me. "Come on let's go."

Sam grabs my hand and starts to drag me out of the prison without saying anything else. I'm so shocked I stumble after him for a few steps before being able to find the words. "What are you doing here?"

"What does it look like I'm doing? I'm rescuing you aint I? Now come on we ain't got time to stand 'ere chatting about it."

Sam once again leads me down the corridor stepping over two more guards who are lying on the floor. I stare at them horrified, "What did you do? Are they dead?"

"No they're not dead, I just slipped them a little something in their ale. They'll wake up in a couple of hours with a sore head but that's it. A lot worse'll happen to us if we get caught 'ere though."

Checking around the corner Sam dashes across to the next door and cautiously creaks it open. He glances around before indicating it's safe to follow. We climb some stairs and then slip out into a courtyard and hesitantly make our way around the edge under cover of an overhanging balcony above us. Taking a quick look up at the walls I see at least six guards on duty and nearly trip over a loose stone before Sam catches my hand and stops me. When we reach the castle's west gate it is clearly locked and more soldiers are stationed just outside.

But Sam wasn't aiming for the west gate itself. He was aiming for the drain next to it. Clearly this is how Sam got into the castle in the first place as the cover is already slightly ajar. Sam swiftly shifts it further out of the way and gestures for me to go first. Trying not to think about it I swing my legs down and lower myself into the darkness. For a moment I just hang there, dangling my legs and not feeling anything below. "Let go" says Sam, so I do and drop only a couple of feet with a small splash into a shallow stream of what I really hope is water but I daren't ask Sam to check.

Sam nimbly lands beside me and then takes my hand once more to lead me through the pitch black tunnel. How Sam knows where he is going is a mystery to me. I just follow him in silence. After a few minutes my eyes adjust to the gloom slightly and I'm at least able to make out the shape of Sam in front of me. Suddenly he stops as we reach a grill covering the entire tunnel and blocking any possible way forward. But then Sam guides my hand to a metal ladder which runs up the wall next to it. He climbs up ahead of me and pushes the drain cover out of the way. I scramble up behind him and we emerge onto a narrow empty street.

Sam replaces the drain cover before starting to move off again. I creep after him but as he pauses at a street corner to look around I have to ask, "Sam, Why are you helping me? I thought you hated me."

"I don't hate you" Sam answers without looking at me.

"But why? I thought you'd left? Why did you come back?" Sam is still trying to drag me down the street but I pull him to a stop. I know we're trying to escape a pretty dire situation but I need to hear the answer. I need to know whether the seed of hope burning in my chest since I first saw Sam is real or not. "Sam, why did you come back? Why did you leave?"

Suddenly Sam stops trying to keep moving and turns back to face me, "Because I love you Cara. I bloody love you. I love you with everything I am but what I am is nothing. A poor travelling showman, an orphan with no standing in the world and you're a bloody princess and how the hell am I supposed to be good enough for you. I can never be good enough for you and it bloody kills me cos I love you so goddamn much. And of course I came back to save you. I promised I wouldn't leave you, din't I? When I saw you being dragged away by them soldiers I swear to God it was like me heart was being ripped out me chest, and I wanted to just jump in and save ya then, but there was too many of them and I hesitated, and then you were gone. N I'm just sorry it took me so god damn long to get to ya, to get you out, but we had to come up with a plan."

It takes me a second to process his words but then relief floods through me. He loves me. I take both his hands in mine and look him straight in the eye so he knows I feel what I'm saying, "Who says you're not good enough for me? Who gets to say that love isn't enough. Because I love you too Sam Gallavantie and that's more than enough for me. You're more than enough for me. Don't you know what you mean to me? You saved me, freed me, gave me a life that I adore. I wouldn't change anything Sam, not one bit of it." I say with tears in my eyes.

Sam looks at me, searching my face for something though I don't know what. Just when I think he isn't going to respond he grabs my face and kisses me. He kisses me like he's never kissed me before. It's a kiss full of every kind of emotion. Love, fear, anger and passion. And I kiss him back with everything I have.

Suddenly he pulls away, "We have to keep moving."

Running hand in hand and sticking to the shadows we reach the city walls at the southern gate. Peaking round the corner though I see the gate is closed and there are at least a dozen guards.

I lean up to Sam's ear and whisper, "How are we going to get past them?"

Sam's turns and looks me straight in the eye. "Do you trust me?"

I nod without any hesitation and Sam immediately gives me a quick kiss and then sets off again, pulling me after him. But he's not running towards the gate, he's running away from it, parallel to the wall.

"Where are we going?" I hiss but he either doesn't hear me or chooses not to answer as we race on. Suddenly he lets go of my hand, stopping at the bottom of a large tree, then, as though it's the easiest thing in the world, he scrambles up the trunk and swings himself into the branches.

Turning around he holds out an arm to me and I somewhat awkwardly follow. "Now what?" I ask but Sam just continues to climb, turning around to help me or point at exactly where I should place my hands or feet. I've never climbed a tree before and I can't say I enjoy the experience. I nearly slip twice but Sam is there each time to steady me.

After a few moments Sam looks around and decides that we are high enough. He points over to the left and I see the city wall running right past our hiding place. Or maybe it's not a hiding place. I watch as Sam crawls along a thick branch which juts out towards the wall. When he's as far out as it's possible to go before the branch starts to get dangerously thin he swings his legs around and then with a leap, drops down onto the top of the wall. I stare at him in horror. He can't seriously expect me to do that. I barely made it up here and now he wants me to jump off. Frantically I shake my head at Sam but he's looking at me and nodding furiously. When I don't move he steps closer and whispers urgently, "Come on, you can do it I promise. It's not as far as you think." I look at the distance again. It definitely is that far. "Cara, you really don't have a choice. The guards are gonna notice you're gone n soon the whole city's gonna start searching for you. We have to go. Come on."

Taking a deep breath I try to focus on one little part at a time. Just like I did with the balcony so many weeks ago when I was escaping an entirely different kind of prison. I made it then, I can make it now, I try to reason with myself. Finally reaching the end and swinging my legs around I try not to think about the next part and just do it. "Really push off hard Cara, you can do it, I'll catch you." Focusing on Sam's words and outstretched hand, I fling myself away from the tree to the wall and actually overdo it a bit, landing on top of Sam and knocking him to the floor.

"Oops sorry." Sam just grins and helps pull me to my feet. "Well done, knew you could do it. Ready for jump number two?"

"Jump number two?"

Sam slowly turns me round away from the tree to see what awaits me on the other side of the wall.

"You have got to be kidding me." I say as I stare down at the huge black gushing river which lies at the bottom of this steep 16 metre drop.

"Nope, time to go." Sam says as he pulls me to the edge.

"No Sam, seriously I can't swim."

"I know," Sam says with a surprisingly soothing calm demeanor when he sees how truely panicked I am, "It's ok. It doesn't matter, you don't need to swim, you just need to float, the current will do the rest. Just lie on your back. I've got you sweetheart, I promise."

Sam takes my hand and gives it a squeeze. "Don't let go," I whisper.

"Never" He says, "Ready? 1 2 3."

Suddenly Sam leaps and pulls me with him. Squeezing my eyes tight shut I feel a rush of wind as the river races up to meet us. As we hit the water I lose Sam's hand and find myself submerged in cold darkness. Flailing around with my arms and legs I can't figure out which way is up. I open my mouth to scream and water rushes in. Terror fills me as I flashback to when I was being tortured in the dungeons. Oh my god, I'm going to die. But then suddenly my head breaks the surface, coughing up water, I just have enough time to pull in one precious lungful of air before I go under again. Frantically kicking my legs again now that I know which way is up I manage to get my head out of the water once more, "Sam!" I scream "Sam!" Abruptly I feel a pair of arms around me and Sam's reassuring voice, "I've got you, it's ok, lie back, I've got you."

Taking lungfuls of deep breaths I lie back onto Sam and the panic recedes slightly as we let the current take us down stream and away from the castle. It feels like we travel like this for ages but I daren't ask Sam what the next part of the plan is in case he doesn't have one. Suddenly Sam starts to try and manoeuvre us towards the river bank, "Kick your legs Cara" he instructs whilst he steers us with one arm and kicks his own legs. For a moment I wonder why Sam's chosen this particular spot but then I see it. A small glowing light up ahead on the south side of the river. Sam calls out and the answering voice nearly makes me burst into tears as Pepe, Dav, Kinken, Luis and Risa come into view. They form a human chain to reach us and somehow drag our heavy soaked bodies up onto the river bank. Instantly Risa is wrapping me in a blanket and pulling me in for a hug. "Oh Cara my love, are you ok? Are you alright? Are you hurt? They didn't hurt you did they?"

Dav kneels down in front of me whilst Pepe is checking on Sam, "Nice to see you again kiddo."

"That was the worst bloody escape plan ever." I stutter as the cold makes my teeth chatter uncontrollably.

Sam laughs, "We escaped, that's the main thing."

Pepe shakes his head, "You escaped the city, we ain't escaped the country yet. Come on we gotta get moving."

Risa pulls me to my feet but when I stumble Dav sweeps me up and carries me to the caravans. I twist around for Sam but he's being helped into Pepe's caravan.

"Let's get you out these wet things and warmed up." says Risa as Dav shuts the door and a moment later the caravan starts to move. As I change into warm dry clothes and get bundled up by even more blankets the swaying caravan tells me we are travelling at a much faster pace than we are used to. I hope the horses can cope. Risa insists that I drink a flask of warm tea, eat some stew and then rest. Truthfully I really wish I was in the same caravan as Sam but I know we can't stop just to allow me to swap so I crawl onto my bunk. With everything that has happened I feel my eyes drifting closed as soon as my head hits the pillow. My last thought is one that makes me smile. They came back for me.

# Chapter 27

---

When I wake up it's to find sunlight streaming through the window and the caravan stationary. Quickly climbing out of bed I race outside to find the Gallavanties all sat around a firepit. Luis is the first to notice I'm awake, "Morning sunshine, or afternoon more accurately."

"It's afternoon, really?" I say as I go and sit down next to Sam who immediately puts his arm around my shoulders and gives me a kiss on the side of my head.

I smile up at him, "Thanks for rescuing me"

"Anytime" he whispers before giving me a proper kiss.

Turning back to the others I thank them too.

"Did you really think we was abandoning yous?" Pepe asks with a wry smile, "Had to come up with a plan didn't we? Much easier to rescue yous when we're not all locked up as well."

"I figured you were leaving me so you could go to Leforth and warn Aleti about the attack."

"Not without you honey." says Risa.

"We'd never leave one of our own behind," adds Dav.

Luis pipes up, "Oh and if you're looking for someone to blame for the whole river swim thing it was all Kinken's idea."

I laugh, "Well I'll forgive you this time Kinken but next time could you come up with a plan that doesn't involve a sixteen metre jump into a freezing cold river?"

"I'll bear that in mind," Kinken says with a smile.

"Right" Dav says, standing with purpose, "We can't rest too long. They'll know you're gone and they'll be looking for ya, and if it were me the first place I'd be looking would be at the people ya came here with so let's get back in Aleti country before they catch up to us."

Pepe pushes himself to his feet before adding, "Cara you'd best stay hidden in the caravan so ya can't be seen by passersby. Sam you stay with her just in case any of the guards caught a glimpse of you last night n all."

Sam nods and we quickly pack up the makeshift camp and reattach the horses to the wagons, although truthfully they could do with a longer break. Climbing back into the caravan Sam and I cuddle up together on the bench. Sam gently starts to stroke my forehead as we set off again.

"I'm so glad you're ok. I'm sorry about our argument." Sam says breaking the comfortable silence. "It was stupid and I didn't mean what I said."

"I know, it was just the shock of finding out. I'm sorry I kept such a big secret from you. I know I should've told you earlier."

Apologies said we let the silence envelop us once more until, "Sam, you know everything you said last night, about me being a princess and you not being good enough?"

"Yeah?"

"Well I meant what I said. I love you and nothing's going to change that. Just because people come from two different worlds doesn't mean it can't work if they want it to. And I want it to, to work between us I mean. I just wanted you to know."

"I love you too and I want it to work as well."

"Then we'll make it work" I smile.

As Sam smiles back at me and moves as though to give me a kiss we suddenly hear a shout and then the distant thunder of approaching horse hooves. Slowly it dawns on me who those horses must belong to and Sam and I stare at each other in horror. "What do we do?" I whisper. Leaping up from the bench Sam pulls at the planks of wood underneath. Clearly on a hidden hinge that I've never noticed the wood swings open to reveal a small hole behind it. "Quick" Sam urges. Throwing myself off the chair I crawl into the now open space underneath. Sam forces himself in with me before pulling the wooden planks back into place with a click. The space is really only designed for one person but lying face to face there's just enough room. Trying to regulate my heavy breathing we both try to listen. There's definitely voices coming from outside though I can't make out what they're saying. Suddenly the caravan door is thrown open and heavy footsteps enter. I daren't breathe. My heart is pounding so loudly I fear that it's going to give us away. As the man with large black boots starts throwing things around, opening cupboards and searching under the beds another one enters. He moves towards our end of the caravan banging on the walls. Through the narrow slates in the wood I watch as he stops right in front of us. He bends down and reaches for the planks of wood in the bench opposite us giving them a sharp tug. Knowing he's about to do the same to our bench I reach out and grab the wood from the inside. Holding it with all my might I manage to keep it in place when the soldier tries to pull it. "Nothing" calls the other guard from the other end of the caravan

"Nothing" our guard echoes back and they both turn to leave. Even when the caravan door shuts I don't dare move, and Sam and I continue to lie in our hiding place for at least another fifteen minutes. I strain to listen to what's going on but can't hear anything now. The sound of the caravan door opening again makes the pair of us jump but we both let out a huge sigh of relief when it's Risa's voice which calls out, "It's ok, they're gone."

Emerging from underneath the bench Pepe fills us in on what happened. "Guards from Otraf caught up with us quicker than we thought. Searched all the caravans and questioned us but we played dumb. Acted as though as far as we were concerned you were still rotting in jail in Otraf, and seeing as when we left quite publically early yesterday you were definitely still locked up they couldn't really doubt us. Still think they were pretty surprised not to find ya here. Good job Sam."

"Well they nearly did find us if Cara hadn't thought to hold the wood from inside."

Pepe nods, "They're ahead of us on the road now though, heading to LeForth. I don't think it's safe to go that way."

"What other way is there?" I ask.

"Through Relad." he answers simply.

"Relad? But can we go that way? I thought the Relad's didn't like it when people entered their land."

"They don't, but I've been through once before and they do make exceptions if you don't mean harm and the need is great, and our need is pretty great don't ya think?"

With the decision made we turn east and follow a smaller dusty road. We travel well past nightfall until Pepe says that we really can't push the horses any further. The tension never leaves us and every sound has us all jumping up in fear, ready to fight or hide from whatever is coming. We take it in turns to sleep so that there's always at least two on guard to watch for anyone approaching. The following day we keep going though it's clear the horses are getting tired with the amount and speed we're asking them to do. Slowly though the mountains start to appear in front of us and grow more distinctive with each passing hour. We're nearly there. Now I just have to hope the arrowmen don't turn us away, or worse, kill us.

# Chapter 28

It's when we're entering the foothills of the mountains that Sam leans over to me and whispers, "Don't look up. We're being watched." Of course instinctively all I want to do is look up now and it takes all my focus to keep my attention on the road ahead. "Where?" I whisper.

"Everywhere" is his answer. Trying to look as though I'm merely stretching my neck I glance up as casually as I can and catch a glimpse. I see at least four of them. Just their outlines in the shadows. Standing on a ridge high up to our left, their bows in hand though not thankfully nocked with arrows. At least they're not attacking us for entering the mountains. Yet. I can't help but think.

We continue on the road for a few more minutes. I can feel their eyes still on us but they make no move. Suddenly Pepe pulls his cart to a halt in front of us. He gets down from the driving seat and leaning forwards I see why. Standing across the road are five Reladians. They stand like an arrowhead, the woman stood at the point clearly the designated leader. Whilst their bows are strung casually across their back they don't reach for them as Pepe approaches.

Looking up again I see that they don't need to. There are at least twenty more Relads visible in the mountains on either side of the pass. Bows drawn, arrows notched, waiting. Heart pounding I watch as Pepe stops in front of the female leader. Will they hear us out? Or shoot us all for entering their land?

It's impossible to hear what Pepe and the Reladian warrior are saying but at one point I clearly see Pepe gesturing at me. The conversation continues and eventually an agreement is obviously reached because the woman nods and Pepe starts to return to his caravan. "We've been granted an audience with the Queen" is all he says before climbing back into his seat and urging Storm on. We follow the Reladians in single file through the mountain range for over an hour before reaching a wider opening where the bowmen indicate that we should stop. With a wave of their hands they signal for us to come down from the caravans. When we've all gathered together, the female leader seems to never take her eyes off of me, she nods and says, "The horses will be cared for. Come." Then she begins to climb the side of the mountain. I glance at Pepe for reassurance but he just starts to follow and so I follow him. Clambering up the steep rocky face I'm out of breath within a few minutes and have cuts on my hands from where I slip and catch the sharp edges of the rocks. Sam tries to help where he can but the land is so slippy and treacherous he really needs to concentrate himself. And still we climb. The Reladians who are leading the way never stop to look back as they negotiate the terrain with ease, although I suppose they do live here and are used to it. After twenty minutes of climbing I have a stitch in my side so painful I'm convinced I can't carry on. Just as I'm moments away from collapsing with exhaustion we finally emerge onto a flat platform which appears to have been cut into the mountainside.

I fall to my knees and take in several deep breaths whilst massaging my aching ribs. The Reladians wait for all of the Gallavanties to make it up onto the platform before gesturing as though to continue. Sam takes my hand and pulls me to my feet, and it's then that I notice the opening in the mountain. A gaping black hole has been carved in the rock. Without hesitation the warriors enter the darkness and we've no choice but to follow. The cold blackness swallows us within our first few steps and I cling on to Sam's hand even tighter as we keep moving. Unable to see even an inch in front of my face I edge forwards slowly. Just as I'm starting to think that the Relads have led us into some sort of trap I'm blinded by the brightness of a dozen lanterns suddenly roaring into life. As my eyes adjust I see that myself and the other Gallavanties are in the centre of a circle of burning torches. Beyond the circle of light stand the famous Relad arrowmen. Hundreds of them. Men, women and children, all armed with a bow in their hands. And right in front of us sits their Queen. Sat in a throne made of rock she listens intently as the female warrior who led us here whispers in her ear.

As we wait nervously Pepe leans over to whisper, "She'll want to speak to you. They only granted us entry when I told them who you were. Answer their questions honestly. Never lie to a Reladian, they can always tell when someone is not being entirely truthful and they do not like dishonesty."

I nod just as the Queen and her warrior finish their discussion and turn to look at me with assessing eyes.

"They claim you are the Princess Elisa of Aleti."

"Yes your majesty," I say giving a curtsey, "I am Princess Elisa Cara Paisley Regal, daughter of King Rafel Javier Shanks Regal, and these are my friends, though I consider them more family, the Gallavanties. I thank you for granting us entry to your sacred land."

"It is not usual for us to permit entry of outsiders and we have never had a visit from another Royal. Why are you here?"

"Your majesty we are travelling from Otraf. Whilst there we learnt of General Srumthro's plans to invade my country of Aleti. We are trying to get back to warn them of the imminent attack. But the General knows of us and there are Karhaner soldiers ahead of us on the road to Leforth. It was not safe to travel that way and so we turned to you, in the hopes that you would grant us safe passage through the mountains."

"And why would we do that? If there is to be a battle between Karhaner and Aleti it is not for us to interfere, we have no wish to end up in the middle of your war."

"I understand your majesty, I know that Relad keeps isolated so as to remain peaceful. Peace is what I want too. It is not my intention to start a war but to prevent one." Taking a deep breath, I decide to take a risk and ask for more than just safe passage. It's unlikely they will agree but right now Aleti is not in a position where potential allies can be ignored. Continuing I step forward and look the Queen directly in the eyes, "I have met the General and seen the madness in his eyes. If we cannot stop him at the beginning, at Leforth, then I fear a long and bloodied war will sweep not only my country but the entire continent. I know that you consider yourselves apart from other nations but I do not think General Srumthro will think that. He is not a man to be satisfied with winning one battle or one country. He will not stop until he has conquered everything in sight.

Thousands of innocent lives will be lost if the General gets his way. Aleti is first and then maybe Navas or Cobback. Maybe you'll be the last place he turns to. Maybe you have years of peace ahead of you before his sights set on you but I believe they will set on you eventually. The only difference then is that we will all be gone, and there will be no allies to aid you. I know I am asking for something that you do not do. But just because you have stood alone for centuries does not mean you must always stand alone. I humbly come here and extend the hand of friendship. Aleti have not been allies to the people of Relad before and you have no reason to trust us or help us now, but I am asking anyway. I believe that though we are different, more unites us than divides us. I believe that we could work together to achieve peace, though I am sure it will not be easy."

Slowly the Queen stands, descending the steps she stops in front of me. She searches my eyes with such intensity I swear it's like her gaze can see into my very soul. With a small smile she nods, "I believe that you believe everything that you say. But as you point out yourself, Aleti have never attempted to become allies with us before, and now you come to us only when you need aid. The timing is suspicious, and though you speak of future benefits how can I be sure that your word will hold? You may be the Princess but you are not the Queen. Not yet. How can you make promises of friendship on behalf of your father?"

I shake my head, "I can't. I do not speak for my father. I can not say what my father would promise. And to tell you the truth I would not trust my father's promises. And I can give you no reason to trust me or mine."

"You do not trust your own father?"

"No. I don't trust him at all. Truth be told I have very little faith in him. But that will not stop me from trying. From trying to do what is right and from trying to convince him to do what is right. For the sake of my country and all the people in it I have to at least try."

The Queen truly smiles at me now, nodding with bright eyes, "Well now you sound like a Queen. A warrior Queen, prepared to defend her country and people. That is a Queen I understand."

She turns and strolls back to her throne, "You and your friends may stay here tonight. I will not promise you an alliance in the coming war but I can offer you help on your journey. The Tarney river begins in these mountains and flows all the way to Carrard. We have boats you can borrow to take you downstream. The river is flowing fast at this time of year, you can reach Carrard in less than two days. I have many skilled boatmen who can accompany you."

It is more than I dared hope for, "Thank you, your majesty. I will not forget your kindness and aid in our time of need." I sweep a low curtsey.

At a signal from their Queen the Relads all relax and restore their arrows to their quivers, swinging their bows back onto their shoulders. As the female warrior who led us here begins to consult with the Queen again everyone else starts to disperse. Two of our escort step forward and bowing to me, they gesture that I should follow them. They lead us further into the cave, taking seemingly random turnings until sunlight up ahead indicates that we are at last returning outside. But as we step out into the late afternoon sun it is as though we have stepped into a whole new world. Behind me Risa gasps at the beauty which lays before us. A huge open expanse of rainforest. An oasis of greenery. A vivid land of colour nestled inside a ring of snowy mountains standing guard around us. To think that no-one knows this is here. The Relads are known for their isolation and they have long been an unsolvable mystery to the rest of the world. I've often wondered how they survived in the cold mountains but now I see the secret they've been keeping. No wonder they are so protective of their home and who enters here. This is wonderful. And I know that for the Queen to allow us to see this is a special gift.

We follow the path down into the valley, attracting many stares from the Reladians whose homes line the way. But they are friendly stares, they smile and nod when I catch their eye. One small girl grins and waves at me whilst another young lad decides to walk beside us. They seem almost as excited for us to be here as we are to be allowed into this incredible place of sanctuary. We come to an open area with logs to sit on and a large fire in the middle. The guards collect some bread and meat sticks from a woman nearby and offer them to us with smiles. As we sit and start to eat, more Reladians gather. The young boy who followed us here is watching Sam intently. Deciding to test the waters he casually kicks a small stone in Sam's direction. With a smile, Sam kicks it back, causing the small boy to break out into a massive grin. He kicks it again and soon a game has started. One young girl offers up a proper ball and Sam and Luis soon have a crowd of small admirers chasing after them as they race across the grass, the ball at their feet. As I laugh at the joyful sight before me Risa approaches the man cooking the skewered meat and begins to ask him questions. I've no doubt that Risa will soon be including these Reladian meat sticks in her recipes. Looking around I see a group of women standing on the opposite side of the fire. Cautiously I approach them, relaxing slightly when they smile and indicate it's ok for me to join them. They all have quivers and bows on their backs. "You can hunt?" I indicate the bows, "Do all women hunt as well as the men?"

"Yes, men, women, children, we all learn to use the bow."

I smile, "Where I come from it is usually only the men who are given weapons."

The women look at me in surprise, "Why?"

"Er, that's a good question. I don't really know. I don't suppose there is a reason, that's just the way it's always been."

"How strange."

"Yes, it is strange when you think about it. Perhaps that can change though. Will you show me how you use it?" I ask.

A young woman nods, "I will teach."

She takes her bow and effortlessly notches an arrow. She takes up a shooting stance and then fires her arrow into the centre of a tree trunk which lies forty metres away. Another woman hands me her bow and so I try to mimic the stance of my tutor. They help me to notch the arrow and then prod me to twist my arm, lower my elbow and widen my stance. They show me how to adjust my fingers and indicate how to draw the string back further. Keeping my eyes on the target tree I release my arrow, but the string catches my holding arm and the arrow drops barely three metres in front of me. I laugh and quickly go to retrieve it, keen to try again. The woman all smile at my poor first effort but step forward to help me again. With my patient tutors I practise for hours, until I can notch my own arrow, draw smoothly and hit the target regularly. By the time the sun sets my fingers are sore but I'm ridiculously pleased with the progress I have made and my new friends are all smiling at me proudly.

We spend the night in borrowed bedding underneath the stars before the first rays of sunshine wake us. The same Reladians who escorted us yesterday are already here to lead us back to where we left the horses and caravans. As we pass back through the same large cavern as before I see the queen once more, standing beside her throne in a deep discussion with someone. Hesitating at first but then deciding it's worth one last try, I approach.

"Your majesty" I curtsey, "I wanted to convey my deepest thanks once more to you for your hospitality and use of your boats. I will be forever grateful. This is a very special place, more special than I could ever have imagined. I understand greatly your wish to protect it. I cannot say what will happen at Leforth, the truth is I fear the Karhaner's numbers are much greater than ours, but if we should prevail know that my offer of friendship and future alliance will still stand. I think we both have similar ambitions and both want the best for our countries and people. I truly do believe that we could work together to achieve those aims, but I understand that trust takes time to build and asking for your support against Karhaner now would be a huge leap of faith for you."

She nods slowly, again watching me thoughtfully with those piercing eyes. I have the uncanny feeling that she is assessing every part of me, though what she is looking for I do not know. "I do hope that you are wrong about General Srumthro's intentions but I do not think you are. I wish you well Princess. I have enjoyed meeting you. I hope that we will meet again."

I smile, "Yes I wish that too. Hopefully in more positive circumstances" I add which raises a smile from her. "Go" she nods, "Your people need you." Giving one last curtsey I quickly return to the Gallavanties and our escorts to begin the climb back down into the valley.

When we get back to the caravans it is a relief to see everything as it was and the horses have been well cared for. We also see three more Reladians waiting for us. They speak briefly with our guards who then translate to us. "There is room for the horses on the boat but not the caravans. Too heavy. They must stay here." I can tell Pepe is reluctant to abandon our homes but with little choice we quickly gather what we can and follow the boatmen. Two large flat boats greet us at the riverside along with a fourth boatman. Their apparent leader indicates that we will need to separate and travel on two seperate boats, "Both go to Carrard?" he asks and Pepe nods in the affirmative. "Wait." I interrupt, "It doesn't make sense for all of us to go to Carrard. We don't know when the attack from Karhaner is going to come and someone should go to Leforth and warn them now."

"She's right," Kinken nods, "I will go to Leforth. But if many of their soldiers are already bound for Albeck we should send someone there too to call them back."

"I can go to Albeck" volunteers Luis. Risa goes to protest but Luis looks determined, "I'm the fastest rider of us all Ri, you know it makes sense. We don't have time to argue about this. I'll be fine. I'll say I'm following the orders of the Princess." He adds with a grin.

Pepe then nods towards Kinken, "I'll go to Leforth with Kinken, if that is where the battle is to be then I'm best placed there."

I nod, "Ok. When you get there go to Lord Francis, he is a reasonable man who distrusts Lord Fagan and already has fears about General Srumthro and Karhaner. I'm sure he will heed your warning."

Pepe looks skeptical, "Will we be able to see him?"

"Tell them you're sent by the Princess but if they still refuse then go to Emily, Lord Francis' daughter. She is a friend. I visited her when we were in Leforth and she knows of you. She will help you gain an audience with her father." I turn to Risa, Sam and Dav but they all start talking before I can say anything.

"Don't even question it kid, I'm sticking with you." Dav growls.

Sam takes my hand, "Not a chance I'm leaving your side."

Risa nods, "We're coming to Carrard."

"And if on this mission we so happen to bump into Lord Fagan and his son Joseph then so much tha' better, I've got a thing or two ta say ta them." Dav adds as he starts to lead Whisper, Storm and Rain onto the boats.

As wrong as it feels to separate from Pepe, Luis and Kinken, I know it gives us the best chance of success. Watching Luis and Risa say goodbye is harder than I thought, and fills me with guilt at the danger I've put them in, but as we push off I know there is no turning back. We travel fast downstream together until a makeshift landing platform appears and then I watch as their boat slows down to dock and allow Luis, Pepe and Kinken to disembark, while our boat continues on. As we watch half our party fade into the distance all I can do is pray that I'm making the right choices and that this isn't the last time I will see them.

# Chapter 29

---

Stepping off the boat into Carrard is a surreal experience. Returning to the city that I once called home, where I first met the Gallavanties and all this began. It's just after noon and the city is a hive of activity, the citizens going about their regular routines. It seems odd to see such normality when I am filled with the knowledge that we are soon to be at war. Dav, Risa, Sam and I head straight for the northern castle gates, walking through the courtyard and approaching the entrance I attempt to walk straight in but a guard steps into my path. "Where'd ya think you're going?"

"To see my father, the King. Now move this is urgent." The guard stares at me for a moment and then bursts out laughing. "Good one, now move along."

I look at him in confusion before realising that he thinks I'm joking, he doesn't recognise me. To be fair to him, glancing down at my dusty clothes, it's not really surprising. I try again, "I realise this is a strange situation but I am Princess Elisa and you are stopping me from entering my own home."

The guard raises his eyebrows, "Do I look stupid to you?" He looks me up and down, "You ain't no princess and anyway, everyone knows the Princess is in Talor. You ain't getting in love."

At this point another soldier wanders over to see what's going on, I try to explain again, with support from Sam, Dav and Risa, but he doesn't seem interested in what he claims is some sort of con. He actually shoves me away, telling me to get lost or he'll have me arrested. Both Dav and Sam step forward in anger but I stop them and drag them both away. I thought the difficult part of the journey was getting to Carrard itself. This problem hadn't even occurred to me. Not being able to get into my own castle.

As we re-group just outside the gates trying to think of another way in, I notice a group of soldiers walking through the courtyard with one familiar face. "Scott!" I yell, "Scott! Over here!" He twists his head round and then I see his eyes widen in recognition. A smile breaks out across my face as he quickly abandons his group and makes his way over. "Who's he?" Sam asks suspiciously.

"A friend of Molly's, he helped get me in and out of the palace before."

"Your highness, what are you doing here? You're supposed to be in Talor, although Molly said that wasn't true. Where have you been? And who are these people?" Scott asks, glancing around at the Gallavanties.

"These are my friends. Listen Scott I need your help. I need to get into the castle but those idiots over there won't let me in. I tried to tell them who I am but they don't recognise me."

"Well you don't exactly look like yourself!" He points out, "I nearly didn't recognise ya. And security's been a lot tighter of late for some reason."

"You can get us in though, right?"

"Maybe." He looks behind him at the guards dotted around the square. "Go to the servants entrance on the east side. I'll go in and find Molly and see if she can get you in that way."

I breathe a sigh of relief, "Thank you Scott."

He nods and then quickly walks away. I grab Sam's hand and lead the way to the same door which I escaped from on my second ever visit to the city. We wait for what seems like ages but is probably more like twenty minutes when a familiar figure suddenly emerges from the door. Her face lights up at the sight of me and before I know it we're both hugging and speaking at once. "Molly it's so good to see you."

"Cara, I can't believe it's you. I almost didn't believe Scott when he told me you were here."

"It feels so strange to be back."

"Are you alright? Why are you back?"

"It's a long story but the short version is we're here to warn my father. Aleti is in danger. General Srumthro is planning to invade from Karhaner. I need to see my father, can you get us inside the palace?"

Molly grimaces and glances at the group, "I don't know about getting all of you in. Since your escape there's been a lot more scrutiny everywhere. There's guards on every entrance, even the service ones." She looks me up and down thoughtfully, "I might be able to sneak you in princess, dressed as you are, I can easily pass you off as a new kitchen girl, but a larger group would be much harder." She looks at Dav's huge muscular frame, "And I don't even know how I would begin to explain your presence."

Sam immediately steps forward, "No way you're going in there alone."

"Sam, if this is the only way then I have to take it. There isn't time to argue about this, the sooner I speak to my father the sooner we can start preparing for war. Once I'm inside I'll be able to get the rest of you inside too. I'll be fine."

Dav points out, "Last time you was in there you were near beaten to a pulp."

"That was different and I won't be alone, I'll be with Molly."

Molly nods, "And Scott. I can get Scott to escort us too. Once people realise she's the princess returned there shouldn't be any problems."

Sam stares at me with an element of panic in his eyes, "I promised I'd never leave you again."

"And you're not leaving me. I have to do this. I promise I'll be as quick as I can and then I'll be back to get you."

Molly gestures Scott over and with one last look of reassurance to Risa and Dav, I squeeze Sam's hand and turn to follow. Molly loops her arm with mine and mutters, "Just act normal, let me do the talking" as we approach the servants entrance and the two guards stationed there. One nods at Scott and Molly, seemingly uninterested in us but the other soldier blocks the way.

"I know you two. Don't recognise you."

Molly grips my arm but answers with a smile, "My cousin, she's new, just got a job in the kitchens so I'm taking her there now."

There's an awkward moment of silence where I don't think they've bought our story but then he gives a shrug and moves out of the way, and we squeeze through. Breathing a sigh of relief we race down the corridor and up the stairs into the main palace hall. As we cross the room Tutor Jenna appears through a set of double doors and does a double take at the sight of me, "Princess Elisa, I did not know you had returned. And what are you wearing?" she sneers in disgust.

Ignoring her shock and question I ask, "Good Afternoon Tutor Jenna, lovely to see you again too, do you know where my father is?"

"I, errr, I believe he is in a council meeting."

"Excellent, thank you." I brush past her and continue up the stairs until Molly pulls me to a stop.

"Wait Cara, you can't just go into the council meeting like that. You saw Tutor Jenna's reaction. I love you an all, but if you want the Lords and your father to take you seriously you need to go in there as Princess Elisa, not as Cara."

Slowly I nod. She's right. I might have loved being Cara for the last few months but right now my country needs its Princess. We take a detour via my old room so that I can change. If it felt strange stepping back into the city entering my room again is a whole other level. Nothing has changed, everything is exactly where I left it, and yet I have changed so much that I feel oddly out of place. Whilst Molly heads straight for my dressing room I slowly take in the place I once called home. Shaking myself out of the moment I follow Molly and change quickly. Putting on a familiar silk dress, Molly does my hair and then insists that I wear my tiara too. Looking at myself in the mirror it's easy to imagine that the last two months haven't happened at all. I can almost feel myself slipping back into my previous self, that ignorant spoilt lonely scared girl. But I am not her any more, straightening my spine and giving myself a determined nod, I turn to Molly and say, "Let's go."

She leads me along the corridor to the Council Chambers, "Good luck" she whispers as I pause outside. I take a deep breath and remind myself what is at stake here. Be confident, be strong, don't let them intimidate me. I fling open the door and stride into the room, interrupting Lord Fagan in mid-speech.

A confused exclaim comes from my father, "Elisa?" as I march straight up to him, ignoring the perplexed looks from the Lords of the council, and the absolutely astounded face of Lord Fagan. "Father, listen, Aleti is in great danger. General Srumthro has built an army and is planning to invade. He intends to attack Leforth any day now. We have to act."

There's an echo of gasps and then concerned mumblings from the Lords at my words. When my father stands to speak I think he's still in shock at my admittedly dramatic appearance, "What are you talking about? General Srumthro? Invasion?"

"I know this might seem sudden but..."

Lord Fagan glares at me as he too stands raising his voice above mine, "This is nonsense. The Princess doesn't know what she is talking about. Please remain calm and ignore the Princess' clearly overactive imagination. I don't know what she is trying to achieve, guards, return the Princess to her room and I will speak..."

Catching Lord Fagan off guard I push him back down into his chair and cut him off. "This is not a rumour, this is not questionable gossip. This is fact. Just four days ago I was imprisoned in Otraf and heard these plans from General Srumthro himself."

There's a moment of stunned silence. My father looks at me in shock, "What do you mean you were in Otraf four days ago? You've been in Talor for the last two months, how did you get imprisoned in Karhaner?"

I turn to Lord Fagan with a slight smile. For the first time I can remember he looks a little uncomfortable, "You know I did wonder, when I heard the lies you'd spread to explain my disappearance, whether my father knew the truth or not, but apparently you lied to him as well."

Addressing the room once more I make sure every Lord hears my words, "Almost eight weeks ago I was told by my father and Lord Fagan that I must marry Joseph Fagan. When I refused I was badly beaten by both Joseph Fagan and Lord Fagan." There's a gasp of horror around the room but I continue, "They attempted to lock me in my room but I escaped and ran away. I have not been in Talor, I've been touring the country in disguise with friends. When we reached Otraf and found out what was happening we planned to return to Carrard to warn the citizens of Aleti, but my identity was discovered and I was captured and tortured by General Srumthro. Thankfully my friends returned to rescue me and we were able to make it back here. I am telling you, Karhaner is coming for us. The General has gathered an army and is preparing to march south as we speak. The attack on Leforth is imminent and we must act now."

As I finish my speech no one makes a sound. Every pair of eyes is on me but for a moment no one moves, seemingly not knowing what to say. Lord Fagan opens his mouth to speak again but I decide I'm not giving him the chance. "I've already sent word to Lord Francis to prepare the Leforth's defenses and another message has been dispatched to Albeck calling back the soldiers who were deployed there." I glare at Lord Fagan as I emphasize my next line, "I don't know why the soldiers were being transferred there in the first place but with luck they are already returning to where they need to be. We must send our own reinforcements from Carrard to join them as soon as possible. Lord Culton can you make that happen?"

Lord Culton glances nervously at first my father and then Lord Fagan but then nods, "Yes your highness, I'll start immediately." He stands and leaves the room quickly as I continue, "If I remember rightly there is mention of aid in the event of an attack in our agreement with Navas, we need that aid now, and whilst recent relations with Cobback are not as they once were they are still our oldest allies, we should send word to them too."

"This is ridiculous." Lord Fagan shouts and rises, walking to stand next to my father. "I don't know what kind of game you're playing or where you are getting your information from but there is no threat from Karhaner and as for this alleged attack on you, that is preposterous."

"And why would I lie, Lord Fagan? Why would I make this up? Ask yourself why would I come back here unless my country truly was in danger? I was perfectly happy in my new life. Trust me, I wouldn't have come back if I didn't have to."

My father looks uncertainly between me and Lord Fagan. Suddenly interrupting our argument, he shouts, "Everyone out." Stunned silence follows. "I said everyone out. Go, leave. I will speak with my daughter and Lord Fagan alone."

Quickly the Lords scramble up from their seats and trip over themselves in their haste to get out.

The door slams closed and a tense silence descends. Lord Fagan opens his mouth to speak but my father raises a hand to stop him, turning back to me instead, "Tell me the truth now Elisa, you can't just burst in here and make declarations of war. Now I need to know, were you in Otraf or were you in Talor?"

Taking my father's hands into mine I emphasise each word, hoping he will listen, "I have not set foot in Talor. I was in Otraf, father. I told you, when you tried to force my hand in marriage and I said no, the Fagans beat me. I ran away and joined a travelling show group. I've been with them for the last two months. We went to Ameve and then Leforth, and then we entered Karhaner and went to Otraf, but when we got there things weren't right. We found out that every man was being called up to join the army. I'm telling the truth, Father. General Srumthro discovered my identity, he imprisoned me and tortured me and he is coming for Aleti, I swear it."

As I stare into my father's eyes, willing him to believe me, once again Lord Fagan attempts to step forward, "I've never heard a more preposterous story in all my life. Surely you can't believe that either I or my son would ever lay a hand on the Princess, your majesty. You know it's not true. I am your most trusted advisor."

My father looks at Lord Fagan with a somewhat calculating look, "You told me my daughter was in Talor. That she needed time away from court to better understand her duties as Princess. Did you lie to me?"

Lord Fagan hesitates in his response. I can almost see his mind whirring, thinking of what to say to get out of this. It's actually quite nice to see him looking so uncomfortable. His eyes twitch in my direction before he gives a dramatic sigh and hangs his head, "Forgive me your majesty, yes I lied. The Princess was never in Talor." I start to smile at his confession but my expression soon turns to outrage as he begins to spin a new tale. "I should have told you the truth from the start but I did not want to worry your majesty. Of course her accusations of abuse are completely untrue but she did indeed disappear while we were on tour in Navas. I have had guards scouring the country for her. I believed her to be kidnapped and thought that making her disappearance known would only encourage the perpetrators. I hoped to find her and bring the villains to justice without causing a scandal for the princess."

I start to try and argue back but my father once again raises his hand to stop me, "You should not have kept my daughter's disappearance from me. I understand why not allowing the news to go public was important but to keep such a thing a secret from the King." My father shakes his head, "We will discuss this further and you must ensure that no secrets are kept from me in the future, do you understand Lord Fagan?" I stare at my father in disbelief, he doesn't actually believe Lord Fagan's version of events does he?

Lord Fagan seems to have regained some of his confidence as he responds, "Of course your majesty, it will never happen again. I am just so pleased that the Princess has returned unharmed. Though clearly she is still angry about the arranged marriage with Joseph and is lying to try and change your mind. This fabrication of war with Karhaner is just that. A way to make a dramatic reappearance and distract you so that you'll forget about the wedding. If General Srumthro was planning something so large as an invasion I would've heard about it. He has not so much as glanced at Aleti in all his time in power, why would he now?"

Getting desperate now I question Lord Fagan, "Why are you so insistent that this isn't true? How can you be so certain what is or isn't happening in Karhaner?"

As Lord Fagan and I face off, my father stood watching, the doors to the chamber suddenly fly open. Four guards enter followed by Sam, Risa and Dav, with more guards following them. "Your Majesty, I beg your pardon for intruding but these people were at the northern gate causing quite a stir, insisting on entry. They say they are with the Princess and that it is a matter of life and death. They say that Aleti is under attack from Karhaner and that..."

My father raises his hand to cut the guards off, whilst I race towards the Gallavanties, "They are with me. Let them go at once."

The guards look skeptically at me before turning their questioning gaze on my father, awaiting his orders. I turn to him too imploringly, "Father, these are my friends, release them."

"Your friends?" my father says, looking the Gallavanties up and down, "By that you mean these are the people you say you have been travelling with?"

"Yes."

"Then these are the people who are responsible for keeping you from your rightful place at the palace, kidnapping and imprisoning you. Arrest them and throw them in the dungeons."

The guards move to do my father's bidding as I shout in protest, "What? No! They did not kidnap me, I ran away, and they did not imprison me, they helped me to escape. They are my family. I will not let you harm them."

The guards continue to drag the Gallavanties from the room despite my pleading and Sam's shouts of protest. It takes six guards to take Dav who is fighting against them.

"They have done nothing wrong. Father please. Why will you not listen to me?"

He turns to me with fake sympathy, looking at me as though I am a fool who has been misled, speaking in such a patronising way, "Daughter, they are common criminals who have kept the princess hostage, they must be punished."

"No! The only person being held hostage here is you! Held hostage by Lord Fagan for years now. Why can you not see it?

See how he manipulates you? How his policies are destroying the country?"

Lord Fagan interrupts, "Because you are just a silly young girl. You do not know the world or understand the way in which a king rules. Your father knows what he is doing and who to trust."

Drawing myself up and looking Lord Fagan in the eye I let him know that I will not be silenced this time and I am not afraid of him, "I am not a silly young girl. Not any more. And I promise you Lord Fagan, you will pay for what you have done to me, to my father and to this country. But not now. Right now I have a war to win against a far bigger enemy than you. So you stay here and hide in this room, whispering your poison words to my father. I'm done with you both. I will defend my country without either of you slowing me down."

Spinning from the room I leave my father and Lord Fagan knowing that they are not the people who can help me now. No doubt I will have to deal with Lord Fagan again at some point but first I need to free Sam, Risa and Dav, and then worry about how we can help Leforth and stop General Srumthro. Racing down the main staircase and along the lower corridor towards the kitchen I go in search of Molly.

Turning the corner I almost crash into her and Scott coming the other way. "Cara, we were just coming to find you. Scott said they've taken the Gallavanties to the dungeons, what happened with the Lords and your father?"

I shrug, "Exactly as you would expect. Lord Fagan told everyone I was lying and my father believed him. It doesn't matter. What matters is we need to free Sam, Risa and Dav."

Scott shakes his head, "Don't know how we do that, there's at least four men guarding them."

"When I was imprisoned in Otraf, Sam did something to the guards, he put something in their drink to make them sleep. Do you know what could do that?"

Molly thinks for a moment and then smiles, "My mum has a draft for when we're poorly or hurt, to numb pain, but it can make you quite drowsy. I bet if you drank more than the usual dose it would put you to sleep pretty quick."

"Perfect, can you get it?"

"I'll go now."

"I need to speak with Lord Culton and then we'll meet back here."

Molly nods already turning to head back towards the kitchen with Scott while I go to Lord Culton's rooms in the east wing.

Knocking on the door, I find him sitting at his desk surrounded by paper and issuing orders to a guard stood beside him.

"Your highness," he quickly rises, "This is Major Divorg from the Carrard garrison. We're just organising plans. I've already sent messages to the Garrison for the men to prepare to march north. We're making arrangements to leave at dawn tomorrow."

I nod, "Excellent work Lord Culton. You know this is not approved by either my father or Lord Culton. They don't believe the threat is real."

"I know. But I do. Since you opened my eyes to Lord Fagan's duplicity I've been paying a lot more attention to what's going on and I don't trust anything that comes out of that man's mouth."

I breathe a sigh of relief, "Thank you. How many men do we have and how quickly can we make it to Leforth?"

"4,000 men but only half have horses as it stands. Those who travel on horseback can make it to Leforth in under three days but for those marching it'll be more like five."

I shake my head in frustration, "That's not enough, General Srumthro is calling up every able bodied man in Karhaner. Where can we get more men and more horses from?"

Lord Culton looks worried, "If we can requisition horses from the merchants of the city that would be enough for the whole garrison here to ride to Leforth. And there's a garrison of 5,000 stationed in Vamanst we can call for but they won't make it to Leforth for at least two weeks at best. The other option is to ask the other Lords. They all have private guards assigned to them and their regions, if we can call together all the soldiers of the Northern Lords who can make it to Leforth in the next few days that would give us another, maybe 2,000."

"Will they do it? Will the Lords agree to it even if the order doesn't come from my father?"

"I think they will if you ask it of them."

"Well we don't have much choice, we must get every man that we can. Can you organise a meeting with all the Lords? Get them all here for me to speak to without my father or Lord Fagan knowing?"

"Yes," Lord Culton glances at the Major still hovering, "I can get word to them."

The Major gives a nod and hurries from the room, presumably to spread the word.

After ensuring that Lord Culton is on top of the army arrangements I leave his rooms and begin to make my way back towards the kitchens, hoping that Molly has been able to get the potion we need. But I've barely made it halfway when a familiar figure steps out into the corridor in front of me. Joseph. His eyes narrow at the sight of me, "I heard you were back."

"Yes, I'm back, now if you'll excuse me" I say, pushing past him, but before I can continue his hand shoots out to grip my upper arm. Squeezing and digging his nails in just like he did before.

"You just sweep back in here and think you can go up against my father. That didn't work out so well for you last time." He snarls in my ear. With sudden speed I twist my arm out of his grasp, grab his thumb and contort it backwards, exactly as Dav taught me. He gasps in pain as I calmly say, "You know if I twist just a little bit more your thumb will dislocate. I've heard it's quite painful." Stepping closer so I can look him straight in the eye I tell him, "I am not the naive spoilt girl who you scared away so easily before. I may have failed to stand up for my country last time but I will not fail again." Quick as lightning I sweep my foot behind his legs and leave him sprawled on the floor. I stride off down the corridor without a backward glance.

Finding Molly and Scott once more I'm relieved to see that Molly was successful. "Mum gave me what she had" she says, showing me two small bottles.

"Is it enough?" I ask.

"Only one way to find out" is Molly's pragmatic response.

Collecting four mugs of ale from the kitchen we divide all of the liquid we have between the four drinks, hoping that the ale will mask the taste of the draught, then Molly takes the tray to deliver to the guards who are stationed at the entrance to the cellar dungeons. Waiting just around the corner with Scott we listen in as Molly approaches.

"Afternoon, brought some ale for ya all."

Whilst some of the guards appear enthusiastic, muttering their thanks and obviously taking the offered drinks, there is one who is clearly a bit more switched on than the others because he questions

Molly. "Why you bringing us drinks? We don't usually get delivery service when we're on duty down here."

Molly acts perplexed, "Don't ask me, I'm just following orders. Take these drinks to the soldiers in the cellar they said, so here I am. If ya don't want it, don't drink it, but don't moan at me if ya down here for hours and don't get offered nothing else." There's a grunt in response and the reluctant guard must have taken the mug of ale because a moment later Molly reappears with an empty tray, a smile and a wink. Still hiding round the corner all three of us hold our breaths whilst we wait for a sign that something has happened. Several minutes pass and the guards are still chatting with each other as normal. Risking a peek around the corner I see the four guards all sat around a table playing some sort of card game, apparently completely unaffected by our drinks.

I lean back and closer to Molly whispering, "It's not working."

She grimaces and murmurs, "Maybe it wasn't enough of the potion between the four of them."

I sigh in annoyance whilst trying to think, "We need another plan. Scott can't you try and distract them, draw them away somehow."

"I told you before, I'm just a foot soldier, they're not gonna listen to me."

"Couldn't you act as though it's on the orders from someone higher up? I know! Major Divorg. Say you've a message from Major Divorg and they're needed back at the garrison."

"All of them? I don't think they'll buy that."

"Just try" urges Molly, giving Scott a little nudge.

With a sigh Scott draws himself up and says, "Alright, I'll try."

He steps around the corner purposefully before immediately coming to a surprising halt. He looks back at us with a laugh, "I don't think we'll be needing plan B."

Peaking around the corner once more reveals four sleeping guards collapsed at the table. I beam at Molly, "It worked."

Scott scoops up the ring of keys which have fallen to the floor and quickly opens up the cell. Before any of its inhabitants have time to react I'm throwing myself into Sam's arms, grabbing Risa and Dav at the same time, "Are you ok? Are you alright? I'm so sorry, I'm so so sorry. I tried to stop them but my father wouldn't listen."

Sam's stroking my face to calm me down, "We're fine, we're fine. Are you ok? What happened?"

Scott interrupts before I can respond, "Hate to break up the reunion but we should go before someone finds out what we did."

"Right, I'll explain on the way." I say grabbing Sam's hand as we make a quick escape and I explain the new plan. With the Gallavanties now free I just have the simple task of arranging an army to try and stop an invasion, whilst a King and chief advisor work against me. Should be easy enough.

# Chapter 30

As I walk along the third floor corridor towards Lord Culton's chamber the mumble of several conversations happening at once grows. Approaching the doorway I can hear heated exchanges as people try to talk over each other, their voices practically shouting to be heard above the din. Pushing the door open I squeeze into the crowded room with Sam, Risa, Dav, Molly and Scott following. Lord Culton's chamber is full to bursting with Lords but as soon as my presence is noticed a deafening silence descends as all eyes turn towards me, just as they did in the Lords Chamber before. Although this time there is less shock and more guarded expressions which greet me. I realise they are all waiting for me to speak but a sudden wash of nervousness pours over me and I'm unsure how to start proceedings. Noticing my hesitation Lord Culton climbs onto his chair so that he can be seen by everyone, "My Lords I thank you for gathering here at such short notice. I realise that the venue is not our usual location for discussing important business but unfortunately the need for secrecy on this occasion meant we could not meet in the Lords Chamber. You have all been asked here because

I believe you all to be trustworthy and true loyalists to our country. I know that you will have many questions but I ask you please to listen to what Princess Elisa has to say."

During Lord Culton's introductory speech Sam has reached for my hand and given it a reassuring squeeze, reminding me to have confidence, or atleast to portray confidence even if I don't really feel it, so as Lord Culton gives me a nod to speak I take a deep breath and climb onto the small end table next to me.

"Thank you Lord Culton and thank you Lords for your time. You were all present in the Lords Chamber when I attempted to warn my father of the threat from Karhaner. As I told you then I have personally bared witness to what is happening in Otraf and heard the plans of invasion from General Srumthro himself. This is not an uncorroborated rumour or hearsay, these are exact words that I heard from him myself. Every able bodied man in Karhaner was being drafted into the army and I saw workshops and blacksmiths all over the city preparing weapons. I do not believe they were far off from being ready to march when I was there but with my escape and the knowledge that I will have returned to Aleti to warn everyone I think we can assume General Srumthro will quickly move his plans forward to give us less time to prepare. Everything is a matter of urgency now. The Carrard garrison is already under orders to prepare to march north tomorrow but we need more men. I ask all the northern Lords to immediately send word to your own soldiers to make their way to Leforth as fast as they are able."

At this statement rapid mumbling instantly breaks out as the Lords react to my plea and several questions are shouted to me from different directions.

"We are expected to just send all our men to Leforth and leave our own provinces unguarded."

"How can we have heard nothing about this gathering army before now?"

"What about the southern lords, are they not expected to contribute?"

"Why are we meeting here and not with the King and Lord Fagan?"

I was hoping to avoid the topic of my Lord Fagan and my father's scepticism but realise it is unavoidable.

I raise my hand for silence. "My father and Lord Fagan are not here because I cannot trust them. They do not believe the threat to be real and as such do not intend to act in any way. To follow their plan, or lack of plan, would be a devastating mistake from which our country cannot recover. It is, simply put, not an option. That is why they are not here and why..."

I try to continue but the grumblings have once again risen as the Lords realise that I am asking them to act against their King. Trying not to get annoyed at the interruptions I attempt to answer their questions whilst pushing forward the notion of marching troops to Leforth.

"If the King and Lord Fagan do not think it to be a true threat."

One Lord whose name I do not know leans forward and suggests. "Perhaps we should send an envoy to Leforth to speak to Lord Francis and corroborate these claims. No sense marching all our men north if we're not sure."

"But I am sure." I want to scream but try to maintain some semblance of calm authority in my attempts to get through to them. "I am sure that by then it will be too late. If we want to stop General Srumthro from completely invading Aleti then we have to stop him at Leforth. If he wins that battle and gains control of the city then he can use that as his springboard to the rest of the country and he will pick off every other city and province one by one. To stand a chance we must come together and defeat him now at the border."

"But the King..."

"The King is wrong." I snap. "My father is lost, too far gone under Lord Fagan's influence. He will not listen to me. He will not deviate from Lord Fagan's commands. I do not know what Lord Fagan's motives or intentions are. I do not understand why he will not heed my warning but he won't. And so it falls to me. To take control where my father will not. To defend my country where my father will not. And I ask you where you intend to stand?" I take a deep breath and try to speak more calmly but I can feel a sense of resignedness taking over. As I begin to speak again I hope it comes across to the Lords as more passionate rather than desperate. Looking them all in the eye I implore them, "Take a moment my Lords to think through what I am telling you and ask yourselves this, why would I lie? Why would I exaggerate or make up this story? Ask yourselves what you have to lose by believing me, and what you have to lose if you don't. If we march north with our men and then no threat comes, then your men return home. You've lost a few weeks of your time and perhaps some extra coin from army expenses but there is no real harm done. But if you don't listen, if we don't march north and the attack does come as I say it will, then we lose Leforth, and then our country, piece by piece we lose everything. Are you willing to take that risk? The risk that I am right? I understand that it is not an easy decision to trust me. I stand before you with no evidence of my claims other than my own eye witness account. I understand that many of you have been a part of the Lords council for many years and that you are used to obeying the orders of my father and Lord Fagan. I understand the power and control that Lord Fagan has, and I understand how brave you must be to go against him. But as Lord Culton says, we asked you here because we thought that you are brave enough. And I believe that every man in this room truly cares about our country and will do what is right. Do you remain loyal to my father and Lord Fagan, bury your head in the sand and hope that I am wrong, or will you take a leap of faith and trust me? Will you stand with me? I am your princess and future queen, and I will defend my country from the threat I know is coming. I intend to ride north and do all I can to fight General Srumthro. I will do it alone if I must, but I would really like to do it with your support."

Lord Colton stands, "My Princess, I have no reason to doubt your word. I trust in you and know you will defend our country against all enemies, from both inside and outside of our realm." He glances around meaningfully before returning his gaze to me. "I will stand with you. I will follow you into battle. I am at your command, your highness." He bows low and I breathe a silent sigh of relief. I swear I could hug him for breaking the awkward silence which had followed my heated speech, instead I give a small smile and regal nod of my head in his direction, "Thank you Lord Culton."

After a moment's pause Lord Adrian stands too, "Your highness, I am with you also."

He is quickly followed by Lord Lijnders and then Lord Klurgen. Slowly one by one, whether through true belief in my words or whether they are merely swept along by others, every Lord in the Chamber bows, pledging me their allegiance. I look at Sam standing beside me and hope starts to bloom. We may have a chance to stop the General after all. If we can make it in time.

With the Lords seemingly onside Lord Culton takes over the meeting to discuss the details and to begin giving more detailed orders. The Lords seem happy to accept his leadership and I for one am certainly grateful. As much as I may have projected confidence during my speech I truthfully don't know the first thing about organising the movement of thousands of men and horses. Whilst I initially contribute by answering a few more questions regarding General Srumthro and his army it soon becomes clear that my presence is no longer really required. When Major Divorg arrives with an update on preparations I take the opportunity to escape by suggesting I go and visit the garrison myself. An idea met with approval by Lord Culton.

Stepping out of the crowded room I finally feel like I can breath again and feel my shoulders sag with relief. Dav gives me a smile and pat on the back, "Ya did good kid."

Risa grins, "You were brilliant, the way you commanded that room, got them all onside, you were like a proper Princess."

I laugh at this, "I am a proper princess."

Whilst Sam smiles at me I can tell something doesn't feel quite right. Noticing my quizzical look, the others quickly move off down the corridor, following Scott and Molly, in order to give us some semblance of privacy. I take his hand and feel a stupid sense of relief when he doesn't pull away, "What's wrong?"

He shakes his head, "Nothing's wrong as such. It was just kinda weird. Seeing you in Princess mode like that. Seeing all those Lords bowing to you. It just kinda reminded me how far apart our worlds are. Kinda scared me to be honest. I know we've talked about this before but it's another thing actually seeing it. I don't wanna lose you."

I pull him to a stop and reach up to cradle his face in my hands, waiting until his eyes settle on mine before I smile, "I love you Sam. Always and forever. That person you saw in there, Princess Elisa, I can't deny that she's a part of me and who I am. But more than anything she's an act, a character that I have to become sometimes. I can't escape that, especially not now when the country needs me, but she is only a small part of me. The part that I show to the Lords and the rest of the world. But you see all of me, you know the real me. Please trust me when I say that nothing is going to change how I feel about you. And as for that nonsense about us being from two different worlds, what a load of rubbish, you are my world Sam."

"And you're mine" he smiles, a real smile this time, and bends to give me a gentle kiss. "Thanks for the reassurance love, I was just having a moment. I love you too." He gives me another kiss before taking my hand again, "Now let's go see this army of yours" making me laugh as we race to catch up with the others who are already leaving the courtyard.

Entering the garrison it looks like organised chaos as men and women run around carrying equipment and shouting commands to each other. A huge pile of arrows is being sorted into bundles and I can see swords being sharpened at the smiths whilst several wagons are being loaded with food. Our presence is noticed but other than sketching bows, everyone continues with their work. A man finishes giving orders to a group of soldiers before approaching. He bows low as he introduces himself, "Your Highness, I am Garrison Sergeant Major Qay."

I nod in acknowledgement, "Major Qay, you have your orders, are preparations going as expected?"

"Yes your highness, things are a little more rushed than normal but we will be ready."

He hesitates as though he wants to say more but then stops himself.

"What is it Major?"

"We received orders from Lord Fagan to stop preparations but Major Divorg said to ignore them."

I nod, "The only orders you are to obey are those that come directly from myself or from Lord Culton. Anything from either my father or Lord Fagan is to be dismissed."

The major gulps and looks confused, "But your highness, we cannot ignore orders from the King."

"You can and you must. Your country's future depends on you doing just that."

It appears that our conversation has been overheard because several men have stopped what they are doing and are now watching us, murmuring amongst themselves.

Dav addresses Major Qay but raises his voice to ensure that he is heard, even by those who are pretending not to listen, "The king is a coward, hidin' in his room and refusin' ta go north and fight in this battle. Lucky we got a Princess who cares and is brave enough to do what he aint."

Molly nods and then also speaks up, "Tortured and imprisoned by General Srumthro and yet still willing to face him on the battlefield. We couldn't ask for a better leader."

"More courage in her little finger than the King and Lord Fagan combined" adds Risa beaming at me.

By now the whole yard has frozen and is listening. Even people in the buildings either side are standing on their balconies or hanging out of windows to hear.

Molly continues, "I am proud to call the Princess a friend, and I trust her. She is riding north to take her place on the front line and lead us into battle to defend her country. Our country. Whilst Lord Fagan and the King hide here."

Scott steps forward too and turns to directly address the whole courtyard, "Many of the Lords are joining her because they believe in her too. I am joining her. She doesn't stand here and command that you fight alongside her. She is asking you. The choice is yours. Stay here if you want. Stay with the King and Lord Fagan in the capital and wait for news of how the battle goes. But I hope that there are at least some among you who are brave enough to fight. Who care enough about our country to want to defend it. "

I nod and somehow find my voice, "Scott speaks true. Any man who wishes to follow the King's orders, remain here and hide with Lord Fagan, is free to do so. For all those brave men who are ready to fight for their country against the evil which is coming to destroy it, ride north with me. We leave at first light tomorrow."

There's a moment's pause as my final words hang in the air, and then a wave of noise swells as the soldiers before me roar and raise their hands in salute, declaring their intent to fight. It seems I have my army.

# Chapter 31

----------------------------------------

We travel fast, pushing the horses as far as we can each day. The weather is kind to us and we make good progress. As each day passes without word from Leforth my optimism that we might arrive in time grows. Each evening myself and the Lords draw up battle plans, discussing defensive strategy and trying to predict General Srumthro's attack. From my brief time with him I think he's arrogant enough not to be subtle about his approach and will simply throw everything on an assault at the main northern gate, but the Lords are keen to discuss every possibility which I suppose is wise. Sam and Dav take part in the meetings too, their knowledge of Leforth's streets proves valuable and their ability to come up with some less orthodox fighting tactics are brilliant. I think the Lords are quite impressed with their suggestions.

They accept their presence and council without any dissent. On our final evening on the road we are all stood around a large map of Leforth. The eastern side of the city is protected by the Reladian mountains. Several times now I've opened my mouth to share my conversation with the Queen of Relad but stop myself. Although I felt like we understood each other and she seemed open to an alliance, the Relads have kept themselves so isolated I cannot expect aid to come after one brief meeting. The Relads rarely leave their mountain territory and to hope they might do so to help defend our city is futile. Still, I think, when we reach Leforth I will find a way to at least get a message to them to ask once more. At this point I will do everything I can to give us the best possible chance. Though we sent urgent messages there is still no word from Navas or Cobback. For now at least it appears we are on our own.

Though we expect the Karhaner army to focus their efforts on breaching the northern gate, the possibility of them circling to the western side of the city is real. The defences there are certainly less substantial. As the Lords suggest ways we can quickly bolster the wall if they do attempt an attack here the discussion is halted by the sound of approaching horse hooves. We turn as one to the sight of a rider charging down the road towards us from the direction of Leforth. He reins his horse in and flings himself off, dashing forwards as he pulls a letter from his pocket. "Your highness" he quickly bows, "A message from Lord Francis. The Karhaner army has been sighted."

There's a gasp from one of the Lords behind me but I'm too busy ripping the letter open to see who it was. Scanning the words quickly I take a deep breath before turning to the Lords who are all staring at me waiting for news. "The army has been sighted by scouts less than a day's march to the north of Leforth. Lord Francis predicts they will reach the city by tomorrow afternoon. He reports they have done all they can to bolster the northern defences but is worried they don't have the men to hold them back. Your men from the northern provinces and returning soldiers from Albeck are still coming in but the scout's report estimates the Karhaner army to be at least 20,000."

"20,000?" Mutters Lord Adrian turning pale. "Even if we arrive in time that only takes our numbers to barely 11,000. They will outnumber us two to one."

"We will arrive in time." Lord Culton says staunchly. "We rise early and push hard, we can make it by early afternoon. If the General chooses to attack immediately our men will have to go into battle without rest but at least we will be there."

I nod, "And Lord Francis says the defences have been strengthened. We have a chance."

"Plus you're only counting the official soldiers" Dav adds gruffly. "Never underestimate ordinary people fighting for their homes and families. You attack a woman's child and they become like a fierce tiger. If you include the citizens of Leforth then we have the numbers."

Sam steps forward, "We should organise for older citizens and those unable to fight to look after the children so everyone who wants to fight is able to."

"Even the women?" Asks Lord Klurgen incredulously.

"Yes the women. I dare say some of them are probably braver than a lot of men. I know some pretty courageous women." I can't help but smile at Sam's response. I slip my hand into his and give it a squeeze. Turning back to the messenger I return Lord Francis' note, "Get some food and rest, and then you must continue on to Carrard as fast as you can. My father must hear this news. Deliver the note directly to him, do not give it to Lord Fagan. Is that clear?" The messenger nods, bows and then leaves. Sam leans forward to whisper in my ear, "Do you think this will finally make your father believe you."

I shrug, "Even if he does it may be too late."

Sam looks at my grim expression then slowly pulls me in for a hug. Wrapping my arms around him tightly I take a moment to just appreciate him being here with me, until an awkward cough makes me pull away. The Lords are all trying to studiously ignore the moment. "Lets all get to bed. Tomorrow is going to be a long day." With bows and nods the Lords begin to disperse. As Sam starts to step away I pull his hand back, "Stay with me tonight." He raises his eyebrow in surprise. "Really? Am I allowed? Won't people say something."

I shake my head, "I don't care. We're going into battle tomorrow and who knows what will happen. We could all die tomorrow. If that's the case I don't want to spend my last night on this earth alone. I want to spend it with the person I love most in this world."

Sam smiles and bends to give me a slow delicious kiss. "I love you too, more than anything, and whilst I am a bit more optimistic about tomorrow, you're right, I don't want to spend any time apart from you if I don't have to."

"Well tonight you don't have to" I lean up to return his kiss and then pull him backwards towards my tent.

As we approach the city walls it's clear the battle has not yet started. There are no sounds of war or evidence of attack. In fact the city looks scarily similar to how it did when the Gallavanties and I approached it not so long ago. But as we lead our army through the open southern gates there's a definite shift in the city, though not the one I was expecting. People race out of their homes onto the street and they start to cheer and clap. I hear cries of 'God Bless you Princess Elisa'.

We continue through the city and a river of cheers greet us wherever we go. I don't understand. They surely know of the impending attack, why are they so happy to see us? And then it hits me. They think we are here to save them. They think we are enough to stop the attack. I can see the hope and relief in their faces as we slowly ride past. Their masks of fear and worry slipping away at the sight of us. An overwhelming sense of guilt and panic starts to fill me up. They don't know that we don't have enough men, that this battle is going to be a very close thing, that there is a very good chance we are going to lose despite the army we bring with us. I feel like I'm giving them false hope but then I think to myself what else can I do. If hope is all I can give them right now then surely that is better than no hope at all.

Still, finally reaching the Leforth Lord Manor House and leaving the crowds behind is a welcome relief and I have to shake my feelings off as I dismount and step forward to greet Lord Francis and several others who are waiting for us in the courtyard. I approach Lord Francis, who offers a low bow, and then opens his mouth to speak but before he can utter a word Luis comes bursting out of the door behind him. In seconds he's wrapping Risa up in a tight hug, lifting her off the ground in his excitement, and I can't help the ear splitting grin that fills my face. Next thing I know I'm receiving the same treatment and giggling as Luis swings me round. It's then I notice that Pepe and Kinken are also there and more hugs are exchanged as we all start talking at once.

Being reunited with everyone feels like coming home and a giddiness lights me up. It's only when I catch sight of Lord Francis' utterly confused expression that I remember I'm supposed to be in Princess mode. Clearing my throat and trying to pretend our exuberant reuniting was totally normal, I give a small smile, "Lord Francis, it's nice to see you again although the circumstances are not happy ones. We have a lot to discuss, are there any updates on the Karhaner army's movements?"

Lord Francis is still giving the Gallavanties odd looks but nods and answers my question, "I can take you to the northern wall where you will see the Karhaner army appear to be setting up camp within sight but not within range. From what our scouts have observed it appears they are making preparations for their attack, we don't think it will be today but at this point we don't know if they are planning to attack at night or wait until tomorrow morning."

"Then we must be vigilant. Let's gather inside with your military leaders to discuss what defenses you have prepared and if there is anything else we can do between now and the attack."

"Yes your highness." As Lord Francis leads us inside he glances at Sam who remains by my side and at the rest of the Gallavanties who are talking amongst themselves as they also follow. I can see the questions bubbling inside his head. Stepping inside the door I'm delighted by another reunion. "Emily!" I hug my friend.

"Boy am I glad to see you" she smiles.

I beam back at her and turn to pull Sam closer, "I believe you've met Pepe, Kinken and Luis but this is the rest of my family, Risa and Dav, and this is Sam."

Emily's eyebrows raise as she looks at Sam, a sly smile sneaking across her face, "So you're Sam, it's very nice to meet you." She winks at me before looking back at Sam appraisingly, "Elisa was right, you are quite cute."

"Emily" I laugh, giving her a friendly smack across the arm. Sam seems quite uncomfortable with Emily's studious attention, "Are you blushing?" I ask, laughing again at Sam's awkwardness.

"No" he mutters, "Anyway I thought we had a meeting to get to, there's a war happening you know."

Emily and I grin at each other but follow after Lord Francis once more. As we step into the dining room which has clearly been turned into some form of headquarters, all smiles and laughter disappear as I observe the table full of city maps and models of soldiers. Settling into a chair at the head of the table I take a deep breath. This is going to be a long and stressful meeting and the fate of our whole country may depend on it. Sam sits beside me and gives my hand a squeeze. I nod to Lord Francis to begin.

Screwing up a fifth piece of paper and throwing it across the room I let out a growl of frustration. "What did that piece of paper ever do to you?" Asks Sam as he slips through the doorway, quietly shutting the door behind him. I sigh rubbing my temples where I can feel a headache coming on.

"I can't do it. I'm trying to write a letter to Queen Kella. After our meeting this afternoon I thought it was worth one last try."

Sam nods, neither one of us commenting on the uncomfortable reality that the war council meeting had taught us about just how high the odds were stacked against us.

"I just can't find the right words. How can I convince her to help when there is no reason for them to do so? A lot of risk and no guaranteed reward. As a Queen she would be mad to agree. It's pointless" I say, throwing down my pen again and sinking my head on to the desk in front of me.

Sam starts massaging my shoulders and drops a kiss on top of my head.

"Worth a try though isn't it? She says no and we've lost nothing. Besides I think she quite liked you. And as independent as Relad has been I don't think she was totally against the idea of an alliance. Lets just write the letter and send it."

"But I don't know what to say" I whine like a petulant child.

"Yes you do, you're good with words. Think about when you spoke to all those Lords and got them all onside, you can do this."

"But I didn't plan any of that, I didn't think about it, it just came out in the moment. And speaking is so much easier than writing it down. When I try to put it down on paper it just doesn't sound right."

"Well forget about writing it down and pretend you're speaking to the Queen right now. Come on, stand up." Sam pushes me to stand and then takes my place at the writing desk, pulling a fresh piece of parchment towards him. "You speak and I'll write. Might need to rewrite it in your handwriting after but at least the words'll be there. Don't think about it, just start speaking." He dips the quill pen into the ink and then waits expectantly.

"I don't even know how to start. How should I address her in the beginning."

"Less thinking" murmurs Sam still waiting with his hand poised above the paper. I sigh and try to clear my head.

"Queen Kella,

I'm sure you already know the purpose of my letter, and I can't deny that this letter is written out of desperation. I said before that to ask for your aid was an unreasonable request and that is still the case. You owe us nothing. In fact we are still indebted to you for the aid you have already provided in our escape from Karhaner. We are not friends or allies. Not at this moment in time. But still here I am, asking. I send this unreasonable request anyway. If you were to offer your aid in our time of crisis," I pause, "gosh I don't even know what to say, I don't want to make promises I can't keep" Sam is still writing away as I pace up and down, "don't write that bit Sam I'm trying to think."

"No it sounds good, it sounds right, the Queen will respond to honesty."

I look at him skeptical but perhaps he is right. I take a deep breath and continue, "but whilst I expect nothing, I hope beyond hope that there is a seed of friendship that can be planted. I think that you and I understand each other, at least a little. I even think that you and I could be friends, but that might not be a future that is open to us. The coming battle will change everything, for my country and for the world. I believe that you could decide in what way, for better or for worse. Truthfully I've run out of words. I don't know what else to say. No matter what happens I do truly thank you for what you did for me and my friends, and for giving us a glimpse of the paradise you call home. I know that that was an honour and something I will never forget. May peace and love be in your path.

Your friend,

Princess Elisa"

I look over at Sam as he ends the letter with the words I know to be a traditional Reladian blessing. He smiles at me, "Perfect. Now rewrite it so it's in you handwriting and I'll find the fastest messenger I can. Don't change a word of it, don't second guess yourself, ok? Trust me. It sounds right, it sounds like you and the Queen will respect that above all else."

I nod and reach over to give Sam a kiss, "Thank you, I don't know what I would do without you."

Sam grins, "Neither do I, now get writing."

Standing on top of the city walls in the moonlight, a soft breeze whispering past my hair, the world feels almost peaceful. If it wasn't for the specs of fires I can clearly see burning from the Karhaner camp which stretches out before me. Something about the darkness makes the approaching storm seem further away. I had tried to sleep but after almost two hours of tossing and turning I had given up. I left Sam sound asleep, nothing would stop that boy from sleeping, and came up here, hoping to clear my mind, but it wasn't really working.

I'd sent my letter to Queen Kella with an urgent messenger hours ago but tried to squash any semblance of hope of aid. I knew in this moment that we had done everything we could, gathered every man that we could, reached out to every possible ally, built up the defenses of Leforth as much as possible. There was nothing left to do but fight, and hope that we had done enough. Taking one last lungful of night air, I move to return to my bedchamber. Even if I couldn't sleep I could watch Sam sleep, maybe for the last time. Immediately scolding myself and brushing that morbid thought aside, I climb into bed and snuggle up to Sam's side. Tomorrow was only a few hours away and then I would face the truth of our future. But not now. Now I close my eyes and sleep.

<h1 style="text-align:right">Chapter 32</h1>

It feels like my eyes have only just closed when the deafening sound of a large horn being blown across the city makes both Sam and I shoot up awake. Seconds later a young Leforth private bursts through the door breathing heavily. He hesitates at the sight of Sam and I but then quickly collects himself and bows as words rush out of his mouth. "Your highness, you're needed."

"Is it starting?" I ask as I immediately jump out of bed and start grabbing clothes and armour.

"Yes your highness" the man is staring at me wide eyed and a blush creeps over his cheeks before he turns away, "I'll wait outside, your highness."

Sam laughs as he climbs out of bed and starts dressing at a much calmer pace than my frantic efforts, "He nearly had a heart attack at the sight of you in your nightgown. He'll be telling everyone this story in future, telling his grandkids all about the time he saw the princess in her nightgown."

"Let's hope he gets the chance to have grandchildren." I mutter as I race towards the door but before I can open it Sam grabs my arm and pulls me back. For a moment he just holds me face and stares into my eyes. Bending down he gives me a fierce passionate kiss that ends far too quickly. "I love you" he breathes.

"I love you too." I whisper in reply. He looks at me for one more moment before giving a decisive nod, grabbing my hand and leading the way out the door.

We race down the stairs and into the dining room where our defense plans still lie all over the table. The mood is sombre and I'm greeted by a grim faced Lord Francis giving a brief nod. "They're moving" he says simply and the breath that I didn't even realise I was holding gets sucked out of my body. "Everyone knows their positions and jobs." Lord Francis continues looking around the room at the Generals gathered. "The gate mustn't fall." He emphasises again, just in case anyone had forgotten this most essential fact. He is greeted with nothing but determined nods. "Well then. May fortune smile on us all. To your zones." He instructs and instantly there's a burst of noise and bustle as everyone starts to leave the room, until it's just the Gallavanties left. Instinctively we've all held back though no-one says anything. The ominous silence makes my eyes begin to well with tears as I look around at my family, knowing this might be the last time we are all here together. "Don't be daft" Pepe breaks the silence gruffly, pulling me in for a quick hug. He slaps Dav on the shoulder and nods at Kinken, "Let's go deal with these pesky Karhaners." And with another quick hug for Sam and a small smile from Kinken they leave the room.

I turn back to Luis, Risa and Dav but can't think of a single thing to say. Dav and Sam will be positioned on the wall close to me but Luis and Risa are stationed together on the western side. Luis had tried to convince Risa to take charge of the citizens who were making their way to the south of the city, so as to be as far away from the fighting as possible, but she had refused. With somewhat pained smiles they simply open their arms and I rush into them, squeezing them both as hard as I can. "I love you guys."

"We love you too" murmurs Risa. And now I can't stop the tears from flowing. Risa wipes them away but more are silently running down my face as she hugs first Dav and then Sam. She whispers something in his ear, which I think is about me judging by the glance he throws my way, but I don't hear what it is. Luis follows Risa with tight hugs and then takes her hand and they walk out the room without a backward glance.

Wiping away my tears with the backs of my hands. I take a deep breath. "Spose we'd better go or they'll start without us." I mumble trying to inject some humour and ignore the fact that I feel like I've just said goodbye. It's not funny but Sam smiles anyway and takes my hand.

We exit the Lord Manor house and quickly make our way north, merging into the chaos that has filled the streets as men and some women with weapons race towards the city wall, while others with young children or elderly relatives race south. Weaving around the bustling carnage we reach the wall and climb the stairs to step out on the battlements. Already the wall is lined with men. Stepping forward to look through a crenel I see a sight that stops my heart. A seemingly never ending stretch of Karhaner soldiers lined up like a twisting snake. My gaze swings from left to right trying to encompass the full army but I can't. Once again fear grips me. But glancing at the soldier to my left, who looks rather like I feel, pale with sweat pouring down his face and a slight tremor wobbling his lip, I realise I cannot let my fear show. Drawing myself up I try to give the soldier a reassuring smile before going to take up my designated position. Dav and Sam do the same, Dav's final message coming out more like a threatening growl, "Stay in sight."

I stand to the east of the northern gate, Sam stands with Dav directly above the gate to my left but still within sight. I grab my bow and look down at the large quiver of arrows in front of me. My heart is pounding and I try to take some deep calming breaths but the adrenaline is flowing. I'm ready. But the Karhaner army still has not moved. The once bare landscape is now lined with large wooden spikes hammered into the ground and pointing at our enemy, hopefully preventing them from full scale charges. They stay in their lines, stretching back so far I'm not sure I can see the end. Five minutes go past, then ten. The tension builds and everyone seems to be growing restless. I can hear soldiers shifting from one foot to the other and murmurs of chatter but my eyes are fixed on the enemy. Waiting.

Suddenly as one the army seems to move, but not forwards. It's a wave that travels from front to back of soldiers lifting their sword arms high into the sky. All the air gets sucked out of my lungs. This is it. But instead of charging forwards like I expect. They swing their swords down against their shields and a resounding boom echoes across the open land between us. Slowly, deliberately they raise their arms again as one, before beating their shields once more. They start to drum a slow, steady, menacing beat. It's almost mesmerising how synchronised the movement is. The loud pulse slowly picks up pace as the drumming continues. A chill creeps down my spine and I try to swallow the dry lump in my throat.

Suddenly, whilst some continue pounding on their shields, a wave of soldiers break ranks and charge towards us. Instinctively I grab my bow from my back, swinging it round and notching an arrow before I realise that the charge has stopped. No longer racing towards us they've halted at the line of wooden spikes and are attacking them with their swords and axes. These men are now within range so an order goes out and we fire. They drop like flies, not defending themselves or stopping to shield, still they continue on. Not getting any closer, only focusing on destroying the spikes in front of us. I stare at them intently. Whilst we hoped that the hurriedly erected spikes would cause a problem for them we didn't expect them to go to such efforts to remove them.

We manage to take down hundreds of them while they're not even really attacking us yet. As I watch them creating a gap directly in line with the northern gate, I know there is a greater purpose to their systematic destruction. Looking back towards the still stationary army dread creeps up my spine. They need to remove the spikes to create room for the huge rolling contraptions which I somehow didn't notice before, so focused on the sheer number of them was I. We expected them to have a battering ram but not like this. Mounted onto some sort of wheeled swing the reinforced steel ram gleams in the early morning sunshine, waiting for its moment. As the gap in the spikes grows and more spaces open up further down the line the real movement seems to happen. Their second wave attacks, this time ignoring the spikes and pouring like a flood towards the wall.

When some reach the wall many of our defense strategies kick in and arrows start flying from the battlements on those below, huge rocks rain down, lifted and dropped onto those who have reached the base of the wall. But still they keep coming, not seemingly phased by those who have fallen. Huge wooden ladders with curved hooks on the end suddenly emerge from the crowd. We expected this and had planned our response so I watch with some satisfaction as the Karhaner attempts to press their ladders to the city walls are thwarted by Leforth men pushing the ladders back each time. A hiss of frustration escapes me when I see that several have managed to get their hooks over the city walls but our back up plan quickly follows as oil is poured from above onto the top rungs and then set a light.

The fire spreads downwards quickly and those Karhaner soldiers who had begun to climb quickly retreat. I breathe again. Another win. But still the Karhaner army keeps coming with relentless predictability. More pitch and oil are poured over the sides splashing across the men below, before flaming arrows rein down to set them ablaze. I can hear the screams of glowing men and the smell of burning flesh from here and it makes me want to throw up. I constantly have to remind myself that these men want to kill us and take our country, and that every gruesome action is necessary.

As the fire engulfs the front line of men and others back away to escape, I wonder if we've actually managed to drive them back but it is only a temporary moment of reprieve. I watch in despair as another wave of men pour forwards from the Karhaner camp line. Dodging through the remaining spike posts, though most have been pushed down now, thousands of them coming like a tidal wave. Taking a deep breath, I reach for my bow.

I try to block out the crescendo of noise and fire arrow after arrow out over the wall, not even taking the time to aim, just raining as many down on to the mass of bodies below as I can. With their shields over their heads I've no idea if what I'm doing is even making an impact. Reaching down to grasp my next arrow my fist closes around thin air and I glance down to find my quiver empty. Spinning around and shouting for more arrows a boy who can't be more than 12 races towards me with a fresh bundle. I briefly wonder why he is here and want to send him back into the city where it is safer, but one look into his determined eyes show me that he wants to be here and contributing to our fight, so I just nod my thanks and turn back to the chaos below.

Looking down at the heaving mass I decide against more random firing. We don't have an unlimited supply of arrows and every arrow needs to count in taking out enemy soldiers when we are so out-numbered. Looking along the wall I see my new strategy. As the army reach the base of the wall, more ladders are being stretched up. These ones appear to have been shortened and don't quite reach the tops of the wall and so can't be pushed away as they were earlier.

But as the men begin to climb their shields have to drop and they are exposed. I aim my bow at the nearest man on the left and fire watching with satisfaction as he takes the hit and then falls from the ladder on to his comrades below. Almost immediately another takes his place. I notch another arrow and fire again before shouting orders down the line to other archers, "Aim for the men on the ladders, they're open on the ladders, aim for the men on the ladders." I can hear the cry being echoed down the line and see the change in tactic being heard as more men fall from more ladders up and down the wall.

It seems to go on for hours. I'm nearing exhaustion but still the battle rages. Somehow we continue to hold them off but the Karhan-er army seems to be never ending. I don't know how much longer I can keep going. Every muscle aches and my fingers are bleeding from pulling back the bow string. I don't know how much longer anyone can go on. Tired pale faces line the walls of men dripping with sweat but refusing to give up. Never stopping their constant vigilance.

What happens when people are simply too exhausted to keep fighting? Thousands of their soldiers lie strewn across the battlefield and in comparison we've lost relatively few, and yet they still outnumber us. After every wave we push back we barely have a moment to catch our breath before the next wave hits. They've given up attempting to climb the wall with ladders and are focusing on battering through the wall instead. The ominous battering ram which had seemed to crawl towards us had finally reached its destination and the incessant thud thud thud of the ram on the outer northern gate has been relentless for nearly an hour. We tried setting the damn thing on fire but they managed to put it out before too much damage was done, and for every soldier we shoot there is another one ready to take their place with the swing ram.

On the left and right sides of the gate where other spaces in the line of spikes were created, the Karhaner army have started using trebuchets to fire huge boulders at the city walls, taking great chunks out each time they hit and causing shockwaves so powerful people on the wall are literally knocked off their feet. Neither of the two slingshot weapons are quite within our range and so there is nothing we can do to stop them and I'm just grateful that they seem to take an age to reload otherwise I fear they would have broken through our walls already.

But then suddenly one of the flying boulders does have its desired effect and breaks through the top of the wall to my right, causing an avalanche to occur and the wall beneath to crumble. I stare in horror at the now gaping hole in our defense. The sight of the gap in our wall has the last remaining Karhanher soldiers who were waiting in reserve charging forwards. Without thinking I run along the wall to the jagged edge, looking down onto the pile of rubble. We have to fill the gap. Yelling to the arrowmen to fire at the charging mass to slow them down I grab a vat of tar and start to drag it towards the hole. A soldier I don't know races to help and we empty the black ooze onto the rocks below.

Two others on the opposite side of the fracture follow our lead before firing a flaming arrow on top. Flames spring to life, creating a wall of fire. Grabbing anything wooden within arms reach I start throwing it down to add more fuel. If we can keep the fire burning then they won't be able to get through. Spinning around I yell down into the courtyard behind the wall for more tar and wood. But I can see that more men have already leapt into action and are racing towards the gap with wagons piled high with large stones, the same ones we were throwing over the wall earlier. Ignoring the searing heat from the fire we started, they begin to pile the stones, rebuilding a makeshift wall, which might not hold for long but would at least slow the Karhaners down further if they do make it through the fire. Glancing back over the northern side of the wall it appears that the flames have at least temporarily driven them back from the gap for now.

Just as I think we've averted the crisis Pepe appears before me, out of breath from running. Sweat and dirt cover his face and he looks exhausted. Urgently he fills me in, "The gate's not gonna hold much longer, we need to counter, try n distract em, buy some time, get em away from the gate for a bit till we can reinforce it more."

Already I'm shaking my head, "It's suicide, we don't have the numbers for an attack outside the walls."

Pepe looks at me grimly, "I know that kid but we need ta reinforce tha gate n we can't do that with them banging away on it. If we open the second gate ta get to the first to reinforce it n they get through..." he breaks off, both of us already knowing what that would mean. The second gate is nowhere near as strong as the first. They would get through it quickly with their ramming machine.

"General Stokes is leading the charge from the western gate. I'm heading there now but you listen kid. If it don't work, if you think they're getting through that gate, you run, ya hear me? If General Srumthro gets ya again you know what he's gonna do. Don't let pride get in the way of running, better to live to fight another day, ya hear me?"

My gut instinct is to shake my head and refuse to run but as Pepe's words sink in, I know he's right. If we lose this fight and the General gains Leforth then there will be many more fights to come.

"Wait, what do you mean you're heading there now? You're not joining the charge? Pepe No!" I grab his arm as though I can somehow hold him here with me but he gently pulls his arm away. "We need every man we can get if we're to stand a chance." He gives me a small smile that doesn't reach his eyes, "Love ya kid." And then he's gone. Running back along the wall. And I can't do anything but stare after his retreating figure.

# Chapter 33

Watching from above our cavalry of men seems pathetically small compared to Karhaner's and I know without a doubt that they are charging into a slaughter house just to try and buy us some more time. I can't help but wince as the two armies collide and I have to look away. I glance at Lord Francis who has appeared beside me. "I think it's time" I murmur, "We need to evacuate the city, send everyone we can south." Lord Francis nods slowly, not taking his eyes off the battle charge below. I turn in search of Sam and Dav but I've not seen either of them since I left my position to deal with the wall breach. I ask Lord Francis if he's seen them and he turns to me so abruptly it makes me jump, a wave of surprise washes over his face before he slowly speaks, "I thought you knew, they all went together, except for the woman, Risa?"

I stare at him uncomprehendingly for a moment, "Went where together?"

He opens his mouth to speak but clearly doesn't know what to say. Then he quietly turns back to the battle scene. For a moment I still don't get it, until my gaze follows his and realisation dawns. "NO" I scream as I race closer to the wall leaning out over the side to look down at the chaos below. It's impossible to distinguish anything from up here but I can't stop my eyes from frantically searching the mass of bodies for a glimpse of them, any of them. How could they do that? How could they send themselves out into certain death?

Our tiny army has nearly reached the northern gate and the swing battering ram but they are now surrounded on all sides. Most seem to have fallen from their horses and are now fighting on the ground. They form a tight circle with their shields creating a barrier. A tiny fly caught in a huge spider's web. Leforth soldiers on the wall try to support their trapped comrades by raining endless arrows down onto the surrounding enemy. But still more of our men fall and the circle gets smaller as they draw back to fill the gaps in the shield wall. Suddenly I'm sure that I spot Dav, in the centre of the circle, shouting orders. "What do we do? What do we do?" I say to no one in particular as sheer panic descends watching the horror unfold, and I start to hyperventilate knowing there is nothing I can do. My entire family are down there and there is nothing I can do.

As I struggle to breath and my vision starts to blur, clutching the top of the wall in an attempt to stay upright, I hear the sound of a horn blast somehow echoing clear and loud across the battlefield. Whipping my head to the right where the sound originated I try to recall what it means. It's not the same horn as before and it's not the bells which mean evacuate. Is it a different signal? I look to Lord Francis but he is also staring east in confusion. Then I hear the beginnings of a cheer. It comes from the east and travels like a wave.

At first I think it's the Karhaners cheering victory, that they've broken through somehow. But then I realise the euphoric whoops are travelling along the top of the wall. It's Aleti soldiers. They're shouting and waving swords and bows in the air but I still don't know why. The battle below seems to have halted at the jubilant sounds pouring down from the wall. As one the mass turns towards the east. And then the Karhaner soldiers are abandoning their attack on the Leforth circle and quickly taking up defensive positions. Leaning out of the wall as far as I can I stare along the wall, trying to see what those in the east have clearly already seen. And then they emerge.

On horseback with bows in hand. Travelling faster than looks possible. The Reladians. In fierce combat attire, with painted faces and black horses frothing at the mouth. They are a terrifying sight. Rising as one on their horses, notching their arrows, they fire with eerie precision. Their range and skills so much greater than ours mean Karhaners start dropping when the Relads are still more than 100 metres away. I stare in wonder at the devastating affect the Relads are having on the enemy. Within seconds it is clear the tide has turned. I could cry with joy. And all I keep thinking is, They came. She came. The queen came. A sob of relief escaping my lips and I have to press a shaking hand over my mouth to prevent more from escaping.

With the Relads cutting through the Karhaners like a hot knife through butter, the small circle of Aleti soldiers are able to make it to the Northern Gate. The Karhaners have abandoned their battering ram and are fleeing in the face of our new allies. Racing back towards their own camp. I've no idea where General Srumthro is but it is clear that his army is retreating. Broken and defeated, they are retreating. Somehow, miraculously, we've done it. We've driven them back. The city was never breached. We've won. Unable to contain myself any longer a hoarse laugh escapes me. Turning to

Lord Francis I pull him into a hug and start spinning around, still laughing uncontrollable.

Lord Francis still seems somewhat stunned, "What happened?" he asks.

"They came. The Reladians came." I beam at him, "Our allies, our new, wonderful, brilliant allies."

Grinning at him again I turn and run back down the inner wall steps and race to the northern gates which are already being pulled open to allow our men back in. But elation at victory quickly goes at the sight of injured men being carried through the entrance. The reality of the cost of the battle hits.

Frozen to the spot I scan the faces of the men as they pour through the gate. I should've known they would be amongst the last through. It's Sam I spot first. There's blood covering half his face but he's walking unaided. Before he even realises I'm there I've launched myself into his arms. For a moment we just hold each other tightly, both grateful to have found the other again. But as I squeeze Sam I look up over his shoulder and my stomach drops. Pepe and Dav are both staggering through the open gate carrying unmoving bodies. Luis and Kinken.

# Chapter 34

-------------------------------------------------------------

The next few minutes go by in a panicked blur as I follow Dav and Pepe to the dance hall which has been turned into a makeshift hospital. I can do nothing but stare at their limp forms. Blood is pouring down one of Kinken's legs while Luis is so deathly pale he almost blends into the white sheet covering the bed which they put him on. Dav is already attempting to tie a tourniquet around the top of Kinken's left thigh while Pepe shouts for help.

Sam says something but I don't hear it until he gives me a gentle shake and moves to stand in front of me, blocking my sight of Luis and Kinken. "Cara, where's Risa?"

"I, I, I don't know."

"Can you find her? She needs to be here."

Slowly I nod, then with a little nudge from Sam, I turn and quickly exit the room, glad to have some sort of purpose. Racing off around the city I try every place that I can think of where she might have gone, but with all the chaos, destroyed buildings and so many peo-ple on the streets I feel like I'm searching for a needle in a haystack. When I do finally set eyes on her I almost wish that I hadn't found her. I freeze to the spot, watching as she hands buckets of water to a line of men who are trying to put out a fire. What on earth do I say? Slowly, hesitantly I approach. She doesn't notice me at first, so absorbed is she with her task, but when she does her face lights up. Just for a second. Then she takes in my expression and I don't have to say anything. She knows. The only reassurance I can give her is that he was alive when I left. Holding hands we race back to the hospital. Luis still looks the same as before, the only movement being the slightest rising and falling of his chest, signalling that he is somehow still with us. As Risa bursts into tears and throws herself onto Luis, I finally let my own silent tears fall too. Without a word Sam wraps his arms around me from behind and I lean back into his touch.

Suddenly glancing around in panic I ask, "Where's Kinken?"

Sam hesitates but then squeezes me tighter as he answers, "They had to take him to the surgeon. They're gonna have to take his leg."

"His leg?"

"He won't survive otherwise. Dav and Pepe went with him."

"What did the doctors say about Luis?"

"Blow to the head. No other injuries they can see but they dunno how bad his head might be." He pauses but then continues in a whisper, "They don't know if he's gonna make it Cara. There's nothing they can do but wait n see."

For the next twelve hours I sit beside Luis, Risa and I each holding one of his hands with our other hands linked together across his chest. Sam tries to convince both of us to get some rest but Risa won't leave him and I won't leave her, so he settles for just keeping us supplied with food and water. At some point Lord Francis comes in to tell me the Karhaner army is in full retreat but I can't muster any sort of joy now. Queen Kella also visits. I seem to take her by surprise when I greet her by throwing my arms around her. I can't do anything but mumble the word 'Thank You' over and over again. Eventually she embraces me back, somewhat awkwardly at first, but then she seems to give in to the contact. Looking around her at our scene beside Luis, she does nothing more than give me an understanding smile and insists that we will talk later after my friend has recovered.

It is dawn again when Pepe and Dav return with Kinken between them on a stretcher. Glimpsing sight of a short stump where his left leg should be makes me want to vomit and I'm grateful when a blanket is placed over him and covers it. Guilt constantly eats away at me. None of the Gallavanties would be here if I hadn't asked them to be. First Dav and then Pepe walk over to hug Risa and then me before sitting down and joining us in our silent vigil.

Eventually exhaustion takes over and though I refuse to leave the hospital I do end up lying down on the floor with Sam. I'm woken up hours later by a commotion taking place above me and the sound of Risa calling Luis' name has me scrambling to my feet.

Luis is awake. He's still as pale as before but his eyes are open. He looks somewhat dazed at the commotion around him. Risa is simultaneously stroking his head whilst crying her eyes out. With a groan he slowly attempts to sit up, quickly helped by Sam and Pepe. Once settled, still lying but now in a more propped up position, he seems more alert to his surroundings. Then with a hoarse whisper he opens his mouth and asks, "Did we win?"

I can't help but laugh as suddenly all the tension seems to flow out of me. Nodding through my laughter I beam at him, "Yes, we won."

"The Reladians came and saved our asses." Sam informs him with a grin.

"That's alright then," he murmurs with a weak smile before turning his attention to Risa, "You can stop crying now love, I'm alright."

She smiles and attempts to wipe away her tears but more quickly take their place, "I was so bloody scared. Don't ever scare me like that again. I thought I was gonna lose you."

"Well you didn't lose me." He whispers, now stroking her face in an attempt to reassure her.

"Good job too, I don't fancy being a single mother." Risa says with a small secretive smile.

Her words instantly register with me and I can't help but gasp. It seems to take Luis a moment longer to catch on as first surprise and then elation light up his face.

"You're... We're..."

"Yep" Risa nods now beaming at him, "We're having a baby."

Unable to contain myself any longer I squeal with excitement and run around the bed to give Risa a hug. Luis still appears to be in shock as Sam, Pepe and Dav offer their congratulations.

"Wait a minute, how long have you known? Did you know before the battle?"

"I've known for sure for about a week."

"Why the blazes didn't you tell me?"

Risa scoffs, "You wouldn't have let me help in the battle if I'd told you and I wasn't about to hide away when I was more than capable of doing my part."

"I can't believe you fought against an invading army whilst you're pregnant" Luis says in horror but Risa only grins even more, "I know right! What a great story to tell our child one day."

I laugh, "I hope it's a girl, we need another girl in the gang."

Dav shakes his head, "You two cause us enough trouble as it is, definitely needs to be a boy."

"Trouble? Us?" I try to feint ignorance but can't help the smile that creeps across my face.

"So much bloody trouble." He murmurs, causing us all to laugh, and just like that everything suddenly feels right with the world again.

Four days after the battle and the clean up operation and repairs are still ongoing. Our scouts have reported the full retreat of the Karhaner army. As we stand around the room which became our command centre Lord Francis and I are outlining the next stage of the city's recovery and ensuring that all the necessary resources are being directed to the right place. Suddenly there's a commotion at the entrance and the double doors fly open. Striding in, looking like he owns the place comes Lord Fagan with my father beside him. Silence descends upon the room as everyone simply stares at the King and Lord Fagan. My father is looking at me and at least has the grace to look somewhat uncomfortable. Lord Fagan, however, has apparently not changed at all. He marches towards the far end of the table, completely ignoring me, "Lord Francis, what's the latest?"

Lord Francis stares at him with an expression of sheer disgust written all over his face, not responding to his question.

Cheerfully I call down the room to him, "Nice of you to join us Lord Fagan, what brings you to Leforth, here for a holiday? You can't be here because of the battle, which you've conveniently missed, because if I remember rightly you quite clearly swore that there was no threat from Karhaner to worry about."

At this Lord Fagan presses his lips together tightly, as though he somehow hoped that his previous words would've been forgotten. "Yes, well, unfortunately the country's intelligence officers were clearly misinformed and unreliable in that respect. A mistake that will not happen again."

I raise an eyebrow sarcastically, "Oh so it's their fault that you ignored me when I stood in front of you and told you General Srumthro's plans?"

"Let us focus on what's important now," Lord Fagan says, clapping his hands together and changing the topic quickly, "Lord Francis, I must congratulate you on your victory. Clearly your defense preparations and our soldiers were enough to drive back the Karhaners and.."

Lord Francis interrupts abruptly, "The only reason we are all stood here now is thanks to Princess Elisa. She came to our aid while you stayed and hid in Carrard like the coward you are. All thanks and praise should be directed towards her and our allies, without whom this war would've been lost."

"Allies?" My father questions, speaking for the first time since entering the room.

I smile at the woman on my right, "Father may I introduce Queen Kella. We owe all our gratitude to her and the Reladians that came to our aid just when it seemed that all was lost."

Queen Kella nods her head respectfully at my father but then turns to address the rest of the room. "Well I think we've covered everything we need to cover for the moment. I shall return home tomorrow, now that we are sure the threat is gone. Princess Elisa I look forward to welcoming you to Relad again soon so that we may continue formalising our Alliance agreement."

"Absolutely," I beam at her. As the room begins to disperse, Lord Fagan looks a little lost, being completely ignored by everyone as he is. It almost brings a small smile to my face and I can only hope that this is a sign that Lord Fagan's grip on power is finally slipping.

"Elisa, may we speak alone." My father asks rather cautiously.

We move into Lord Francis' study, which has sort of become my office over the last week, and I calmly take a seat behind the desk, leaving my father to lower himself into the chair opposite.

My father is staring at me as though he doesn't recognise the woman in front of him. I simply raise my eyebrows in question and wait for him to speak.

He sighs and looks down at his fingers in his lap, "I want to apologise..."

"Go on then." I say bluntly.

He looks up at me sharply, surprised by the command in my tone, before sighing deeply again, "I am sorry. I am sorry I did not listen to you when you told me about the threat. I should have listened."

"Yes, you should have. You had my family thrown in jail," I remind him.

"Your family?" He questions before realising who I mean, he nods slowly, "Yes, that was wrong."

"There were a lot of things that were wrong father."

"Yes, I see that now, we'll talk about it, and I promise I will listen to your suggestions."

I draw myself up, leaning forwards and stare him in the eye, "They will not be suggestions father. Things will change. So much needs to change. For starters, Lord Fagan needs to go, the curfew and his oppressive rules and punishments along with him. We should be working with the people, not against them. A new alliance will be made with Relad and our old friendship with Cobback re-established if they'll have us."

"Elisa, I understand your present anger and untrust of Lord Fagan but he has been a good advisor to me for many years and one mistake..."

"Not a suggestion father. He no longer commands the Lords Chamber and he cannot stay. Oh and another thing, I will marry whomever I want, the choice is wholly mine to make."

"Elisa..."

"And I can tell you now it won't be Joseph Fagan."

"I understand that Elisa but there are limits, you can't marry a commoner you met in the street." He pleads before I cut him off, "I will marry the person I love with all my heart and you will learn to accept it."

There's a cold tension as we warily watch each other, neither one of us wanting to be the one who blinks first. Finally he looks away with a sigh, "Marriage is still more than a year away, we can talk about this later."

I let his comment slide knowing that whether we discuss it now or in a year's time the end result will be the same. One day marrying Sam is something that I won't compromise on.

# Epilogue

W e stay in Leforth for another 3 weeks, ensuring the city walls and gates are all fully repaired, and that reports of the Karhaner army's total retreat are fully confirmed. Sources from within Otraf seem to indicate that there may well be a rebellion against General Srumthro brewing. I certainly hope those rumours are true. Alliance meetings take place with Queen Kella and although both my father and Lord Fagan are at the negotiations, it is I who leads on it all. Though there are no words to express my gratitude towards Queen Kella and the Reladians for the leap of faith they took in coming to our aid, I am determined to make good on my promise and form a long lasting bond between our nations, based on mutual prosperity, and I think the true respect and friendship that Queen Kella and I are developing reflects that with which our countries will follow.

Leaving behind half of the Carrard garrison to continue to help with the rebuilding of the city and ensure that the newly repaired walls remain well guarded, we return to Carrard. Luis is now fully recovered and him and Risa appear in a constant state of happiness as they look forward to their future. Kinken is adapting well to his new crutches though I still haven't yet got used to the sight of him with his missing leg.

Our return into the city is greeted with overwhelming crowds of cheering people, waving flags and throwing flowers, as we ride past. It annoys me that my father and Lord Fagan lead the way and wave at the people as though accepting their thanks, when they did nothing to earn it, but there's no doubt that the screams get louder when the Gallavanties and I follow, and I can clearly hear my name being called from all directions. Perhaps if I have earnt some semblance of trust or respect from the city folk they will accept me in my efforts to undo the damage done in the last few years by Lord Fagan. After the deafening welcome and so many months away it seems unbelievably strange to find myself sitting at my old dining table in my old room with the Gallavanties, Molly and Scott. Laughing and joking as we casually eat our supper, with Sam's arm resting on the back of my chair, absentmindedly twirling a piece of my hair, I want to capture and hold on to this memory forever. But then my moment of bliss shatters as I overhear the conversation between Pepe, Dav and Kinken.

"I say stick with the route we were on, east to Albeck and then on to Cobback."

"Ah but I fancy some sun, why not head south to Esland and Toria and then we can loop back up to Cobback later in the year."

"If we head south first we'll be in Andrent for turtle hatching season. I always love watching these tiny little things scrabbling to make their way into the sea."

"And it'll be the right time for dolphins too."

"Wow, dolphins. I've never seen dolphins" Molly pipes up.

"Oh you have to see them one day, gorgeous things, never fail to put on a show, leaping out the water, they come right up to the boats too."

"Molly, Scott, have you guys ever thought of travelling?" Risa asks across the table.

"Oh yeah, I've always wanted to travel" Scott answers, "See the world."

Molly seems a bit more thoughtful with her reply, "To be honest the idea of even leaving Carrard would have seemed mad to me a few months ago, but after hearing everything Cara has seen and done, maybe an adventure would be exciting."

At Molly's response Risa gives Luis a little smile and wink but then the conversation moves on, and whilst everyone else still seems to be having a good time I can't shift the heavy feeling that has come over me, like a stone in my stomach.

Lieing in bed that night I can't sleep.

"What's wrong?" Sam murmurs beside me, clearly sensing my agitation.

Unable to hold my thoughts inside my head any longer, the most important question bursts out of me, "What are you going to do now?"

He rolls over so that we are facing each other, "What do you mean?"

"I heard Pepe and Dav and Kinken at dinner, they were talking about travel plans. Getting on the road again, where to take the show next." I pause but there's no response from Sam so after a moment's hesitation I just ask, "Are you leaving? Are you going with them?"

I hold my breath as I wait for his answer. With a small smile he gently strokes his hand along my cheek, "Haven't I already told you that I'm not leaving you again? Didn't I promise? I'm not going anywhere, not without you."

I sigh with relief and lean forward to give him a gentle kiss, "Everyone else will leave though won't they." I mutter glumly.

"It's what they do Cara, it's who they are. They'll be back though."

"It won't be the same."

"No it won't be but maybe that's a good thing. Sometimes change is ok. We've got a lot of changes to make here after all."

"We?" I ask with a smile.

"Yes, we. Always we from now on." He murmurs, "Now stop stressing and go to sleep."

I laugh and snuggle closer, knowing that everything will be ok so long as Sam is by my side.

And so two weeks later it's with a heavy heart that I stand at the castle gate, waving goodbye as the Gallavanties caravans disappear down the road before me. Sam stands on my left waving madly as well but the thing that has truly made me able to cope with the departure of half of my family are the couple standing to my right. Risa and Luis decided to stay too, wanting to set down roots and a permanent home for their baby. I couldn't have been happier and have already insisted they take the palace apartment right next door to my room. Whether they will stay there or eventually find their own place I don't know but knowing they're staying in the city fills me with joy. Keeping Risa and Luis did mean saying goodbye to another set of friends though. When the Gallavanties realised they needed more recruits, Molly and Scott decided to answer the call, and although I'll miss them I know that they're going to love life on the road.

As the caravans finally drift out of sight, I can't help but look around at my surroundings and think back. "This is where it all started" I murmur, "These are the gates that I stood outside of all those months ago before I met you, before I first decided to run away and explore the city."

Sam grins, "Best decision you ever made."

My answering smile adds a twinkle to his eye, "Yes, yes I believe it was."